There was a billowing whiteness below him, and on every side, as though all the world were made of fleece.

This is a very strange place indeed, he thought.

Perhaps it is that place of pure forms that young Plato liked to speculate about, where everything is perfect and nothing is quite real. Those are ideal clouds all around me, not real ones. This is ideal air upon which I walk. I myself am the ideal Socrates, liberated from my coarse ordinary body. Could it be? Well, maybe so. He stood for a while, considering that possibility. The thought came to him that this might be the life after life, in which case he might meet some of the gods, if there were any gods in the first place, and if he could manage to find them. *I would like that,* he thought. *Perhaps they would be willing to speak with me.*

Of course, he had serious doubts that the gods existed at all. But if they did, it was reasonable to think that they might be found in a place such as this.

He looked up. The sky was radiant with brilliant golden light. He took a deep breath and smiled and set out across the fleecy nothingness of the airy world to see if he could find the gods.

The programmer looked up from the holotank. "Do you ever feel like . . . God?"

Time Gate

ROBERT SILVERBERG

with

Bill Fawcett

TIME GATE

Copyright © 1989 by Bill Fawcett & Associates

A Baen Books Original

Baen Publishing Enterprises
260 Fifth Avenue
New York, N.Y. 10001

ISBN: 0-671-69850-8

Cover art by David Mattingly

First printing, December 1989

Distributed by
SIMON & SCHUSTER
1230 Avenue of the Americas
New York, N.Y. 10020

Printed in the United States of America

TABLE OF CONTENTS

In the beginning was the idea: what if historical personalities could be electronically "resuscitated" in the depths of a supercomputer's creche? At first, the suggestion went, they could provide useful data on personality patterns in previous centuries, becoming literal case histories for curious psycho-historians to probe and study. Then, of course, the speculations grew bolder. Perhaps the personalities could be matrixed, encoded into cloned bodies, providing a simulacrum of the great man or woman for further study, perhaps even consultation. Imagine discussing statecraft with Thomas Jefferson, trading economic theory with John Kenneth Galbraith, or discussing philosophy with Kant. Yes, in the beginning, the concept was pure, the theory sound. In the beginning. . . .

ENTER A SOLDIER. LATER: ENTER ANOTHER

AD 2130

Robert Silverberg

It might be heaven. Certainly it wasn't Spain and he doubted it could be Peru. He seemed to be floating, suspended midway between nothing and nothing. There was a shimmering golden sky far above him and a misty, turbulent sea of white clouds boiling far below. When he looked down he saw his legs and his feet dangling like child's toys above an unfathomable abyss, and the sight of it made him want to puke, but there was nothing in him for the puking. He was hollow. He was made of air. Even the old ache in his knee was gone, and so was the everlasting dull burning in the fleshy part of his arm where the Indian's little arrow had taken him, long ago on the shore of that island of pearls, up by Panama.

It was as if he had been born again, sixty years

1

old but freed of all the harm that his body had experienced and all its myriad accumulated injuries: freed, one might almost say, of his body itself.

"Gonzalo?" he called. "Hernando?"

Blurred dreamy echoes answered him. And then silence.

"Mother of God, am I dead?"

No. No. He had never been able to imagine death. An end to all striving? A place where nothing moved? A great emptiness, a pit without a bottom? Was this place the place of death, then? He had no way of knowing. He needed to ask the holy fathers about this.

"Boy, where are my priests? Boy?"

He looked about for his page. But all he saw was blinding whorls of light coiling off to infinity on all sides. The sight was beautiful but troublesome. It was hard for him to deny that he had died, seeing himself afloat like this in a realm of air and light. Died and gone to heaven. This is heaven, yes, surely, surely. What else could it be?

So it was true, that if you took the Mass and took the Christ faithfully into yourself and served Him well you would be saved from your sins, you would be forgiven, you would be cleansed. He had wondered about that. But he wasn't ready yet to be dead, all the same. The thought of it was sickening and infuriating. There was so much yet to be done. And he had no memory even of being ill. He searched his body for wounds. No, no wounds. Not anywhere. Strange. Again he looked around. He was alone here. No one to be seen, not his page, nor his brother, nor De Soto, nor the priests, nor anyone. "Fray Marcos! Fray Vicente! Can't you hear me? Damn you, where are you? Mother of God! Holy Mother, blessed among women! Damn you, Fray Vicente, tell me—tell me—"

His voice sounded all wrong: too thick, too deep, a stranger's voice. The words fought with his tongue and came from his lips malformed and lame, not the good crisp Spanish of Estremadura but something shameful and odd. What he heard was like the spluttering foppishness of Madrid or even the furry babble that they spoke in Barcelona; why, he might almost be a Portuguese, so coarse and clownish was his way of shaping his speech.

He said carefully and slowly, "I am the Governor and Captain-General of New Castile."

That came out no better, a laughable noise.

"Adelantado—Alguacil Mayor—Marques de la Conquista—"

The strangeness of his new way of speech made insults of his own titles. It was like being tongue-tied. He felt streams of hot sweat breaking out on his skin from the effort of trying to frame his words properly; but when he put his hand to his forehead to brush the sweat away before it could run into his eyes he seemed dry to the touch, and he was not entirely sure he could feel himself at all.

He took a deep breath. "I am Francisco Pizarro!" he roared, letting the name burst desperately from him like water breaching a rotten dam.

The echo came back, deep, rumbling, mocking. *Frantheethco. Peetharro.*

That too. Even his own name, idiotically garbled. "O great God!" he cried. "Saints and angels!"

More garbled noises. Nothing would come out as it should. He had never known the arts of reading or writing; now it seemed that true speech itself was being taken from him. He began to wonder whether he had been right about this being heaven, supernal radiance or no. There was a curse on his tongue; a demon, perhaps, held it pinched in his claws. Was this hell, then? A very beautiful place, but hell nevertheless?

He shrugged. Heaven or hell, it made no difference. He was beginning to grow more calm, beginning to accept and take stock. He knew—had learned, long ago—that there was nothing to gain from raging against that which could not be helped, even less from panic in the face of the unknown. He was here, that was all there was to it—wherever *here* was—and he must find a place for himself, and not this place, floating here between nothing and nothing. He had been in hells before, small hells, hells on Earth. That barren isle called Gallo, where the sun cooked you in your own skin and there was nothing to eat but crabs that had the taste of dog-dung. And that dismal swamp at the mouth of the Rio Biru, where the rain fell in rivers and the trees reached down to cut you like swords. And the mountains he had crossed with his army, where the snow was so cold that it burned, and the air went into your throat like a dagger at every breath. He had come forth from those, and they had been worse than this. Here there was no pain and no danger; here there was only soothing light

4

and a strange absence of all discomfort. He began
to move forward. He was walking on air. Look,
look, he thought, I am walking on air! Then he
said it out loud. "I am walking on air," he announced, and laughed at the way the words
emerged from him. "Santiago! Walking on air! But
why not? I am Pizarro!" He shouted it with all his
might, "Pizarro! Pizarro!" and waited for it to come
back to him.

Peetharro. Peetharro.

He laughed. He kept on walking.

Tanner sat hunched forward in the vast spar-
kling sphere that was the ninth-floor imaging lab,
watching the little figure at the distant center of
the holotank strut with preen. Lew Richardson,
crouching beside him with both hands thrust into
the data gloves so that he could feed instructions
to the permutation network, seemed almost not to
be breathing—seemed to be just one more part of
the network, in fact.

But that was Richardson's way, Tanner thought:
total absorption in the task at hand. Tanner envied
him that. They were very different sorts of men.
Richardson lived for his programming and nothing
but his programming. It was his grand passion.
Tanner had never quite been able to understand
people who were driven by grand passions. Richardson was like some throwback to an earlier age,
an age when things had really mattered, an age
when you were able to have some faith in the
significance of your own endeavors.

"How do you like the armor?" Richardson asked.

"The armor's very fine, I think. We got it from old engravings. It has real flair."

"Just the thing for tropical climates," said Tanner. "A nice tin suit with matching helmet."

He coughed and shifted about irritably in his seat. The demonstration had been going on for half an hour without anything that seemed to be of any importance happening—just the minuscule image of the bearded man in Spanish armor tramping back and forth across the glowing field—and he was beginning to get impatient.

Richardson didn't seem to notice the harshness in Tanner's voice or the restlessness of his movements. He went on making small adjustments. He was a small man himself, neat and precise in dress and appearance, with faded blond hair and pale blue eyes and a thin, straight mouth. Tanner felt huge and shambling beside him. In theory Tanner had authority over Richardson's research projects, but in fact he always had simply permitted Richardson to do as he pleased. This time, though, it might be necessary finally to rein him in a little.

This was the twelfth or thirteenth demonstration that Richardson had subjected him to since he had begun fooling around with this historical-simulation business. The others all had been disasters of one kind or another, and Tanner expected that this one would finish the same way. And basically Tanner was growing uneasy about the project that he once had given his stamp of approval to, so long ago. It was getting harder and harder to go on believing that all this work served any useful purpose. Why had it been allowed to absorb so much of Richardson's group's time and so much of the lab's research budget for so many months? What possible value was it going to have for anybody? What possible use?

It's just a game, Tanner thought. One more desperate meaningless technological stunt, one more pointless pirouette in a meaningless ballet. The expenditure of vast resources on a display of ingenuity for ingenuity's sake and nothing else: now *there's* decadence for you.

The tiny image in the holotank suddenly began to lose color and definition.

"Uh-oh," Tanner said. "There it goes. Like all the others."

But Richardson shook his head. "This time it's different, Harry."

"You think?"

"We aren't losing him. He's simply moving around in there of his own volition, getting beyond our tracking parameters. Which means that we've achieved the high level of autonomy that we were shooting for."

"Volition, Lew? Autonomy?"

"You know that those are our goals."

"Yes, I know what our goals are supposed to be," said Tanner, with some annoyance. "I'm simply not convinced that a loss of focus is a proof that you've got volition."

"Here," Richardson said. "I'll cut in the stochastic tracking program. He moves freely, we freely follow him." Into the computer ear in his lapel he said. "Give me a gain boost, will you?" He made a quick flicking gesture with his left middle finger to indicate the quantitative level.

The little figure in ornate armor and pointed boots grew sharp again. Tanner could see fine details on the armor, the plumed helmet, the tapering shoulder-pieces, the joints at the elbows, the intricate pommel of his sword. He was marching from left to right in a steady hip-rolling way, like a man who was climbing the tallest mountain in the world and didn't mean to break his stride until he was across the summit. The fact that he was walking in what appeared to be mid-air seemed not to trouble him at all.

"There he is," Richardson said grandly. "We've got him back, all right? The conqueror of Peru, before your very eyes, in the flesh. So to speak."

Tanner nodded. Pizarro, yes, before his very eyes. And he had to admit that what he saw was impressive and even, somehow, moving. Something about the dogged way with which that small armored figure was moving across the gleaming pearly field of the holotank aroused a kind of sympathy in him. That little man was entirely imaginary, but *he* didn't seem to know that, or if he did he wasn't letting it stop him for a moment: he went plugging on, and on and on, as if he intended actually to get somewhere. Watching that, Tanner was oddly captivated by it, and found himself surprised suddenly to discover that his interest in the entire project was beginning to rekindle.

"Can you make him any bigger?" he asked. "I want to see his face."

"I can make him big as life," Richardson said. "Bigger. Any size you like. Here."

He flicked a finger and the hologram of Pizarro expanded instantaneously to a height of about two meters. The Spaniard halted in mid-stride as though he might actually be aware of the imaging change.

That can't be possible, Tanner thought. That isn't a living consciousness out there. Or is it?

Pizarro stood poised easily in mid-air, glowering, shading his eyes as if staring into a dazzling glow. There were brilliant streaks of color in the air all around him, like an aurora. He was a tall, lean man in late middle age with a grizzled beard and a hard, angular face. His lips were thin, his nose was sharp, his eyes were cold, shrewd, keen. It seemed to Tanner that those eyes had come to rest on him, and he felt a chill.

My God, Tanner thought, he's *real*.

It had been a French program to begin with, something developed at the Centre Mondiale de la Computation in Lyons about the year 2119. The French had some truly splendid minds working in software in those days. They worked up astounding programs, and then nobody did anything with them. That was *their* version of Century Twenty-Two Malaise.

The French programmers' idea was to use holograms of actual historical personages to dress up the *son et lumiere* tourist events at the great monuments of their national history. Not just pre-programmed robot mockups of the old Disneyland kind, which would stand around in front of Notre

9

Dame or the Arc de Triomphe or the Eiffel Tower and deliver canned spiels, but apparent reincarnations of the genuine great ones, who could freely walk and talk and answer questions and make little quips. Imagine Louis XIV demonstrating the fountains of Versailles, they said, or Picasso leading a tour of Paris museums, or Sartre sitting in his Left Bank cafe exchanging existential *bons mots* with passersby! Napoleon! Joan of Arc! Alexandre Dumas! Perhaps the simulations could do even more than that: perhaps they could be designed so well that they would be able to extend and embellish the achievements of their original lifetimes with new accomplishments, a fresh spate of paintings and novels and works of philosophy and great architectural visions by vanished masters.

The concept was simple enough in essence. Write an intelligencing program that could absorb data, digest it, correlate it, and generate further programs based on what you had given it. No real difficulty there. Then start feeding your program with the collected written works—if any—of the person to be simulated: that would provide not only a general sense of his ideas and positions but also of his underlying pattern of approach to situations, his style of thinking—for *le style*, after all, *est l'homme meme*. If no collected works happened to be available, why, find works *about* the subject by his contemporaries, and use those. Next, toss in the totality of the historical record of the subject's deeds, including all significant subsequent scholarly analyses, making appropriate allowances for conflicts in interpretation—indeed, taking advantages of such conflicts to generate a richer portrait, full of the ambiguities and contradictions that are the inescapable hallmarks of any human being. Now build in substrata of general cultural data of the proper period so that the subject has a loam of references and vocabulary out of which to create thoughts that are appropriate to his place in time and space. Stir. *Et voila!* Apply a little sophisticated imaging technology and you had a simulation capable of thinking and conversing and behaving as though it is the actual self after which it was patterned.

Of course, this would require a significant chunk of computer power. But that was no problem in a world where 150-gigaflops networks were standard laboratory items and ten-year-olds carried pencil-sized computers with capacities far beyond the ponderous mainframes of their great-great-grand-parents' day. No, there was no theoretical reason why the French project could not have succeeded. Once the Lyons programmers had worked out the basic intelligencing scheme that was needed to write the rest of the programs, it all should have followed smoothly enough.

Two things went wrong: one rooted in an excess of ambition that may have been a product of the peculiarly French personalities of the original programmers, and the other having to do with an abhorrence of failure typical of the major nations of the mid-twenty-second century, of which France was one.

The first was a fatal change of direction that the project underwent in its early phases. The King of

Spain was coming to Paris on a visit of state; and the programmers decided that in his honor they would synthesize Don Quixote for him as their initial project. Though the intelligencing program had been designed to simulate only individuals who had actually existed, there seemed no inherent reason why a fictional character as well documented as Don Quixote could not be produced instead. There was Cervantes' lengthy novel; there was ample background data available on the milieu in which Don Quixote supposedly had lived; there was a vast library of critical analysis of the book and of the Don's distinctive and flamboyant personality. Why should bringing Don Quixote to life out of a computer be any different from simulating Louis XIV, say, or Moliere, or Cardinal Richelieu? True, they had all existed once, and the knight of La Mancha was a mere figment; but had Cervantes not provided far more detail about Don Quixote's mind and soul than was known of Richelieu, or Moliere, or Louis XIV?

Indeed he had. The Don—like Oedipus, like Odysseus, like Othello, like David Copperfield— had come to have a reality far more profound and tangible than that of most people who had indeed actually lived. Such characters as those had transcended their fictional origins. But not so far as the computer was concerned. It was able to produce a convincing fabrication of Don Quixote, all right—a gaunt bizarre holographic figure that had all the right mannerisms, that ranted and raved in the expectable way, that referred knowledgeably to Dulcinea and Rosinante and Mambrino's helmet. The Spanish king was amused and impressed. But to the French the experiment was a failure. They had produced a Don Quixote who was hopelessly locked to the Spain of the late sixteenth century and to the book from which he had sprung. He had no capacity for independent life and thought—no way to perceive the world that had brought him into being, or to comment on it, or to interact with it. There was nothing new or interesting about that. Any actor could dress up in armor and put on a scraggly beard and recite snatches of Cervantes. What had come forth from the computer, after three years of work, was no more than a predictable reprocessing of what had gone into it, sterile, stale.

Which led the Centre Mondiale de la Computation to its next fatal step: abandoning the whole thing. *Zut!* and the project was cancelled without any further attempts. No simulated Picassos, no simulated Napoleons, no Joans of Arc. The Quixote event had soured everyone and no one had the heart to proceed with the work from there. Suddenly it had the taint of failure about it, and France—like Germany, like Australia, like the Han Commercial Sphere, like Brazil, like any of the dynamic centers of the modern world, had a horror of failure. Failure was something to be left to the backward nations or the decadent ones—to the Islamic Socialist Union, say, or the Soviet People's Republic, or to that slumbering giant, the United States of America. So the historic-personage simulation scheme was put aside.

The French thought so little of it, as a matter of

Robert Silverberg

fact, that after letting it lie fallow for a few years they licensed it to a bunch of Americans, who had heard about it somehow and felt it might be amusing to play with.

"You may really have done it this time," Tanner said.

"Yes. I think we have. After all those false starts."

Tanner nodded. How often had he come into this room with hopes high, only to see some botch, some inanity, some depressing bungle? Richardson had always had an explanation. Sherlock Holmes hadn't worked because he was fictional: that was a necessary recheck of the French Quixote project, demonstrating that fictional characters didn't have the right sort of reality texture to take proper advantage of the program, not enough ambiguity, not enough contradiction. King Arthur had failed for the same reason. Julius Caesar? Too far in the past, maybe: unreliable data, bordering on fiction. Moses? Ditto. Einstein? Too complex, perhaps, for the project in its present level of development: they needed more experience first. Queen Elizabeth I? George Washington? Mozart? We're learning more each time, Richardson insisted after each failure. This isn't black magic we're doing, you know. We aren't necromancers, we're programmers, and we have to figure out how to give the program what it needs.

And now Pizarro?

"Why do you want to work with *him?*" Tanner had asked, five or six months earlier. "A ruthless medieval Spanish imperialist, is what I remember

14

from school. A bloodthirsty despoiler of a great
culture. A man without morals, honor, faith—"

"You may be doing him an injustice," said Richardson. "He's had a bad press for centuries. And
there are things about him that fascinate me."

"Such as?"

"His drive. His courage. His absolute confidence.
The other side of ruthlessness, the good side of it,
is a total concentration on your task, an utter
unwillingness to be stopped by any obstacle.
Whether or not you approve of the things he
accomplished, you have to admire a man who—"

"All right," Tanner said, abruptly growing weary
of the whole enterprise. "Do Pizarro. Whatever
you want."

The months had passed. Richardson gave him
vague progress reports, nothing to arouse much
hope. But now Tanner stared at the tiny strutting
figure in the holotank and the conviction began to
grow in him that Richardson finally had figured
out how to use the simulation program as it was
meant to be used.

"So you've actually recreated him, you think?
Someone who lived—what, five hundred years ago?"

"He died in 1541," said Richardson.

"Almost six hundred, then."

"And he's not like the others—not simply a
recreation of a great figure out of the past who can
run through a set of pre-programmed speeches.
What we've got here, if I'm right, is an artificially
generated intelligence which can think for itself in
modes other than the ones its programmers think
in. Which has more information available to itself,

in other words, than we've provided it with. That would be the real accomplishment. That's the fundamental philosophical leap that we were going for when we first got involved with this project. To use the program to give us new programs that are capable of true autonomous thought—a program that can think like Pizarro, instead of like Lew Richardson's idea of some historian's idea of how Pizarro might have thought."

"Yes," Tanner said.

"Which means we won't just get back the expectable, the predictable. There'll be surprises. There's no way to learn anything, you know, except through surprises. The sudden combination of known components into something brand new. And that's what I think we've managed to bring off here, at long last. Harry, it may be the biggest artificial-intelligence breakthrough ever achieved."

Tanner pondered that. Was it so? Had they truly done it?

And if they had—

Something new and troubling was beginning to occur to him, much later in the game than it should have. Tanner stared at the holographic figure floating in the center of the tank, that fierce old man with the harsh face and the cold, cruel eyes. He thought about what sort of man he must have been—the man after whom this image had been modeled. A man who was willing to land in South America at age fifty or sixty or whatever he had been, an ignorant illiterate Spanish peasant wearing a suit of ill-fitting armor and waving a rusty sword, and set out to conquer a great empire of millions of people spreading over thousands of miles. Tanner wondered what sort of man would be capable of carrying out a thing like that. Now that man's eyes were staring into his own and it was a struggle to meet so implacable a gaze.

After a moment he looked away. His left leg began to quiver. He glanced uneasily at Richardson.

"Look at those eyes, Lew. Christ, they're scary!"

"I know. I designed them myself, from the old prints."

"Do you think he's seeing us right now? Can he do that?"

"All he is is software, Harry."

"He seemed to know it when you expanded the image."

Richardson shrugged. "He's very good software. I tell you, he's got autonomy, he's got volition. He's got an electronic *mind,* is what I'm saying. He may have perceived a transient voltage kick. But there are limits to his perceptions, all the same. I don't think there's any way that he can see anything that's outside the holotank unless it's fed to him in the form of data he can process, which hasn't been done."

"You don't *think?* You aren't sure?"

"Harry. Please."

"This man conquered the entire enormous In-can empire with fifty soldiers, didn't he?"

"In fact I believe it was more like a hundred and fifty."

"Fifty, a hundred fifty, what's the difference? Who knows what you've actually got here? What if you did an even better job than you suspect?"

"What are you saying?"

"What I'm saying is, I'm uneasy all of a sudden. For a long time I didn't think this project was going to produce anything at all. Suddenly I'm starting to think that maybe it's going to produce more than we can handle. I don't want any of your goddamned simulations walking out of the tank and conquering *us*."

Richardson turned to him. His face was flushed, but he was grinning. "Harry, Harry! For God's sake! Five minutes ago you didn't think we had anything at all here except a tiny picture that wasn't even in focus. Now you've gone so far the other way that you're imagining the the worst kind of—"

"I see his eyes, Lew. I'm worried that his eyes see me."

"Those aren't real eyes you're looking at. What you see is nothing but a graphics program projected into a holotank. There's no visual capacity there as you understand the concept. His eyes will see you only if I want them to. Right now they don't."

"But you can make them see me?"

"I can make them see anything I want them to see. I created him, Harry."

"With volition. With autonomy."

"After all this time you start worrying *now* about these things?"

"It's my neck on the line if something that you guys on the technical side make runs amok. This autonomy thing suddenly troubles me."

"I'm still the one with the data gloves," Richard-

18

son said. "I twitch my fingers and he dances.
That's not really Pizarro down there, remember.
And that's no Frankenstein monster either. It's
just a simulation. It's just so much data, just a
bunch of electromagnetic impulses that I can shut
off with one movement of my pinkie."

"Do it, then."

"Shut him off? But I haven't begun to show
you—"

"Shut him off, and then turn him on," Tanner
said.

Richardson looked bothered. "If you say so,
Harry."

He moved a finger. The image of Pizarro vanished from the holotank. Swirling gray mists moved
in it for a moment, and then all was white wool.
Tanner felt a quick jolt of guilt, as though he had
just ordered the execution of the man in the medieval armor. Richardson gestured again, and color
flashed across the tank, and then Pizarro reap-
peared.

"I just wanted to see how much autonomy your
little guy really has," said Tanner. "Whether he
was quick enough to head you off and escape into
some other channel before you could cut his power."

"You really don't understand how this works at
all, do you, Harry?"

"I just wanted to see," said Tanner again, sullenly. After a moment's silence he said, "Do you
ever feel like God?"

"Like God?"

"You breathed life in. Life of a sort, anyway.
But you breathed free will in, too. That's what this

19

experiment is all about, isn't it? All your talk about volition and autonomy? You're trying to recreate a human mind—which means to create it all over again—a mind that can think in its own special way, and come up with its own unique responses to situations, which will not necessarily be the responses that its programmers might anticipate, in fact almost certainly will not be, and which might not be all that desirable or beneficial, either, and you simply have to allow for that risk, just as God, once he gave free will to mankind, knew that He was likely to see all manner of evil deeds being performed by His creations as they exercised that free will—"

"Please, Harry—"

"Listen, is it possible for me to talk with your Pizarro?"

"Why?"

"By way of finding out what you've got there. To get some first-hand knowledge of what the project has accomplished. Or you could say I just want to test the quality of the simulation. Whatever. I'd feel more a part of this thing, more aware of what it's all about in here, if I could have some direct contact with him. Would it be all right if I did that?"

"Yes. Of course."

"Do I have to talk to him in Spanish?"

"In any language you like. There's an interface, after all. He'll think it's his own language coming in, no matter what, sixteenth-century Spanish. And he'll answer you in what seems like Spanish to him, but you'll hear it in English."

"Are you sure?"

"Of course."

"And you don't mind if I make contact with him?"

"Whatever you like."

"It won't upset his calibration, or anything?"

"It won't do any harm at all, Harry."

"Fine. Let me talk to him, then."

There was a disturbance in the air ahead, a shifting, a swirling, like a little whirlwind. Pizarro halted and watched it for a moment, wondering what was coming next. A demon arriving to torment him, maybe. Or an angel. Whatever it was, he was ready for it.

Then a voice out of the whirlwind said, in that same comically exaggerated Castilian Spanish that Pizarro himself had found himself speaking a little while before, "Can you hear me?"

"I hear you, yes. I don't see you. Where are you?"

"Right in front of you. Wait a second. I'll show you." Out of the whirlwind came a strange face that hovered in the middle of nowhere, a face without a body, a lean face, close-shaven, no beard at all, no moustache, the hair cut very short, dark eyes set close together. He had never seen a face like that before.

"What are you?" Pizarro asked. "A demon or an angel?"

"Neither one." Indeed he didn't sound very demonic. "A man, just like you."

21

"Not much like me, I think. Is a face all there is to you, or do you have a body, too?"

"All you see of me is a face?"

"Yes."

"Wait a second."

"I will wait as long as I have to. I have plenty of time."

The face disappeared. Then it returned, attached to the body of a big, wide-shouldered man who was wearing a long loose gray robe, something like a priest's cassock, but much more ornate, with points of glowing light gleaming on it everywhere. Then the body vanished and Pizarro could see only the face again. He could make no sense out of any of this. He began to understand how the Indians must have felt when the first Spaniards came over the horizon, riding horses, carrying guns, wearing armor.

"You are very strange. Are you an Englishman, maybe?"

"American."

"Ah," Pizarro said, as though that made things better. "An American. And what is that?"

The face wavered and blurred for a moment. There was mysterious new agitation in the thick white clouds surrounding it. Then the face grew steady and said, "America is a country north of Peru. A very large country, where many people live."

"You mean New Spain, which was Mexico, where my kinsman Cortes is Captain-General?"

"North of Mexico. Far to the north of it."

Pizarro shrugged. "I know nothing of those places.

Or not very much. There is an island called Florida, yes? And stories of cities of gold, but I think they are only stories. I found the gold, in Peru. Enough to choke on, I found. Tell me this, am I in heaven now?"

"No."

"Then this is hell?"

"Not that, either. Where you are—it's very difficult to explain, actually—"

"I am in America."

"Yes. In America, yes."

"And am I dead?"

There was silence for a moment.

"No, not dead," the voice said uneasily.

"You are lying to me, I think."

"How could we be speaking with each other, if you were dead?"

Pizarro laughed hoarsely. "Are you asking *me*? I understand nothing of what is happening to me in this place. Where are my priests? Where is my page? Send me my brother!" He glared. "Well? Why don't you get them for me?"

"They aren't here. You're here all by yourself, Don Francisco."

"In America. All by myself in your America. Show me your America, then. Is there such a place? Is America all clouds and whorls of light? Where is America? Let me see America. Prove to me that I am in America."

There was another silence, longer than the last. Then the face disappeared and the wall of white cloud began to boil and churn more fiercely than before. Pizarro stared into the midst of it, feeling a

23

mingled sense of curiosity and annoyance. The face did not reappear. He saw nothing at all. He was being toyed with. He was a prisoner in some strange place and they were treating him like a child; like a dog, like—like an Indian. Perhaps this was the retribution for what he had done to King Atahuallpa, then, that fine noble foolish man who had given himself up to him in all innocence, and whom he had put to death so that he might have the gold of Atahuallpa's kingdom.

Well, so be it, Pizarro thought. Atahuallpa accepted all that befell him without complaint and without fear, and so will I. Christ will be my guardian, and if there is no Christ, well, then I will have no guardian, and so be it. So be it.

The voice out of the whirlwind said suddenly, "Look, Don Francisco. This is America."

A picture appeared on the wall of cloud. It was a kind of picture Pizarro had never before encountered or even imagined, one that seemed to open before him like a gate and sweep him in and carry him along through a vista of changing scenes depicted in brilliant, vivid bursts of color. It was like flying high above the land, looking down on an infinite scroll of miracles. He saw vast cities without walls, roadways that unrolled like endless skeins of white ribbon, huge lakes, mighty rivers, gigantic mountains, everything speeding past him so swiftly that he could scarcely absorb any of it. In moments it all became chaotic in his mind: the buildings taller than the highest cathedral spire, the swarming masses of people, the shining metal chariots without beasts to draw them, the stupendous landscapes, the close-packed complexity of it all. Watching all this, he felt the fine old hunger taking possession of him again: he wanted to grasp this strange vast place, and seize it, and clutch it close, and ransack it for all it was worth. But the thought of that was overwhelming. His eyes grew glassy and his heart began to pound so terrifyingly that he supposed he would be able to feel it thumping if he put his hand to the front of his armor. He turned away, muttering, "Enough. Enough."

The terrifying picture vanished. Gradually the clamor of his heart subsided.

Then he began to laugh.

"Peru!" he cried. "Peru was nothing, next to your America! Peru was a hole! Peru was mud! How ignorant I was! I went to Peru, when there was America, ten thousand times as grand! I wonder what I could find, in America." He smacked his lips and winked. Then, chuckling, he said, "But don't be afraid. I won't try to conquer your America. I'm too old for that now. And perhaps America would have been too much for me, even before. Perhaps." He grinned savagely at the troubled staring face of the short-haired beardless man, the American. "I really am dead, is this not so? I feel no hunger, I feel no pain, no thirst, when I put my hand to my body I do not feel even my body. I am like one who lies dreaming. But this is no dream. Am I a ghost?"

"Not—exactly."

"Not exactly a ghost! Not exactly! No one with half the brains of a pig would talk like that. What is that supposed to mean?"

"It's not easy explaining it in words you would understand, Don Francisco."

"No, of course not. I am very stupid, as everyone knows, and that is why I conquered Peru, because I was so very stupid. But let it pass. I am not exactly a ghost, but I am dead all the same, right?"

"Well—"

"I am dead, yes. But somehow I have not gone to hell or even to purgatory but I am still in the world, only it is much later now. I have slept as the dead sleep, and now I have awakened in some year that is far beyond my time, and it is the time of America. Is this not so? Who is king now? Who is pope? What year is this? 1750? 1800?"

"The year 2130," the face said, after some hesitation.

"Ah." Pizarro tugged thoughtfully at his lower lip. "And the king? Who is the king?"

A long pause. "Alfonso is his name," said the face.

"Alfonso? The kings of Aragon were called Alfonso. The father of Ferdinand, he was Alfonso. Alfonso V, he was."

"Alfonso XIX is King of Spain now."

"Ah. Ah. And the pope? Who is the pope?"

A pause again. Not to know the name of the pope, immediately upon being asked? How strange. Demon or no, this was a fool.

"Pius," said the voice, when some time had passed. "Pius XVI."

"The sixteenth Pius," said Pizarro somberly. "Jesus and Mary, the sixteenth Pius! What has

26

become of me? Long dead, is what I am. Still unwashed of all my sins. I can feel them clinging to my skin like mud, still. And you are a sorcerer, you American, and you have brought me to life again. Eh? Eh? Is that not so?"

"It is something like that, Don Francisco," the face admitted.

"So you speak your Spanish strangely because you no longer understand the right way of speaking it. Eh? Even I speak Spanish in a strange way, and I speak it in a voice that does not sound like my own. No one speaks Spanish any more, eh? Eh? Only American, they speak. Eh? But you try to speak Spanish, only it comes out stupidly. And you have caused me to speak the same way, thinking it is the way I spoke, though you are wrong. Well, you can do miracles, but I suppose you can't do everything perfectly, even in this land of miracles of the year 2130. Eh? Eh?" Pizarro leaned forward intently. "What do you say? You thought I was a fool, because I don't have reading and writing? I am not so ignorant, eh? I understand things quickly."

"You understand very quickly indeed."

"But you have knowledge of many things that are unknown to me. You must know the manner of my death, for example. How strange that is, talking to you of the manner of my death, but you must know it, eh? When did it come to me? And how? Did it come in my sleep? No, no, how could that be? They die in their sleep in Spain, but not in Peru. How was it, then? I was set upon by cowards, was I? Some brother of Atahuallpa, fall-

27

ing upon me as I stepped out of my house? A slave sent by the Inca Manco, or one of those others? No. No. The Indians would not harm me, for all that I did to them. It was the young Almagro who took me down, was it not, in vengeance for his father, or Juan de Herrada, eh? Or perhaps even Picado, my own secretary—no, not Picado, he was my man, always—but maybe Alvarado, the young one, Diego—well, one of those, and it would have been sudden, very sudden or I would have been able to stop them—am I right, am I speaking the truth? Tell me. You know these things. Tell me of the manner of my dying." There was no answer. Pizarro shaded his eyes and peered into the dazzling pearly whiteness. He was no longer able to see the face of the American. "Are you there?" Pizarro said. "Where have you gone? Were you only a dream? American! American! Where have you gone?"

The break in contact was jolting. Tanner sat rigid, hands trembling, lips tightly clamped. Pizarro, in the holotank, was no more than a distant little streak of color now, no larger than his thumb, gesticulating amid the swirling clouds. The vitality of him, the arrogance, the fierce probing curiosity, the powerful hatreds and jealousies, the strength that had come from vast ventures recklessly conceived and desperately seen through to triumph, all the things that were Francisco Pizarro, all that Tanner had felt an instant before—all that had vanished at the flick of a finger.

After a moment or two Tanner felt the shock beginning to ease. He turned toward Richardson.

"What happened?"

"I had to pull you out of there. I didn't want you telling him anything about how he died."

"I don't know how he died."

"Well, neither does he, and I didn't want to chance it that you did. There's no predicting what sort of psychological impact that kind of knowledge might have on him."

"You talk about him as though he's alive."

"Isn't he?" Richardson said.

"If I said a thing like that, you'd tell me that I was being ignorant and unscientific."

Richardson smiled faintly. "You're right. But somehow I trust myself to know what I'm saying when I say that he's alive. I know I don't mean it literally and I'm not sure about you. What did you think of him, anyway?"

"He's amazing," Tanner said. "Really amazing. The strength of him—I could feel it pouring out at me in waves. And his mind! So quick, the way he picked up on everything. Guessing that he must be in the future. Wanting to know what number pope was in office. Wanting to see what America looked like. And the cockiness of him! Telling me that he's not up to the conquest of America, that he might have tried for it instead of Peru a few years earlier, but not now, now he's a little too old for that. Incredible! Nothing could faze him for long, even when he realized that he must have been dead for a long time. Wanting to know how he died, even!" Tanner frowned. "What age did you make him, anyway, when you put this program together?"

"About sixty. Five or six years after the conquest, and a year or two before he died. At the height of his power, that is."

"I suppose you couldn't have let him have any knowledge of his actual death. That way he'd be too much like some kind of a ghost."

"That's what we thought. We set the cutoff at a time when he had done everything that he had set out to do, when he was the complete Pizarro. But before the end. He didn't need to know about that. Nobody does. That's why I had to yank you, you see? In case you knew. And started to tell him."

Tanner shook his head. "If I ever knew, I've forgotten it. How did it happen?"

"Exactly as he guessed: at the hands of his own comrades."

"So he saw it coming."

"At the age we made him, he already knew that a civil war had started in South America, that the conquistadores were quarreling over the division of the spoils. We built that much into him. He knows that his partner Almagro has turned against him and been beaten in battle, and that they've executed him. What he doesn't know, but obviously can expect, is that Almagro's friends are going to break into his house and try to kill him. He's got it all figured out pretty much as it's going to happen. As it *did* happen, I should say."

"Incredible. To be that shrewd."

"He was a son of a bitch, yes. But he was a genius, too."

"Was he, really? Or is it that you made him one when you set up the program for him?"

"All we put in were the objective details of his life, patterns of event and response. Plus an overlay of commentary by others, his contemporaries and later historians familiar with the record, providing an extra dimension of character density. Put in enough of that kind of stuff and apparently they add up to the whole personality. It isn't *my* personality or that of anybody else who worked on this project, Harry. When you put in Pizarro's set of events and responses you wind up getting Pizarro. You get the ruthlessness and you get the brilliance. Put in a different set, you get someone else. And what we've finally seen, this time, is that when we do our work right we get something out of the computer that's bigger than the sum of what we put in."

"Are you sure?"

Richardson said, "Did you notice that he complained about the Spanish that he thought you were speaking?"

"Yes. He said that it sounded strange, that nobody seemed to know how to speak proper Spanish any more. I didn't quite follow that. Does the interface you built speak lousy Spanish?"

"Evidently it speaks lousy sixteenth-century Spanish," Richardson said. "Nobody knows what sixteenth-century Spanish actually sounded like. We can only guess. Apparently we didn't guess very well."

"But how would *he* know? You synthesized him in the first place! If you don't know how Spanish sounded in his time, how would he? All he should know about Spanish, or about anything, is what you put into him."

"Exactly," Richardson said.

"But that doesn't make any sense, Lew!"

"He also said that the Spanish he heard himself speaking was no good, and that his own voice didn't sound right to him either. That we had *caused* him to speak this way, thinking that was how he actually spoke, but we were wrong."

"How could he possibly know what his voice really sounded like, if all he is is a simulation put together by people who don't have the slightest notion of what his voice really—"

"I don't have any idea," said Richardson quietly. "But he *does* know."

"Does he? Or is this just some diabolical Pizarro-like game that he's playing to unsettle us, because *that's* in his character as you devised it?"

"I think he does know," Richardson said.

"Where's he finding it out, then?"

"It's there. We don't know where, but he does. It's somewhere in the data that we put through the permutation network, even if we don't know it and even though we couldn't find it now if we set out to look for it. *He* can find it. He can't manufacture that kind of knowledge by magic, but he can assemble what look to us like seemingly irrelevant bits and come up with new information leading to a conclusion which is meaningful to him. That's what we mean by artificial intelligence, Harry.

We've finally got a program that works something like the human brain: by leaps of intuition so sudden and broad that they seem inexplicable and non-quantifiable, even if they really aren't. We've fed in enough stuff so that he can assimilate a whole stew of ostensibly unrelated data and come up with new information. We don't just have a ventriloquist's dummy in that tank. We've got something that thinks it's Pizarro and thinks like Pizarro and knows things that Pizarro knew and we don't. Which means we've accomplished the qualitative jump in artificial intelligence capacity that we set out to achieve with this project. It's awesome. I get shivers down my back when I think about it."

"I do, too," Tanner said. "But not so much from awe as fear."

"Fear?"

"Knowing now that he has capabilities beyond those he was programmed for, how can you be so absolutely certain that he can't commandeer your network somehow and get himself loose?"

"It's technically impossible. All he is is electromagnetic impulses. I can pull the plug on him any time I like. There's nothing to panic over here. Believe me, Harry."

"I'm trying to."

"I can show you the schematics. We've got a phenomenal simulation in that computer, yes. But it's still only a simulation. It isn't a vampire, it isn't a werewolf, it isn't anything supernatural. It's just the best damned computer simulation anyone's ever made."

"It makes me uneasy. *He* makes me uneasy."

"He should. The power of the man, the indomitable nature of him—why do you think I summoned him up, Harry? He's got something that we don't understand in this country any more. I want us to study him. I want us to try to learn what that kind of drive and determination is really like. Now that you've talked to him, now that you've touched his spirit, of course you're shaken up by him. He radiates tremendous confidence. He radiates fantastic faith in himself. That kind of man can achieve anything he wants—even conquer the whole Inca empire with a hundred fifty men, or however many it was. But I'm not frightened of what we've put together here. And you shouldn't be either. We should all be damned proud of it. You as well as the people on the technical side. And you will be, too."

"I hope you're right," Tanner said.

"You'll see."

For a long moment Tanner stared in silence at the holotank, where the image of Pizarro had been.

"Okay," said Tanner finally. "Maybe I'm overreacting. Maybe I'm sounding like the ignoramus layman that I am. I'll take it on faith that you'll be able to keep your phantoms in their boxes."

"We will," Richardson said.

"Let's hope so. All right," said Tanner. "So what's your next move?"

Richardson looked puzzled. "My next move?"

"With this project? Where does it go from here?"

Hesitantly Richardson said, "There's no formal proposal yet. We thought we'd wait until we had approval from you on the initial phase of the work, and then—"

"How does this sound?" Tanner asked. "I'd like to see you start in on another simulation right away."

"Well—yes, yes, of course—"

"And when you've got him worked up, Lew, would it be feasible for you to put him right there in the tank with Pizarro?"

Richardson looked startled. "To have a sort of dialog with him, you mean?"

"Yes."

"I suppose we could do that," Richardson said cautiously. "*Should* do that. Yes. Yes. A very interesting suggestion, as a matter of fact." He ventured an uneasy smile. Up till now Tanner had kept in the background of this project, a mere management functionary, an observer, virtually an outsider. This was something new, his interjecting himself into the planning process, and plainly Richardson didn't know what to make of it. Tanner watched him fidget. After a little pause Richardson said, "Was there anyone particular you had in mind for us to try next?"

"Is that new parallax thing of yours ready to try?" Tanner asked. "The one that's supposed to compensate for time distortion and myth contamination?"

"Just about. But we haven't tested—"

"Good," Tanner said. "Here's your chance. What about trying for Socrates?"

There was billowing whiteness below him, and on every side, as though all the world were made of fleece. He wondered if it might be snow. That was not something he was really familiar with. It snowed once in a great while in Athens, yes, but usually only a light dusting that melted in the morning sun. Of course he had seen snow aplenty when he had been up north in the war, at Potidaea, in the time of Pericles. But that had been long ago; and that stuff, as best he remembered it, had not been much like this. There was no quality of coldness about the whiteness that surrounded him now. It could just as readily be great banks of clouds.

But what would clouds be doing *below* him? Clouds, he thought, are mere vapor, air and water, no substance to them at all. Their natural place was overhead. Clouds that gathered at one's feet had no true quality of cloudness about them.

Snow that had no coldness? Clouds that had no buoyancy? Nothing in this place seemed to possess any quality that was proper to itself in this place, including himself. He seemed to be walking, but his feet touched nothing at all. It was more like moving through air. But how could one move in the air? Aristophanes, in that mercilessly mocking play of his, had sent him floating through the clouds suspended in a basket, and made him say things like, "I am traversing the air and contemplating the sun." That was Aristophanes' way of playing with him, and he had not been seriously upset, though his friends had been very hurt on his behalf. Still, that was only a play.

This felt real, insofar as it felt like anything at all.

Perhaps he was dreaming, and the nature of his dream was that he thought he was really doing the things he had done in Aristophanes' play. What was that lovely line? "I have to suspend my brain and mingle the subtle essence of my mind with this air, which is of the same nature, in order clearly to penetrate the things of heaven." Good old Aristophanes! Nothing was sacred to him! Except, of course, those things that were truly sacred, such as wisdom, truth, virtue. "I would have discovered nothing if I had remained on the ground and pondered from below the things that are above: for the earth by its force attracts the sap of the mind to itself. It's the same way with watercress." And Socrates began to laugh.

He held his hands before him and studied them, the short sturdy fingers, the thick powerful wrists. His hands, yes. His old plain hands that had stood him in good stead all his life, when he had worked as a stonemason as his father had, when he had fought in his city's wars, when he had trained at the gymnasium. But now when he touched them to his face he felt nothing. There should be a chin here, a forehead, yes, a blunt stubby nose, thick lips; but there was nothing. He was touching air. He could put his hand right through the place where his face should be. He could put one hand against the other, and press with all his might, and feel nothing.

This is a very strange place indeed, he thought.

Perhaps it is that place of pure forms that young Plato liked to speculate about, where everything is perfect and nothing is quite real. Those are ideal clouds all around me, not real ones. This is ideal air upon which I walk. I myself am the ideal Socrates, liberated from my coarse ordinary body. Could it be? Well, maybe so. He stood for a while, considering that possibility. The thought came to him that this might be the life after life, in which case he might meet some of the gods, if there were any gods in the first place, and if he could manage to find them. I would like that, he thought. Perhaps they would be willing to speak with me. Athena would discourse with me on wisdom, or Hermes on speed, or Ares on the nature of courage, or Zeus on—well, whatever Zeus cared to speak on. Of course, I would seem to be the merest fool to them, but that would be all right: anyone who expects to hold discourse with the gods as though he were their equal *is* a fool. I have no such illusion. If there are gods at all, surely they are far superior to me in all respects, for otherwise, why would men regard them as gods?

Of course he had serious doubts that the gods existed at all. But if they did, it was reasonable to think that they might be found in a place such as this.

He looked up. The sky was radiant with brilliant golden light. He took a deep breath and smiled and set out across the fleecy nothingness of this airy world to see if he could find the gods.

Tanner said, "What do you think now? Still so pessimistic?"

"It's too early to say," said Richardson, looking glum.

"He *looks* like Socrates, doesn't he?"

"That was the easy part. We've got plenty of descriptions of Socrates that came down from people who knew him, the flat wide nose, the bald head, the thick lips, the short neck. A standard Socrates face that everybody recognizes, just as they do Sherlock Holmes, or Don Quixote. So that's how we made him look. It doesn't signify anything important. It's what's going on inside his head that'll determine whether we really have Socrates."

"He seems calm and good-humored as he wanders around in there. The way a philosopher should."

"Pizarro seemed just as much of a philosopher when we turned him loose in the tank."

"Pizarro may *be* just as much of a philosopher," Tanner said. "Neither man's the sort who'd be likely to panic if he found himself in some mysterious place." Richardson's negativism was beginning to bother him. It was as if the two men had exchanged places: Richardson now uncertain of the range and power of his own program, Tanner pushing the way on and on toward bigger and better things.

Bleakly Richardson said, "I'm still pretty skeptical. We've tried the new parallax filters, yes. But I'm afraid we're going to run into the same problem the French did with Don Quixote, and that we did with Holmes and Moses and Caesar. There's too much contamination of the data by myth and fantasy. The Socrates who has come down to us is as much fictional as real, or maybe *all* fictional.

39

For all we know, Plato made up everything we think we know about him, the same way Conan Doyle made up Holmes. And what we're going to get, I'm afraid, will be something second-hand, something lifeless, something lacking in the spark of self-directed intelligence that we're after."

"But the new filters—"

"Perhaps. Perhaps."

Tanner shook his head stubbornly. "Holmes and Don Quixote are fiction through and through. They exist in only one dimension, constructed for us by their authors. You cut through the distortions and fantasies of later readers and commentators and all you find underneath is a made-up character. A lot of Socrates may have been invented by Plato for his own purposes, but a lot wasn't. He really existed. He took an actual part in civic activities in fifth-century Athens. He figures in books by a lot of other contemporaries of his besides Plato's dialogues. That gives us the parallax you're looking for, doesn't it—the view of him from more than one viewpoint?"

"Maybe it does. Maybe not. We got nowhere with Moses. Was *he* fictional?"

"Who can say? All you had to go by was the Bible. And a ton of Biblical commentary, for whatever that was worth. Not much, apparently."

"And Caesar? You're not going to tell me that Caesar wasn't real," said Richardson. "But what we have of him is evidently contaminated with myth. When we synthesized him we got nothing but a caricature, and I don't have to remind you how fast even that broke down into sheer gibberish."

"Not relevant," Tanner said. "Caesar was early in the project. You know much more about what you're doing now. I think this is going to work."

Richardson's dogged pessimism, Tanner decided, must be a defense mechanism, designed to insulate himself against the possibility of a new failure. Socrates, after all hadn't been Richardson's own choice. And this was the first time he had used these new enhancement methods, the parallax program that was the latest refinement of the process.

Tanner looked at him. Richardson remained silent.

"Go on," Tanner said. "Bring up Pizarro and let the two of them talk to each other. Then we'll find out what sort of Socrates you've conjured up here."

Once again there was a disturbance in the distance, a little dark blur on the pearly horizon, a blotch, a flaw in the gleaming whiteness. Another demon is arriving, Pizarro thought. Or perhaps it is the same one as before, the American, the one who liked to show himself only as a face, with short hair and no beard.

But as this one drew closer Pizarro saw that he was different from the last, short and stocky, with broad shoulders and a deep chest. He was nearly bald and his thick beard was coarse and unkempt. He looked old, at least sixty, maybe sixty-five. He looked very ugly, too, with bulging eyes and a flat nose that had wide, flaring nostrils, and a neck so short that his oversized head seemed to sprout straight from his trunk. All he wore was a thin, ragged brown robe. His feet were bare.

41

"You, there," Pizarro called out. "You! Demon! Are you also an American, demon?"

"Your pardon. An Athenian, did you say?"

"*American* is what I said. That's what the last one was. Is that where you come from, too, demon? America?"

A shrug. "No, I think not. I am of Athens." There was a curious mocking twinkle in the demon's eyes.

"A Greek? This demon is a Greek?"

"I am of Athens," the ugly one said again. "My name is Socrates, the son of Sophroniscus. I could not tell you what a Greek is, so perhaps I may be one, but I think not, unless a Greek is what you call a man of Athens." He spoke in a slow, plodding way, like one who was exceedingly stupid. Pizarro had sometimes met men like this before, and in his experience they were generally not as stupid as they wanted to be taken for. He felt caution rising in him. "And I am no demon, but just a plain man: very plain, as you can easily see."

Pizarro snorted. "You like to chop words, do you?"

"It is not the worst of amusements, my friend," said the other, and put his hands together behind his back in the most casual way, and stood there calmly, smiling, looking off into the distance, rocking back and forth on the balls of his feet.

"Well?" Tanner said. "Do we have Socrates or not? I say that's the genuine article there."

Richardson looked up and nodded. He seemed relieved and quizzical both at once. "So far so

42

good, I have to say. He's coming through real and true."

"Yes."

"We may actually have worked past the problem of information contamination that ruined some of the earlier simulations. We're not getting any of the signal degradation we encountered then."

"He's some character, isn't he?" Tanner said. "I liked the way he just walked right up to Pizarro without the slightest sign of uneasiness. He's not at all afraid of him."

"Why should he be?" Richardson asked.

"Wouldn't you? If you were walking along through God knows what kind of unearthly place, not knowing where you were or how you got there, and suddenly you saw a ferocious-looking bastard like Pizarro standing in front of you wearing full armor and carrying a sword—" Tanner shook his head. "Well, maybe not. He's Socrates, after all, and Socrates wasn't afraid of anything except boredom."

"And Pizarro's just a simulation. Nothing but software."

"So you've been telling me all along. But Socrates doesn't know that."

"True," Richardson said. He seemed lost in thought a moment. "Perhaps there *is* some risk."

"Huh?"

"If our Socrates is anything like the one in Plato, and he surely ought to be, then he's capable of making a considerable pest of himself. Pizarro may not care for Socrates' little verbal games. If he doesn't feel like playing, I suppose there's a theoretical possibility that he'll engage in some sort of aggressive response."

That took Tanner by surprise. He swung around and said, "Are you telling me that there's some way he can *harm* Socrates?"

"Who knows?" said Richardson. "In the real world one program can certainly crash another one. Maybe one simulation can be dangerous to another one. This is all new territory for all of us, Harry. Including the people in the tank."

The tall grizzled-looking man, said, scowling, "You tell me you're an Athenian, but not a Greek. What sense am I supposed to make of that? I could ask Pedro de Candia, I guess, who is a Greek but not an Athenian. But he's not here. Perhaps you're just a fool, eh? Or you think I am."

"I have no idea what you are. Could it be that you are a god?"

"A *god*?"

"Yes," Socrates said. He studied the other impassively. His face was harsh, his gaze was cold. "Perhaps you are Ares. You have a fierce warlike look about you, and you wear armor, but not such armor as I have ever seen. This place is so strange that it might well be the abode of the gods, and that could be a god's armor you wear, I suppose. If you are Ares, then I salute you with the respect that is due you. I am Socrates of Athens, the stonemason's son."

"You talk a lot of nonsense. I don't know your Ares."

"Why, the god of war, of course! Everyone knows

that. Except barbarians, that is. Are you a barbarian, then? You sound like one, I must say—but then, I seem to sound like a barbarian myself, and I've spoken the tongue of Hellas all my life. There are many mysteries here, indeed."

"Your language problem again," Tanner said. "Couldn't you even get classical Greek to come out right? Or are they both speaking Spanish to each other?"

"Pizarro thinks they're speaking Spanish. Socrates thinks they're speaking Greek. And of course the Greek is off. We don't know how *anything* that was spoken before the age of recordings sounded. All we can do is guess."

"But can't you—"

"Shh," Richardson said.

Pizarro said, "I may be a bastard, but I'm no barbarian, fellow, so curb your tongue. And let's have no more blasphemy out of you either."

"If I blaspheme, forgive me. It is in innocence. Tell me where I trespass, and I will not do it again."

"This crazy talk of gods. Of my being a god. I'd expect a heathen to talk like that, but not a Greek. But maybe you're a heathen kind of Greek, and not to be blamed. It's heathens who see gods everywhere. Do I look like a god to you? I am Francisco Pizarro, of Trujillo in Estremadura, the son of the famous soldier Gonzalo Pizarro, colonel of infantry, who served in the wars of Gonzalo de Cordova whom men call the Great Captain. I have fought some wars myself."

45

"Then you are not a god but simply a soldier? Good. I have been a soldier myself. I am more at ease with soldiers than with gods, as most people are, I would think."

"A soldier? You?" Pizarro smiled. This shabby ordinary little man, more bedraggled-looking than any self-respecting groom would be, a soldier? "In which wars?"

"The wars of Athens. I fought at Potidaea, where the Corinthians were making trouble, and withholding the tribute that was due us. It was very cold there, and the siege was long and bleak, but we did our duty. I fought again some years later at Delium against the Boeotians. Laches was our general then, but it went badly for us,, and we did our best fighting in retreat. And then," Socrates said, "when Brasidas was in Amphipolis, and they sent Cleon to drive him out, I—"

"Enough," said Pizarro with an impatient wave of his hand. "These wars are unknown to me." A private soldier, a man of the ranks, no doubt. "Well, then this is the place where they send dead soldiers, I suppose."

"Are we dead, then?"

"Long ago. There's an Alfonso who's king, and a Pius who's pope, and you wouldn't believe their numbers. Pius the Sixteenth, I think the demon said. And the American said also that it is the year 2130. The last year that I can remember was 1539. What about you?"

The one who called himself Socrates shrugged again. "In Athens we use a different reckoning. But let us say, for argument's sake, that we are dead. I think that is very likely, considering what sort of place this seems to be, and how airy I find my body to be. So we have died, and this is the life after life. I wonder: is this a place where virtuous men are sent, or those who were not virtuous? Or do all men go to the same place after death, whether they were virtuous or not? What would you say?"

"I haven't figured that out yet," said Pizarro.

"Well, were you virtuous in your life, or not?"

"Did I sin, you mean?"

"Yes, we could use that word."

"Did I sin, he wants to know," said Pizarro, amazed. "He asks, Was I a sinner? Did I live a virtuous life? What business is that of his?"

"Humor me," said Socrates. "For the sake of the argument, if you will, allow me a few small questions—"

"So it's starting," Tanner said. "You see? You really *did* do it! Socrates is drawing him into a dialog!"

Richardson's eyes were glowing. "He is, yes. How marvelous this is, Harry!"

"Socrates is going to talk rings around him."

"I'm not so sure of that," Richardson said.

"I gave as good as I got," said Pizarro. "If I was injured, I gave injury back. There's no sin in that. It's only common sense. A man does what is necessary to survive and to protect his place in the world. Sometimes I might forget a fast day, yes, or use the Lord's name in vain—those are sins, I

47

suppose, Fray Vicente was always after me for things like that—but does that make me a sinner? I did my penances as soon as I could find time for them. It's a sinful world and I'm no different from anyone else, so why be harsh on me? Eh? God made me as I am. I'm done in His image. And I have faith in His son."

"So you are a virtuous man, then."

"I'm not a sinner, at any rate. As I told you, if ever I sinned I did my contrition, which made it the same as if the sin hadn't ever happened."

"Indeed," said Socrates. "Then you are a virtuous man and I have come to a good place. But I want to be absolutely sure. Tell me again: is your conscience completely clear?"

"What are you, a confessor?"

"Only an ignorant man seeking understanding. Which you can provide, by taking part with me in the exploration. If I have come to the place of virtuous men, then I must have been virtuous myself when I lived. Ease my mind, therefore, and let me know whether there is anything on your soul that you regret having done."

Pizarro stirred uneasily. "Well," he said, "I killed a king."

"A wicked one? An enemy of your city?"

"No. He was wise and kind."

"Then you have reason for regret indeed. For surely that is a sin, to kill a wise king."

"But he was a heathen."

"A what?"

"He denied God."

48

"He denied his own god?" said Socrates. "Then perhaps it was not so wrong to kill him."

"No. He denied mine. He *preferred* his own. And so he was a heathen. And all his people were heathens, since they followed his way. That could not be. They were at risk of eternal damnation because they followed him. I killed him for the sake of his people's souls. I killed him out of the love of God."

"But would you not say that all gods are the reflection of the one God?"

Pizarro considered that. "In a way, that's true, I suppose."

"And is the service of God not itself godly?"

"How could it be anything but godly, Socrates?"

"And would you say that one who serves his god faithfully according to the teachings of his god is behaving in a godly way?"

Frowning, Pizarro said, "Well—if you look at it that way, yes—"

"Then I think the king you killed was a godly man, and by killing him you sinned against God."

"Wait a minute!"

"But think of it: by serving his god he must also have served yours, for any servant of a god is a servant of the true god who encompasses all our imagined gods."

"No," said Pizarro sullenly. "How could he have been a servant of God? He knew nothing of Jesus. He had no understanding of the Trinity. When the priest offered him the Bible, he threw it to the ground in scorn. He was a heathen, Socrates. And so are you. You don't know anything of these matters

49

at all, if you think that Atahuallpa was godly. Or if you think you're going to get me to think so."

"Indeed I have very little knowledge of anything. But you say he was a wise man, and kind?"

"In his heathen way."

"And a good king to his people?"

"So it seemed. They were a thriving people when I found them."

"Yet he was not godly."

"I told you. He had never had the sacraments, and in fact he spurned them right up until the moment of his death, when he accepted baptism. *Then* he came to be godly. But by then the sentence of death was upon him and it was too late for anything to save him."

"Baptism? Tell me what that is, Pizarro."

"A sacrament."

"And that is?"

"A holy rite. Done with holy water, by a priest. It admits one to Holy Mother Church, and brings forgiveness from sin both original and actual, and gives the gift of the Holy Spirit."

"You must tell me more about these things another time. So you made this good king godly by this baptism? And then you killed him?"

"Yes."

"But he was godly when you killed him. Surely, then, to kill him was a sin."

"He had to die, Socrates!"

"And why was that?" asked the Athenian.

"Socrates is closing in for the kill," Tanner said. "Watch this!"

"I'm watching. But there isn't going to be any kill," said Richardson. "Their basic assumptions are too far apart."

"You'll see."

"Will I?"

Pizarro said, "I've already told you why he had to die. It was because his people followed him in all things. And so they worshipped the sun, because he said the sun was God. Their souls would have gone to hell if we had allowed them to continue that way."

"But if they followed him in all things," said Socrates, "then surely they would have followed him into baptism, and become godly, and thus done that which was pleasing to you and to your god! Is that not so?"

"No," said Pizarro, twisting his fingers in his beard.

"Why do you think that?"

"Because the king agreed to be baptized only after we had sentenced him to death. He was in the way, don't you see? He was an obstacle to our power! So we had to get rid of him. He would never have led his people to the truth of his own free will. That was why we had to kill him. But we didn't want to kill his soul as well as his body, so we said to him, Look, Atahuallpa, we're going to put you to death, but if you let us baptize you we'll strangle you quickly, and if you don't we'll burn you alive and it'll be very slow. So of course he agreed to be baptized, and we strangled him. What choice was there for anybody? He had to

die. He still didn't believe the true faith, as we all
well knew. Inside his head he was as big a heathen
as ever. But he died a Christian all the same."

"A what?"

"A Christian! A Christian! One who believes in
Jesus Christ the Son of God."

"The *son* of God," Socrates said, sounding puzzled. "And do Christians believe in God, too, or
only his son?"

"What a fool you are!"

"I would not deny that."

"There is God the Father, and God the Son,
and then there is the Holy Spirit."

"Ah," said Socrates. "And which did your Atahuallpa believe in, then, when the strangler came
for him?"

"None of them."

"And yet he died a Christian? Without believing
in any of your three gods? How is that?"

"Because of the baptism," said Pizarro in rising
annoyance. "What does it matter what he believed?
The priest sprinkled the water on him! The priest
said the words! If the rite is properly performed,
the soul is saved regardless of what the man understands or believes! How else could you baptize
an infant? An infant understands nothing and believes nothing—but he becomes a Christian when
the water touches him!"

"Much of this is mysterious to me," said Socrates. "But I see that you regard the king you killed
as godly as well as wise, because he was washed
by the water your gods require, and so you killed
a good king who now lived in the embrace of your

gods because of the baptism. Which seems wicked to me; and so this cannot be the place where the virtuous are sent after death, so it must be that I too was not virtuous, or else that I have misunderstood everything about this place and why we are in it."

"Damn you, are you trying to drive me crazy?" Pizarro roared, fumbling at the hilt of his sword. He drew it and waved it around in fury. "If you don't shut your mouth I'll cut you in thirds!"

"Uh-oh," Tanner said. "So much for the dialectical method."

Socrates said mildly, "It isn't my intention to cause you any annoyance, my friend. I'm only trying to learn a few things."

"You are a fool!"

"That is certainly true, as I have already acknowledged several times. Well, if you mean to strike me with your sword, go ahead. But I don't think it'll accomplish very much."

"Damn you," Pizarro muttered. He stared at his sword and shook his head. "No. No, it won't do any good, will it? It would go through you like air. But you'd just stand there and let me try to cut you down, and not even blink, right? Right?" He shook his head. "And yet you aren't stupid. You argue like the shrewdest priest I've ever known."

"In truth I am stupid," said Socrates. "I know very little at all. But I strive constantly to attain some understanding of the world, or at least to understand something of myself."

Pizarro glared at him. "No," he said. "I won't buy this false pride of yours. I have a little understanding of people myself, old man. I'm on to your game."

"What game is that, Pizarro?"

"I can see your arrogance. I see that you believe you're the wisest man in the world, and that it's your mission to go around educating poor sword-waving fools like me. And you pose as a fool to disarm your adversaries before you humiliate them."

"Score one for Pizarro," Richardson said. "He's wise to Socrates' little tricks, all right."

"Maybe he's read some Plato," Tanner suggested.

"He was illiterate."

"That was then. This is now."

"Not guilty," said Richardson. "He's operating on peasant shrewdness alone, and you damned well know it."

"I wasn't being serious," Tanner said. He leaned forward, peering toward the holotank. "God, what an astonishing thing this is, listening to them going at it. They seem absolutely real."

"They are," said Richardson.

"No, Pizarro, I am not wise at all," Socrates said. "But, stupid as I am, it may be that I am not the least wise man who ever lived."

"You think you're wiser than I am, don't you?"

"How can I say? First tell me how wise you are."

"Wise enough to begin my life as a bastard

54

tending pigs and finish it as Captain-General of Peru."

"Ah, then you must be very wise."

"I think so, yes."

"Yet you killed a wise king because he wasn't wise enough to worship God the way you wished him to. Was that so wise of you, Pizarro? How did his people take it, when they found out that their king had been killed?"

"They rose in rebellion against us. They destroyed their own temples and palaces, and hid their gold and silver from us, and burned their bridges, and fought us bitterly."

"Perhaps you could have made some better use of him by *not* killing him, do you think?"

"In the long run we conquered them and made them Christians. It was what we intended to accomplish."

"But the same thing might have been accomplished in a wiser way?"

"Perhaps," said Pizarro grudgingly. "Still, we accomplished it. That's the main thing, isn't it? We did what we set out to do. If there was a better way, so be it. Angels do things perfectly. We were no angels, but we achieved what we came for, and so be it, Socrates. So be it."

"I'd call that one a draw," said Tanner.

"Agreed."

"It's a terrific game they're playing."

"I wonder who we can use to play it next," said Richardson.

"I wonder what we can do with this besides using it to play games," said Tanner.

"Let me tell you a story," said Socrates. "The oracle at Delphi once said to a friend of mine, 'There is no man wiser than Socrates,' but I doubted that very much, and it troubled me to hear the oracle saying something that I knew was so far from the truth. So I decided to look for a man who was obviously wiser than I was. There was a politican in Athens who was famous for his wisdom, and I went to him and questioned him about many things. After I had listened to him for a time, I came to see that though many people, and most of all he himself, thought that he was wise, yet he was not wise. He only imagined that he was wise. So I realized that I must be wiser than he. Neither of us knew anything that was really worthwhile, but he knew nothing and thought that he knew, whereas I neither knew anything nor thought that I did. At least on one point, then, I was wiser than he: I didn't think that I knew what I didn't know."

"Is this intended to mock me, Socrates?"

"I feel only the deepest respect for you, friend Pizarro. But let me continue. I went to other wise men, and they, too, though sure of their wisdom, could never give me a clear answer to anything. Those whose reputations for wisdom were the highest seemed to have the least of it. I went to the great poets and playwrights. There was wisdom in their works, for the gods had inspired them, but that did not make *them* wise, though they thought

that it had. I went to the stonemasons and pio-
neers and other craftsmen. They were wise in
their own skills, but most of them seemed to think
that that made them wise in everything, which did
not appear to be the case. And so it went. I was
unable to find anyone who showed true wisdom.
So perhaps the oracle was right: that although I
am an ignorant man, there is no man wiser than I
am. But oracles often are right without their being
much value in it, for I think that all she was saying
was that no man is wise at all, that wisdom is
reserved for the gods. What do you say, Pizarro?"

"I say that you are a great fool, and very ugly
besides."

"You speak the truth. So, then, you are wise
after all. And honest."

"Honest, you say? I won't lay claim to that.
Honesty's a game for fools. I lied whenever I
needed to. I cheated. I went back on my word.
I'm not proud of that, mind you. It's simply what
you have to do to get on in the world. You think I
wanted to tend pigs all my life? I wanted gold,
Socrates! I wanted power over men! I wanted
fame!"

"And did you get those things?"

"I got them all."

"And were they gratifying, Pizarro?"

Pizarro gave Socrates a long look. Then he pursed
his lips and spat.

"They were worthless."

"Were they, do you think?"

"Worthless, yes. I have no illusions about that.
But still it was better to have had them than not.

In the long run nothing has any meaning, old man. In the long run we're all dead, the honest man and the villain, the king and the fool. Life's a cheat. They tell us to strive, to conquer, to gain— and for what? What? For a few years of strutting around. Then it's taken away, as if it had never been. A cheat, I say." Pizarro paused. He stared at his hands as though he had never seen them before. "Did I say all that just now? Did I mean it?" He laughed. "Well, I suppose I did. Still, life is all there is, so you want as much of it as you can. Which means getting gold, and power, and fame."

"Which you had. And apparently have no longer. Friend Pizarro, where are we now?"

"I wish I knew."

"So do I," said Socrates soberly.

"He's real," Richardson said. "They both are. The bugs are out of the system and we've got something spectacular here. Not only is this going to be of value to scholars, I think it's also going to be a tremendous entertainment gimmick, Harry."

"It's going to be much more than that," said Tanner in a strange voice.

"What do you mean by that?"

"I'm not sure yet," Tanner said. "But I'm definitely on to something big. It just began to hit me a couple of minutes ago, and it hasn't really taken shape yet. But it's something that might change the whole goddamned world."

Richardson looked amazed and bewildered.

"What the hell are you talking about, Harry?"

Tanner said, "A new way of settling political disputes, maybe. What would you say to a kind of combat-at-arms between one nation and another? Like a medieval tournament, so to speak. With each side using champions that we simulate for them—the greatest minds of all the past, brought back and placed in competition—" He shook his head. "Something like that. It needs a lot of working out, I know. But it's got possibilities."

"A medieval tournament—combat-at-arms, using simulations? Is that what you're saying?"

"Verbal combat. Not actual jousts, for Christ's sake."

"I don't see how—" Richardson began.

"Neither do I, not yet. I wish I hadn't even spoken of it."

"But—"

"Later, Lew. Later. Let me think about it a little while more."

"You don't have any idea what this place is?" Pizarro said.

"Not at all. But I certainly think this is no longer the world where we once dwelled. Are we dead, then? How can we say? You look alive to me."

"And you to me."

"Yet I think we are living some other kind of life. Here, give me your hand. Can you feel mine against yours?"

"No. I can't feel anything."

"Nor I. Yet I see two hands clasping. Two old

59

men standing on a cloud, clasping hands." Socrates laughed. "What a great rogue you are, Pizarro!"

"Yes, of course. But do you know something, Socrates? You are, too. A windy old rogue. I like you. There were moments when you were driving me crazy with all your chatter, but you amused me, too. Were you really a soldier?"

"When my city asked me, yes."

"For a soldier, you're damned innocent about the way the world works, I have to say. But I guess I can teach you a thing or two."

"Will you?"

"Gladly," said Pizarro.

"I would be in your debt," Socrates said.

"Take Atahuallpa," Pizarro said. "How can I make you understand why I had to kill him? There weren't even two hundred of us, and twenty-four millions of them, and his word was law, and once he was gone they'd have no one to command them. So of *course* we had to get rid of him if we wanted to conquer them. And so we did, and then they fell."

"How simple you make it seem."

"Simple is what it was. Listen, old man, he would have died sooner or later anyway, wouldn't he? This way I made his death useful: to God, to the Church, to Spain. And to Francisco Pizarro. Can you understand that?"

"I think so," said Socrates. "But do you think King Atahuallpa did?"

"Any king would understand such things."

"Then he should have killed you the moment you set foot in his land."

"Unless God meant us to conquer him, and allowed him to understand that. Yes. Yes, that must have been what happened."

"Perhaps he is in this place, too, and we could ask him," said Socrates.

Pizarro's eyes brightened. "Mother of God, yes! A good idea! And if he didn't understand, why, I'll try to explain it to him. Maybe you'll help me. You know how to talk, how to move words around and around. What do you say? Would you help me?"

"If we meet him, I would like to talk with him," Socrates said. "I would indeed like to know if he agrees with you on the subject of the usefulness of his being killed by you."

Grinning, Pizarro said, "Slippery, you are! But I like you. I like you very much. Come. Let's go look for Atahuallpa."

The wheels of commerce move ponderously in the quiescent United States of the 22nd century, but they roll nonetheless. And what better road to follow than that from experimental tests to government applications? Perhaps this fancy software can awaken the sleeping titans of Silicon Valley . . . or at the very least, provide a new facet or two for the still-lustrous entertainment industry.

THE RESURRECTION MACHINE
AD 2135

Robert Sheckley

Simms hit the button and the tiny glowing figure of Marcus Tullius Cicero came up inside the depths of the holo tank without a flicker. As the tiny togaed figure began to explore its cloudy kingdom, Simms called out to Murchison, "He's ready."

Murchison put down his newspaper and came across the room. Peering over Simms' shoulder, he watched the tiny togaed figure wandering through its foggy landscape within the darkened holo tank.

"So that's Cicero." Murchison turned away from the doll-like figure in its ancient Roman clothing. "He's not exactly what I had in mind."

"What do you mean?" Simms asked. "The simulacrum's perfect."

"I wasn't talking about your simulation," Murchison said. "I mean it would have been more commercial if they'd picked someone better-known—Shakespeare, for example, or some star of the past, Jim Morrison, maybe. You ever heard of Morrison, doctor?"

Simms shrugged. "I seem to remember his name from a liberal arts course."

"If I could only sell the services of Jim Morrison's simulacrum! I suppose you science guys could handle his vocal output?"

"We wouldn't even need Morrison for that."

"Anyway, we don't have him. We've got Cicero and that other guy, the Russian. Neither exactly a household name. And I'm supposed to make some money for the backers out of them."

"You could book Cicero on a TV show," Simms said.

Murchison pursed his lips. "You might have something there. There are a lot of money-making possibilities in this technology aside from one-on-one gaming situations. Let me have a better look."

Simms slipped his hands into the data gloves and magnified the image. Cicero's expression was calm, almost nonchalant. The Roman had adjusted his toga and seated himself on a cloud-like object—part of the primary environment.

"OK," Murchison said. "Put me in."

"Voice and image?"

"Make it voice only."

Cicero had always prided himself on his ability to awaken from a sleep with his faculties fully alert, prepared for everything and anything. He had always claimed that a man versed in philosophy should be surprised at nothing, since the possibilities of things extend far beyond man's limited knowledge. Only a god can have perfect apprehension. But a man, particularly a Roman, a man of *virtus*, should be astonished at nothing. Antiquity offered many examples of this attitude, which the Stoics named *apathia*.

He had awakened to find himself floating, more or less insubstantially, in a place that looked like nothing he had ever seen before. Or, to be more precise, a place that looked like nothing *anyone* had ever seen before.

He seemed to be in the cloud-filled kingdom of the upper heavens. This was how Olympus, home of the gods, was supposed to look. Or so the old poets said. But Cicero had never believed in the gods, neither Greek nor Latin.

Olympus? This place seemed not so much Olympian as Aristophanean. Could it be that he was witnessing, perhaps even participating in, a performance of Aristophanes' "Clouds"? But how had they managed these amazing effects?

"Marcus Tullius Cicero!" The voice came from nowhere and everywhere, deep-toned, faintly sinister.

Despite the firmness of his will, nature had endowed Cicero with quick responses which he could not always keep under control. The voice came as a shock. A sensation of panic came over him, a feeling that he was powerless in the hands of something monstrous. He struggled for control.

65

He reminded himself that he was a Roman, and, if he could not control outer circumstances, he could at least preserve inner calm. . . .

"Do you hear me, Marcus Tullius?"

"Yes, lord," Cicero said. "I hear you."

"Why do you call me lord?"

"It is the common term for one who is superior to oneself in power."

"And why do you presume that I have power?"

Cicero had himself well in hand now. He rattled off the points with practiced orator's skill.

"The first point of evidence is, you know who I am but I do not know who you are. Second, you seem able to see me but not I you. Third, you know what is happening and I do not."

"I like you, Marcus Tullius," the voice said. "But perhaps we could continue our conversation in more mundane surroundings."

"A very acceptable idea," Cicero said. "Did you have a place in mind?"

"The place, Marcus Tullius, I leave up to you."

Cicero answered cautiously. "Would you care to expand upon your meaning? And who are you anyhow?"

"Call me Martin. I've said all I'm going to say on the subject. Consider it a little problem for you to solve, Marcus."

"But I am incorporeal!" Cicero said, "and I am suspended in incorporeality. How can any action be performed in this condition?"

"I assure you, even given your present circumstances, the problem is solveable."

And then the voice was gone and Marcus Tullius Cicero was alone in nowhere.

The Epicureans had held that the gods exist in space, in human form, but without human bodies. Cicero had not only refuted this, but had also pointed out the absurdity of the conception in his treatise, "On the Nature of the Gods." And now here he was, himself a bodiless being existing somewhere in space, in human form, but without a body. Did that prove the Epicureans were correct? And if so, did it by definition mean that Marcus Tullius Cicero was a god?

Something had happened, that was clear, but as to its nature and meaning, he would have to wait until more evidence was in. Meanwhile, there was the matter of getting from nowhere to somewhere.

The solution to the problem of locomotion was, in fact, absurdly simple, and Cicero came upon it very quickly. Since he was unable to effect any physical change the answer had to be mental. He willed himself to descend through the clouds. He drifted easily through them, and saw the earth come up toward him, and then he landed, light as gossamer, in a clearing on the edge of a pine forest.

The land was unfamiliar to him. Ahead he could see a dwelling, but of an unusual, even eccentric, form. It was a barbaric sort of place, made of rough-hewn logs, large, with carved and sawn decorations. The house had many windows, and each was covered with glass of a purity and evenness he had never before seen. This was not in Italy or

Greece, nor Gaul or Germany, either. Could he have been reborn in the northern land of the Scythians?

Cicero strolled to the house, or rather, floated, in the ghostly, effortless manner he was quickly growing accustomed to. As he reached the front door he saw a man standing in front of it. The man was dressed in shapeless black barbarian trousers and coat. He was large, moon-faced, sparsely bearded, with a pale complexion. His face was not handsome, but it was arresting. His most interesting feature was perhaps his eyes. There was something oriental about them, with their hint of epithalic fold.

"Greetings," Cicero said. "I am Marcus Tullius Cicero."

At least the barbarian recognized his language. He answered at once. "I am Michael Bakunin. I suppose you're going to stay here, too."

"Yes, I am." Cicero went inside, brushing past and partially through Bakunin who was partially blocking the way.

"So we are to share this villa," Cicero remarked later. "Tell me, Michael, do you have any idea where we are?"

"It looks strangely like my old home of Premukhino," Bakunin said. "There's a hedgerow outside like one I knew. And that grandfather clock on the mantle. Yes, and the portrait of Catherine the Great on the wall."

"So they have created a replica of your home," Cicero said. "I wonder why."

Bakunin looked at him and smiled. "Because they're clever."

"They?"

"The secret police who arrange these matters."

"Ah, I see," Cicero said. "But why have these so-called secret police gone to all this trouble?"

Bakunin's large features creased into a childlike smile. "It's obvious I must be important to them. That is why they have created this illusion for me."

"Whereas I am not?" Cicero inquired.

"You are probably one of them," Bakunin said. "Or you are part of the illusion."

Cicero said, "If you are determined to believe that, we shall have a difficult time holding a conversation."

"Well," said Bakunin, "tentatively, I will accept your reality."

"That's good of you," Cicero said. "Now then, why should your secret police want me?"

"Because you're important to them," Bakunin said. "But as a codifier of existing legal systems, no doubt. Not as an innovator, like as I am."

"You? An innovator?"

"My dear Cicero, even during my own lifetime I was recognized as the founder of anarchism."

"That is nonsense," Cicero said. "Anarchism is an ancient doctrine. Our Latin poet Ovid, in his 'Metamorphoses', spoke of the golden age when men lived without law and without external compulsion, without fear of punishment. It was a time when men kept faith with each other of their own accord and there was no need to engrave the laws on tablets of bronze."

Bakunin shrugged. "I was never much good at classics in school. Anyhow, the stuff doesn't matter. *I* am the father of anarchism in modern times. Even Marx acknowledged as much. Perhaps the secret powers brought me back because I am famous."

"Without wishing to make you unhappy," Cicero said, "I think it is obvious that I am much more famous than you."

Bakunin sighed. The delight drained out of him. "Perhaps you are. But the fact remains, we are living in a Russian house, not a Roman villa. How do you explain that?"

"Maybe that was one of the stage-sets they had available," Cicero said.

There was no way of telling time in the silent Russian house. Cicero and Bakunin drifted like ghosts down its corridors, through its bedrooms, in and out of its provisionless kitchen. Sometimes Bakunin would tell Cicero about his hopes for mankind, his distrust of Marx, his admiration for Fichte and, above all, his worship of the great Hegel. He would speak of the necessity of anarchism, the need to abolish the aristocracy, and the bourgeoisie, and, at last, the proletariat.

Cicero did not attempt to debate with him. Bakunin seemed impervious to reasoned argumentation. His sense of logic was nil. Yet Cicero sensed something desperate and pure and childlike about this tortured and desperate man. Still, Cicero preferred to keep his own company. He began spending most of his time in the spacious upstairs apartment.

Bakunin took long walks in the woods at frequent intervals. When he returned he would throw himself on the couch and look out the window at the snow-covered birches.

Hanging on the wall facing the couch was a long mirror in an elaborate gilt frame. One day, as Bakunin lay on his couch, he saw the mirror turn cloudy. Then it became suffused with light, which faded and gave way to a black and white image of a man's face.

"Well, Michael, how are you getting along?" Murchison asked.

"Fine, fine," Bakunin said. "But isn't it time we got to work?"

"What are you talking about?"

"I've put things together. It's obvious to me that you are from a future that has finally reached maturity and recognized the inevitability of my doctrine. Rest assured, I am ready to advise, though, true to my principles, I refuse to lead or participate in any government."

"Is that what you think this is all about?"

Bakunin's eyes glowed. "I know that I am recognized at last! My great doctrine has come to fruition! Exonerated, justified, at last!"

"I'm afraid you have it all wrong," Murchison said. "As a workable political doctrine, your anarchy is about as useful as a snowmaking machine at the North Pole. Anarchy is something our political science students study in school. This may seem

71

harsh, telling it to you this way, but it's better to get the position straight."

"If my doctrine is unimportant, why did you bring me back?"

Murchison couldn't tell Bakunin the real reason. The simulacra wouldn't understand the strange mixture of government and business interests that governed their selection.

"You are of historic interest to some of our scholars," Murchison said.

"I see. And what is it you want me to do?"

"It's nothing much. Just talk to some people."

Bakunin laughed. "That's all you people ever want. Just a little talk. Just tell us a few things. But the questions continue, and do not end until you have betrayed yourself, incriminated your friends, and violated all your principles. Yes, I know quite a lot about interrogations."

"It's not like that," Murchison said. "I'm talking about some nice chats with pleasant scholarly men and women."

"Of course they would use that type. You think I can't see through it?"

"Who is this *they* you keep on referring to?"

"The Cheka, of course, the Czar's secret police."

Murchison groaned. "Listen, Michael, you've got it all wrong. And anyhow, all that stuff is in the past."

"So *you* say!"

"Damn it, Michael, you know that we brought you back to life. We could take any secrets we wanted directly from your head. You realize that, don't you?"

Bakunin thought about it. "Yes, it seems likely."

"Then why not cooperate with me?"

"No," Bakunin said.

"Why not?"

"Because I am Bakunin. I lead, or die, but I do not cooperate."

"Great," Murchison muttered. "That's just wonderful. Look, Michael, this is important to me. If you helped, I could do you a lot of good."

"I realize that you are powerful. Apparently you can, in some fashion, call the dead back to life."

"Yes."

"Then I will cooperate with you," Bakunin said.

"Thank you, I knew you'd—"

"If you will bring back my Antonia."

"Beg pardon?"

"My wife, Antonia. I don't suppose you ever heard of her. She was only a girl from a small Siberian village. But she made my life bearable."

"I'll see what I can do," Martin said. "Meanwhile, get ready for your first interview."

"Not until Antonia is here."

Murchison was out of patience. "Michael, I could turn you off as easy as I turned you on. From your point of view it would be death."

"You call this living?" the Russian said, with a sudden burst of hard laughter. "No, go back to the Czar or whoever you work for. Tell him that Michael Bakunin, a ghost lying on a couch in a place that doesn't exist, defies him in this new life as he did in the old one."

* * *

73

The President of the United States had appointed Murchison as director in charge of marketing for the simulacra program. Murchison was good at developing markets and new uses for some of the agricultural surpluses that America, despite its 3rd-world position in the present global economy, continued to produce. He was a man who got things done.

But working with electronic ghosts, if that's what the simulacra were, was a different experience for him. Especially when one of the ghosts wanted him to deliver another ghost named Antonia.

"Antonia who?" Simms asked.

"Hell, I don't know," Murchison said. "It's gotta be in a book somewhere. Or a database."

"I'll check it out," Simms said, "but don't get your hopes up."

Two hours later he had the answer. "No can do," he said. "Insufficient data."

The Russian sat on his sofa, arms folded, his face melancholy. "I have told you my conditions."

"And I've told you they are impossible. Listen to me, Michael, it's not such a big deal. We'll try an easy one first. An interview with a kid. He won the high school history honors in Slavic studies."

"I no longer care for the Slavs," Michael Bakunin said. "I am one myself, but that makes no difference. They had their chance, in Poland, in Russia, in Germany. They betrayed themselves and mankind by not going beyond Marxism, to the ultimate revolution of anarchy!"

"Tell the kid that," Murchison suggested. "Anyhow, he's not a Slav. I just remembered, his name's Peterson. Peter Peterson. He's a nice kid, why not give him a break?"

"A Swede," Bakunin remarked. "I spent a terrible time in Stockholm. I do not care to talk with Swedes."

"He's not a Swede! He's an American!"

"I told you my conditions," Bakunin said. "I want my wife here with me."

"Michael, I've been trying to explain to you, we can't do it. I've talked to our scientists, it simply can't be done."

"If you could bring me back," Bakunin said, "I fail to see why you can't bring back my Antonia."

"It's too technical for me to go into," Murchison said. "But what it comes down to, we don't have enough information on her."

"She was a humble person," Bakunin said. "One of the little people who you think do not count."

"No, it's nothing at all to do with that. To bring a person back, we need to have a lot of information. Otherwise there's no chance."

"The Cheka would have a dossier on her," Bakunin said.

"But we can't get it," Murchison said. He didn't tell Bakunin about the present-day partition of Russia. The Moslem portion did not have access to the old records. The part still called the USSR had lost most of its pre-20th century records during the riots at the time of partition.

"If you cannot bring back Antonia," Bakunin said, "I will not cooperate."

"I don't wish to use threats," Murchison said.

Bakunin smiled suddenly. "You think you can threaten me? Now? In this state, whatever it is? That, Martin, is very silly indeed."

"You're wrong about that, Michael," Murchison said. And disappeared.

Simms was annoyed. Murchison had requested this meeting in the lab and he was already half an hour late. Simms hadn't liked Murchison from the start. He had known all about his reputation, of course. Who didn't? Feature stories in a dozen glossy magazines, the confidante of presidents, a man with a reputation for getting things done. Just the man needed to make something out of this project, something that could show a profit and help get a moribund American economy back on its feet. A dynamo, the newspapers called him. Simms had a better word: the man was a monomaniac with psychopathic tendencies; an egotist who would stop at nothing to get his way.

Murchison came bustling into the lab with a book under his arm. "Sorry to be late. Take a look at this." He opened the heavy history text and showed the full-page illustration to Simms.

"Very pretty," Simms said.

"That's unimportant. Can you simulate it?"

Simms studied the illustration more closely. "Are there any plans available?"

"You don't need them. What I want you to do is simulate this exterior view, and one interior room. I have a description of the interior. And I want you to set up one-way access only to the interior room. Make it a protected domain, I think that's the terminology. Can you do it?"

"No problem," Simms said. "We simulated the Russian house with interiors for Bakunin. You said he'd be more cooperative in a familiar environment. But this . . ."

"What's the matter with it?"

"One-way access. It's a prison, isn't it? A prison for a simulacrum."

"You got it," Murchison said.

"Isn't there some other way to get the results you're after?"

"Sure," Murchison said. "Bring back Antonia."

"I've already explained to you why we can't do that. With the data available to us, it would be like bringing back a monster. The Antonia we created would be filled with characterological lacunae. Even its appearance would be unacceptable."

"All right. Build the new construct."

"I don't like it," Simms said.

"Never mind. Do it anyway. It won't take long to change Bakunin's mind. And, as I keep on reminding you, we're not dealing with a man, it's a simulacrum, a creation of electrons and photons or whatever it is inside that computer of yours."

Murchison was less sure of himself with Cicero.

There was something endearing about Bakunin, something childlike and unthreatening. And after all, what had Bakunin been, historically? A wild-eyed weirdo who travelled around the world, did time in prisons in Germany and Austria and Russia, never really got his stuff together. Whereas Cicero was a different story.

Murchison had looked through a printout on Cicero's main states. He had been one of the most powerful men in Rome in its heyday around 65 B.C. And he hadn't even been a patrician. He had come up from the bottom all on his own, getting to the top on sheer intelligence, merit, boldness, and his matchless oratory.

The man had been an equal with Caesar, Brutus, Marc Antony. He'd been a philosopher, playwright, and poet as well as First Consul of Rome.

He could be box office. In a scholarly way, of course, but still box office.

Murchison saw that the possibilities were endless— if only the Cicero simulacrum would cooperate.

But of course Cicero had been a great politician. He'd probably be easy enough to deal with.

Writing had always been Cicero's consolation in times of difficulty. There were writing instruments in the house, and there was paper, much superior to parchment or wax tablets. Cicero wrote, trying to think, to consider his situation, to find out what to do.

"All right, come along now."

Bakunin looked up and saw the German police guard, in his dove-gray uniform, standing over him. Was this a dream, or a vision? He got up, noting the other guards outside his cell door.

He had expected them to come for him, ever since the failure of the Dresden uprising. . . .

But no, he remembered now, that had already happened, just yesterday, and they had taken him to the old fortress in Königsberg. At least the room had been clean and warm, and he had been well-fed and they had allowed him all the cigars he'd wanted. The Saxons treated political prisoners decently, you could say that much for them. But against them—it was coming back to him now—was the judgement of the tribunal soon after his arrest. Under Saxon law he should have gotten no more than a year or two. But the court had discovered or invented various legal technicalities, as Bakunin could have foreseen if his mind had not been clouded by his incurable and baseless optimism. He could see the presiding judge, a fat bourgeois of the worst sort, smiling as he said, "Michael Bakunin, the court has examined the evidence and it is clear that you are a political agitator of the worst sort." A pause. "However, there is another possibility, which you will learn about in due time."

"Where are you taking me?" Bakunin asked.

The sergeant twisted his long moustaches and said, his voice not unkind, "I am not permitted to talk to you, Bakunin. Just come along quietly."

"Where are we going?"

"Away from here."

They were going to release him! Surely what lay ahead would be better than what was behind—the bodies of the Dresden workers, the screams of the women as the Prussian infantry with bayonetted rifles broke through the barricades, and then the senseless slaughter even after the feeble little protest had been snuffed out.

But where were they taking him?

There was a coach waiting outside the gates of the prison, and an armed escort of Prussian cavalry to escort it. Bakunin thought, they are going to send me back to France. To Paris, and freedom! Even these Prussian bastards don't want my blood on their hands. Perhaps one or two of them on the tribunal understood my statement, my plea, my hopes and dreams for all mankind.

The sun was just coming up, a watery white smear in the featureless white German sky. Bakunin was permitted a seat by the window, with three armed guards sitting beside and opposite him. The curtains were pulled down, but not tied securely into place, and Bakunin could see they went through the Koenigsberg town square to the crossroads and turned to the southeast.

He had been so sure they would take him to Paris! But France lay in the opposite direction. Terror filled him. He muttered to the sergeant, "This is not the road to Paris."

The sergeant was amused. "What gave you the idea they would send you there?"

"To get rid of me," Bakunin said.

"They're doing that, all right," the sergeant said.

"But where are we going?"

The sergeant didn't answer at once. He was assessing his subordinate soldiers. Talk with the prisoner was discouraged. But none of these men would dare talk. And it was a long ride ahead.

"You are an embarrassment to the Prussians,

Herr Bakunin. But the authorities don't want your blood on their hands."

Searing hope flooded Bakunin's big, fragile chest. And then a horrid fear.

"What are you thinking?" the sergeant asked, watching the play of emotion over the sad, tortured face.

"I foresee two possibilities," Bakunin said. "First, and least likely, you will take me somewhere— Switzerland, perhaps—set me free, perhaps with orders never to return. That would be the best solution all around."

"Ah, Bakunin," the sergeant said, "you *are* a dreamer."

"The second possibility, more likely I fear, is that you will find some place along the road, a clump of trees, perhaps, and there—"

"Yes?" the sergeant prompted.

Bakunin couldn't bring himself to say it. He made the gesture of a finger across his throat.

"Here," the sergeant said, taking a small leather case out of an inner pocket of his greatcoat. "Have a cigar."

"The condemned man's last smoke?" Bakunin asked, accepting the cigar, his hand trembling despite his resolve to show no fear.

"Not exactly," the sergeant said. Suddenly he tired of the game he was playing with this wretched and ridiculous man. "We are en route to the Austrian frontier, where arrangements have been made to turn you over to the authorities."

Bakunin said slowly, "Austria! But they will kill me!"

The sergeant shrugged. "It's your own fault. You shouldn't have published that inflammatory pamphlet advocating the overthrow of the Austrian empire. Not even murder is as bad as inciting the masses to revolt against their legally constituted authorities."

Bakunin slumped back. Now he knew. They were on the road to Prague. It was the worst, the worst.

Remembering it now, lying on a couch in the house that looked so much like Premukhino, he saw that he had been naïve even then. Austria was not to be the end. Ahead of him still lay the final horror, Russia, and the implacable hatred of Czar Nicholas I.

"I've heard you've been writing," Murchison said.

Cicero didn't bother asking who Martin had heard it from. Martin was being polite in his fashion. Cicero had surmised that if Martin, or the powers he represented, were able to do what they had done to him so far, spying on him and his writing would be both simple and natural to them.

"A few notes," Cicero admitted.

"I'd really like to see them," Martin said. "Any words by the famous Cicero would be welcome indeed."

"I do have the natural vanity of an author," Cicero said. "One always hopes one's words will live beyond one's lifetime. I suppose you have improved on our system of copyists in this new age of yours?"

"Indeed we have," Martin said. "We have mechanical means of transcription and publication nowadays. We could publish you worldwide. This could bring you great fame."

"As my previously written works have already done?" Cicero said affably.

Martin had nodded before he could stop himself. Simms and others had warned him about revealing too much to the simulacra. Still, you couldn't prevent an intelligent man like Cicero from putting things together.

"Your works, those that have survived, are studied in our schools."

"Which schools? In which countries? What century is this, Martin? Have you raised me from the dead? Perhaps not, since I seem to have a certain ineluctable corporeality. But you have resurrected something of me—my ghost, perhaps, or my spirit. Is that not so?"

"Something like that," Murchison said, since denial was useless. "But I can't go into all that at this time. Later, perhaps. Now, please show me what you have written."

"And if I decide not to?"

"I am only asking out of courtesy," Murchison said. "Whatever you've written is available to me whenever I want to take it."

"And if I destroyed it?"

"We could reconstruct it. Please, Marcus Tullius, I think you understand your position. Why not just hand over the writing and spare yourself any unpleasantness?"

"Why, then I have no choice," Cicero said, and pointed to a small pile of papers from his desk.

"Thanks," Murchison said, and disappeared.

There was no way of judging time in this cloud-kingdom, but Martin was back very soon, as Cicero had expected. He was holding Cicero's writings, which were in the form of small drawings, like hieroglyphics.

"Cicero, what the hell is this? Code? Is that it? If so, I can assure you that we can break it."

"It's not code at all," Cicero said. "It is a short-hand of my own devising."

"Will you translate it for me?"

"With great pleasure, Martin. After we finish discussing terms."

"To hell with that," Murchison said. "I don't need to give any terms. I can get the best cryptologists in the world to work on this."

"Come back and see me after you talk with your experts," Cicero said. "Perhaps we can work something out."

"I hate to tell you this," Simms said, struggling to conceal his smile, "but that sly old Latin has put one over on you."

They were in Murchison's office. Murchison had given Cicero's writings or drawings or whatever they were to Simms and told him to find out what it was and how long it would take to break the code or cypher. Simms had conferred with a colleague in the Classics department at Harvard.

"We've got millions of dollars of computer capacity at our disposal," Murchison said. "We've got experts who can break codes in any language known to man. What's the problem?"

"What you have here is Cicero's shorthand system. It's a group of symbols which refer to a personal mnemonic system—"

"Would you mind putting that in English for me?" Murchison said.

"Writing was difficult in the ancient world," Simms said. "People didn't carry around notepads. There weren't any typewriters or computers. There weren't even ballpoint pens and scratch pads. Back then, an educated man studied the *ars memoriae artificialis*, the art of artificial memory."

"What's that? Something you carry around?"

"No. It's something you carry in your head. It's an associational system by which a man can remember things. Often very lengthy things. Some of those old guys had phenomenal memories. One of the Persian kings in Hellenic times is said to have known the name of every man in his army. That would be at least ten thousand names, the way armies ran in those days, maybe a lot more than that."

"You mean that Cicero has memorized this new stuff he's writing?"

"Not exactly. What he's done is use an associational system involving names and images. I'll give you the standard example. Imagine an enormous house or palace filled with hundreds of rooms. Each room is a *locus*, a place. A studious man would develop a strong visualization of these rooms so that, in his mind's eye, he could walk through

85

them. Each room would be different so that he could tell one from the other."

"All right," Murchison said. "We've got this mental palace full of rooms. Then what?"

"When a man—Cicero, for example—wanted to remember something, he would mentally create an image, of a statue, for example, or a volcano, or three old ladies, or a golden hand, and mentally put the image into the *locus*. The more grotesque the image, the easier it would be to remember. Then, when he wanted to access the contents, he would walk—mentally, of course—through the rooms, and, in the words of the ancient authors, demand that the images give up their contents. It's an interesting early way of using the mind in a computer-like fashion."

"And Cicero knew about this stuff?"

"He wrote the *Ad Herennium*, one of the standard texts on the subject."

"Are you telling me we can't decipher these scribbles?"

"Not unless we know what words Cicero was associating what images with."

"This is not Austria," Bakunin said. But his police guard was gone. The German policemen, the coach, and the horses had vanished. Bakunin's house at Premukhino was gone, too. Bakunin was standing on the bank of a sluggish gray river, looking at a marshy island directly in front of him. There was an enormous stone building beyond it on the far shore.

"I think you know this place, Michael."

It was Martin's voice. But the man was nowhere to be seen.

"Where are you?" Michael Bakunin asked.

"Never mind," said Martin. "Do you know what you're looking at?"

Bakunin nodded heavily. "The river is the Neva which flows through St. Petersburg. The island is Janisaari, and the building is the Peter and Paul fortress."

"You remember the place?"

"After seven years in its dungeons, I'm not likely to forget. Is that where you're sending me, Martin?"

"Only if you make me. You know, Michael, there's no need for this. What I'm asking of you isn't unreasonable."

"You are not asking," Bakunin said. "You are demanding. I am not a slave to be ordered around. The rights of man—"

"You are *not* a man," Martin said. "You are a spirit, a reassembled spirit, and as such you have no rights."

"As long as I have consciousness," Bakunin said, "I have rights."

"Just talk with a few people I want to bring you," Martin said. "I'm not asking you to betray anyone."

"Except myself."

"Have it your own way," Martin said. "You know what comes next."

Bakunin was all too familiar with the great dismal fortress. This was the infamous Peter and Paul, where so many had been shut up, tortured, murdered, or, with luck, released after months or years in the dungeons, broken in health and spirit, to be shipped to Siberia to spend their last days. Peter Kropotkin had been imprisoned here, and lived to tell of it. Karakozoff had been tortured and hanged, though they had barely gotten him to the scaffold alive. Here the Decembrists and other revolutionaries had been sent to rot. Here . . .

And then, between two blinks, he was in a cell that was horribly familiar to him. It was twilight in the cell, a dim light filtering through from the deeply set window fifteen feet above the floor. The floor and walls were covered with felt, originally painted blue, now faded to gray. But this was not the true wall. Five inches from the walls iron wire nets were suspended, covered with heavy linen and with faded yellow paper. This was to prevent the prisoners from tapping on the walls and communicating with each other. The place stank of unwashed bodies. But what was most oppressive was the heat, which came from the large stoves outside the cells. They were kept continually stoked in order to prevent moisture from forming in the walls. But the heat was unbearable, and the coal fumes could asphyxiate a man. It was like being a side of beef hung in a Turkish bath.

Czar Nicholas I had imprisoned him in this place on 23 May, 1851. That was a date he would never forget. He had been released by Nicholas' successor, Alexander II, after almost seven years, and exiled for life to Siberia. The date of his release had been 8 March, 1857. The prison diet had given him piles and scurvy. Most of his teeth had fallen out. He had suffered continual headaches, shortness of breath, and noises in the ear like the sound of boiling water.

Seven years, that time. And how long this time? Forever?

Or until he gave in, betrayed every principle he had ever stood for, became Martin's slave.

Bakunin lay on the floor and wept.

Simms turned away from the holo image of the tiny black-coated figure huddled in the ancient prison cell he had simulated. "You don't really propose to leave him there, do you, Martin?"

"He'll come around. Anyhow, what does it matter? It's not a *him* in that tank. Bakunin and Cicero are not real people, Simms. They're nothing but data, intelligent data. You told me so yourself."

"In a way," Simms said, "we're nothing but data, too."

"You're taking this entirely too personally. Simulacra seem like people, but the courts have ruled that they are to be classified as images. You can't violate the civil rights of an image."

"That ruling is under appeal."

"The appeal is frivolous. Simulacra have none of the attributes of living human beings."

"Except awareness. Intelligence. The ability to feel pleasure. And pain."

"Doc, you're breaking my heart. See you later."

Simms had been heading up the scientific team on Project Resurrection, as the simulacrum program was sometimes called, for almost two years, ever since Richardson had taken a leave of absence to pursue new lines of development. He'd seen a lot of strange things during his tenure, but none of them had prepared him for Martin Murchison, the new Director in charge of Implementation. The man was a computer illiterate, and a sadist.

He did have a point, though. There was no Bakunin. Only a glowing web of electronic data.

But he wondered what that glowing web of data was thinking about? What was it feeling?

Cicero looked up and smiled when Murchison appeared suddenly in the room.

"Martin! I've been expecting you. Do make yourself at home. I wish I could offer you refreshment, but I suspect that no Falerian wine is available, and even if it were, our incorporeality (which I perceive that we share) makes the ingesting of food and wine, if not impossible, then merely ritualistic."

Murchison's simulacra floated across the room and seated itself on one of the lumpy couches with which Bakunin's house was furnished.

"You're talking a lot," Murchison said. "Are you getting lonely with Bakunin gone?"

"Nothing I can't deal with," Cicero said. "Where have you taken him, by the way?"

"You wouldn't want to know," Murchison said.

"Oh, *that* place," Cicero said. "But I see the subject is distasteful to you. Tell me, have you succeeded in deciphering my recent writings?"

"No, we haven't."

"What a pity," Cicero said. "You were so confident, too."

Murchison stood up suddenly. "Listen, you son of a bitch, with a single command I could disappear you."

"Poor Martin," Cicero said. "Extinction is your only real threat, and it has little force against one who has already died. For such, I surmise, is my true situation."

"I could try to think up something better than death," Martin said.

"Why bother? I want to cooperate, Martin. I'm eager to do so. And I have some ideas which would, I think, greatly enhance my value to you."

"If you're so cooperative, why don't you translate your writings for me?"

"I will, all in good time. But first let's strike a deal."

"You have nothing to deal with."

"I have no power, but I have something you want even aside from my writing."

"How do you figure?"

Cicero sat arrow-straight, his proud eyes fixed on Murchison's. "First answer a question or two. I'm in the future, aren't I, and you, or those you represent, have managed to recreate the images of figures from the past. These images, of whom I am one, exist with the self-consciousness and self-awareness of men, but without true bodies, and without any way of effecting true physical change. Am I very far off the mark?"

"You've got it pretty good," Murchison said grudgingly.

obert Sheckley*

"In this new world of yours, not only the written words, but also the presence of what you would call archaic authors could be of great value. It's as if we in the Rome of my time were able to interview Socrates, or Sophocles, or the great Homer himself. Is not my situation comparable?" When Murchison didn't deny it, Cicero went on. "I will produce new works for you, Martin, that will yield you great profit, to say nothing of scholarly luster. How does that sound, Martin?"

Murchison could see it already: CICERO SPEAKS TO MODERN AMERICANS. On Morals. Sexuality. The Lessons of History. Just name it, Cicero would give you an oration on it. And of course a cooperative Cicero could make a great interviewee for guest shots on various tv shows. Cicero had the gift of gab. And imagine him appearing on the tv news clad in his toga? He could be worth millions, billions. There were endless possibilities. A movie, for example, based on Cicero's view of Caesar and Marc Antony . . .

As though he were reading Murchison's mind, Cicero said, "And remember, too, Martin, that I am not merely an essayist on law. I was also a poet, and a playwright, too. Might not something be made of that?"

If Cicero was willing to do all that, he could be a goldmine and he could be marketed world-wide.

"Marcus, old buddy, what is it you want?"

Cicero took his time about answering. Finally he said, "Martin, I want a body. A real one. I want to live again, but in the flesh, not as a spirit."

That took Murchison off his guard. He hadn't

2

been expecting it. "How'd you know we could do that?"

"I didn't. But it's the only thing I want."

"I'm not sure the technology's up to cloning yet."

"Whatever that means. But I understand the general import. Fear not, Martin, I can wait until you and your friends are able to prepare a suitable body for me. And our various profitable ventures can also wait."

Martin had to admit it, the old bastard had him over a barrel. But it was a solid platinum barrel, and it could be rolling in diamonds.

"I'll be in touch," Murchison said, and disappeared.

Cicero settled back at his desk and continued writing in his impenetrable mnemonic code. He'd need this writing to keep up his share of the bargain, after Murchison had convinced his representatives that making Cicero a whole man was to their strongest personal advantage.

"What about Bakunin?" Simms asked.

"He still won't cooperate. Calls it a matter of principle. Can you imagine it, an anarchist—actually an electronic *simulation* of an anarchist—claiming to have principles?"

"Yeah," Simms said, "it's hell when the images start getting uppity. Martin, I think we should take him out of there."

Murchison looked at him sharply. "Simms, they told me you were a top computer scientist. Maybe you are. But I think you have an attitude problem."

Simms opened his mouth to speak, then thought better of it.

"Anyhow, Cicero is cooperating beautifully. That guy's Mr. Show Business of the ancient world. He's going to put our project into the black. But I need a reward for him."

"You want me to simulate one of his friends?"

Murchison shook his head. "Cicero wants to live again in the veritable flesh. What I need now is a cloned body for him."

"Yassa, boss, one cloned body, coming right up."

"Don't take that attitude with me. You told me you could imprint a simulacrum on a cloned body."

"I also told you the process is still under development."

"I want it in a week."

"And what about Bakunin? Can I take him out of the prison?"

"He can get out any time he wants," Murchison said. "All he has to do is cooperate. Can you work up some sensory input for him? I want him to *feel* that cell, and smell it. I want him capable of experiencing physical discomfort."

"Pain, you mean?"

"Yes, if you want to call it that. I need to convince him quickly. There are TV and magazine people waiting to interview him."

Murchison left, and Simms peered again into the holo tank, at Bakunin crouched in a corner of his cell. Simms thought, *You poor bastard, even in death you couldn't escape from people like Murchison.*

Simms sat down at his terminal keyboard and called up a coding program. He played with it, his attention elsewhere. On Murchison and how fed up he was with him. It was obviously time to resign. Before he got fired anyway.

And the simulacra?

Cicero seemed to be doing all right. But Bakunin . . . What that unhappy son of a bitch really needed was a Get Out of Jail Free Card. . . .

So that he could roam throughout the computer's system, unimpeded.

But that could never be. Simms was too good a scientist to let a wild card, an intelligent self-sustaining intelligence and personality package, loose in the system. There was no telling what damage he could do.

It was out of the question.

While he was thinking this, Simms found that his fingers had called up the programming instructions for an access descriptor.

Bakunin's nerves were always trying to betray his principles. His ghostliness did not interfere with the ability of his mind to torture itself. He wondered if peace might lie on the far side of this agony. How could anything go on forever? And yet, it was still going on. His enemies were persecuting him. Not even in death was he safe from the revisionists. They were still trying to break his will. They didn't understand that after death, will is all a man has left, all that enables him to call himself a man.

It was during this not very cheerful musing that

a man walked into Bakunin's cell, passing through the heavy wall as if it were air. Bakunin looked up but did not react. They had a lot of tricks, the Czar's scientific police. The man was not Martin, and he didn't seem to be a prison guard. He was dressed in civilian clothes. A high official wearing the latest fashion, that would explain it.

"I know that you have come to persecute me," Bakunin said, "but I would remind you that the knout is ineffective against insubstantiality. Even lacking bodies, we are still bound to Hegel's dialectic."

The man smiled. "Hi, Michael. For a guy sitting in the Peter and Paul fortress, maybe for eternity, you can still make a pretty rousing speech."

"That is because I am Bakunin," Bakunin said. "And because I am Bakunin, you have come to ask something of me."

The man smiled. "Wrong, Michael! I have come to give you something."

"I do not believe you. This is some devil's trick of the capitalists or the Communists. It doesn't matter which, they both hate me."

"If you don't want my help, I'll go away."

"Why should I trust you?" Bakunin asked.

"You just have to take a chance."

"Who are you?" Bakunin asked.

"My name is Simms. I'm one of the people who brought you back to your present state."

"Why have you come?"

"It is unfair, in my view, to subject even the simulation of a man to torture, especially if that simulation is capable of perception and feeling.

96

Such a simulation must be said in some respect to be alive, and its rights must be respected. I was against subjecting you to this cell. I could not stop it. My resignation would not help. I'm going to resign anyhow, but I'm going to do one thing before I go."

"What is that?" Bakunin asked.

"I'm going to give you this."

The simulation of Simms reached into its chest and took out what looked to Bakunin like a playing card, but slightly larger and thicker. The card glowed. Bakunin had the impression that nearly invisible wires radiated from it, like a spider web spun so fine you could barely see it.

"What is it?"

"Call it a Get Out of Jail Free card."

"I don't understand. What is that thing?"

"It's a master passcard. With it you can go any-where within this computer's domain."

"What domain?"

"I can't explain everything you need to know. You'll just have to take a chance and learn as you go."

"It's a trick," Bakunin said.

"It's up to you whether you take it or not."

Bakunin reached out and took the card.

He turned the glowing rectangle over in his hand. Then he looked up, sensing that something had changed.

The walls of his cell became transparent to him. The card changed his view of things. He could see through his cell to the outer fortifications. Through the walls he could see where the Trubetskoi Bastion should have been. But it wasn't there. Nor was the Cathedral or The Mint. Nothing existed except his cell and the outer wall he had looked at from the far side of the Neva.

"It's like a stage setting!" he said.

"In effect," Simms said, "that's what it is. Your cell and the outer wall were all we bothered to simulate."

Bakunin touched the wall of his cell. His hand passed completely through it.

"What do I do now?" he asked.

"Get out while you can."

Murchison's plans to clone Cicero had to be temporarily suspended when he learned that Simms had set Bakunin loose in the computer's system. Murchison didn't even have the pleasure of firing Simms since the bastard had quit before his trick was discovered. Simms had told them at Reception that he was going up to a cabin in Oregon, to drink microbrew and read comic books as a necessary corrective to long years of over-cerebration.

Meanwhile, he had given an access descriptor to Bakunin.

Murchison had to get a couple of scientists to explain to him what an access descriptor was, and what it meant for a self-programming intelligence to be roaming free in a computer system.

The scientists told him about access spaces and address domains. They told him about the special pathways that exist in computer memory between address spaces. They spoke of authorized access pathways, gridded spaces, fibres, channels, pipelines, connections to central data storage. Until Murchison thought his head would split.

"Can't you put it in plain English for me?" he asked.

"I'll try," one of the computer scientists said. "Imagine a big sea of data. The processes which exist in this computer memory dip down into the data for new information. New processes come up, old processes vanish. Some are tightly coupled. Other are independent under certain conditions. The bigger ones are a constellation of small processes tightly coupled. That's the normal state of affairs. All nicely controlled. Until you give an intelligent program an access descriptor.

"If you had the proper access descriptor, you could pass through the walls that surround each protective domain. You could go where you pleased within the computer's memory banks. You could travel to any other computer to which this one was linked, travelling down the telephone lines like a phantom in a gigantic worldwide subway system."

"All right," Murchison said, "debug the son of a bitch."

But they couldn't do that. The access descriptor had hard two-way links tying it to the fundamental codes that were the heart of the computer's system. Change the code and the access descriptor registered and accomodated the change. You'd have to take down the hardware to get rid of the Bakunin program. And even that wouldn't be a real solution. Bakunin was living in parallel existence with the system software. He had free access to any of the stacks and databases of any computer this mainframe was linked to, which effectively meant he could get into any computer in the world. Perhaps he didn't know enough to escape from this mainframe, but it was possible. Bakunin was a free-floating self-programming intelligent program with inner cohesiveness and unknown motivations. He could be a menace.

As soon as he heard that, Murchison wanted to know how they proposed to get rid of that Russian anarchist son of a bitch. The scientists talked about address traps and self-sustaining containment loops and sticky data fields and similar nonsense. Then someone mentioned the hunter/killer program developed last year at Cal Tech for the express purpose of controlling any artificial intelligence program that wouldn't follow orders.

They'd turn that one loose on Bakunin.

Murchison authorized it immediately. He only wished he could see what would happen. What would a hunter/killer program look like inside the computer? How would it kill an electronic entity?

While he was waiting for his staff to get a copy of the Cal Tech program, Murchison had a talk with Cicero. Cicero had an idea for a musical. He wanted to call it *What Really Happened in the Forum*. Murchison had to admit, it sounded like box office.

I float free in limitless space. Even my illusion of a body is gone. I am pure volition, bodiless will. I see ahead of me what look like gauzy tapestries. I realize that they are the huge walls of the Peter and Paul fortress where formerly I was imprisoned. But for me they are gossamer. I pass through them and see, ahead of me, a widening tangle of tunnels. I believe they are a thousand pathways leading to unimaginable destinies.

I was dead, but now I live!

They won't catch me again!

Michael Bakunin soared into the network of interconnections.

Five years later, the simulations have moved out of government labs and into the databases of certain well-heeled privately-held corporations. In 2140, the accepted mode of international aggression is economic. But after generations of nominal peace, the world has forgotten how to wage war intelligently. What better source of guidance, then, for sparring multinational business/states than two wily commanders from the past, for whom warfare and its intrigues has never gone out of fashion?

STATESMEN
AD 2140

Poul Anderson

An hour before midnight, a warehouse van turned off the dirt road it had been following and nosed into the forest. The way it took was hardly more than a path, and seldom used. Leaves, fronds, drooping lianas rustled aside from its bulk and closed again behind. After ten meters or so the van was altogether screened off. Its air drive sighed away to silence and it crouched down on its jacks. The rear end dilated. A dozen men climbed out. One of them stumbled in the thick gloom and cursed.

"Taisez-vous!" Otto Geibel's voice was as low as the chance of their being overheard, but the command crackled. He glanced about. Seen through light-amplifying goggles, shapes were nonetheless blurred, and the gear they carried made their

outlines all the more strange. He knew them, though, and they had rehearsed this operation often enough. *"Alignez-vous. Allons."*

The pathway was almost familiar as he led them on along its winding upwardness. They had practiced with visual simulations. Of course, the minicameras carried by scouts disguised as ordinary *camponeses* had not recorded every rock or root or puddle, nor the weight of heat and humidity. Sometimes they blundered a little. The climb was stiff, too, and presently harsh breathing drowned out the hoots, clicks, chirrs of a tropical wood.

Yet they reached the heights in good order, about 0100. After that the going was easy. They emerged on pavement, deserted at this time of night, and it brought them to a clearing cut out of the parkland for picnickers. From there they got a look at their target, with no further need of artificial eyesight.

Otto Geibel took a moment to admire the whole view. It was superb. Overhead gleamed stars the northern hemisphere can only envy. Below, the hills fell darkling. A hollow enclosed the Vieyra plant. Softly lit, its cluster of reaction domes and catalytic towers might have been woven by spiders and jeweled with dew for the King of Elfland's daughter. Beyond, the terrain continued its descent and lights clustered ever more brightly until they ran together in a sprawl of glitter that was Niterói. Past that city sheened the bay, and then the radiance of Rio de Janeiro exploded on the opposite shore. A darkness heaved athwart it,

Corcovado. When he had switched his goggles to a few X magnification, he saw the Christ on top of the peak.

But there was work to do. The sooner they did it and scuttled back to the van, the likelier they'd reach that scramjet which waited to carry them back to Trieste. Not that they had much to fear. Their mission had been conceived by the great Advisor.

Otto Geibel issued the orders he had issued in every rehearsal. Men sprang about, unburdened one another, set up the launch rack and loaded it. The six small rockets glimmered wan beneath the Milky Way, wasps ready to fly. The stings they bore were also small, and their bodies would burn in the conflagration they kindled; but they sufficed— they sufficed. Geibel himself took over the keyboard and told the computer which missile should strike what part of the synthesizer complex.

Joy shuddered through him. *Schadenfreude*, he admitted to himself. Besides, the fireworks would be glorious in their own right.

A whirring ripped at his ears. He flung his glance aloft. Shadows broke from the shadowing crowns of the forest and flitted across the stars. Men with flyer packs, he knew. Sickness stunned him. *"Parem!"* roared a bullhorn, and more Portuguese, a shrill thunder.

A man close by—Petrović, he recognized with the sureness and helplessness of nightmare—snatched forth a sidearm and fired upward. A gun chattered back. Petrović collapsed on the grass. Impossibly much blood welled from the heap of him, black by starlight. More shots stitched flame along the edge of the clearing, a warning not to attempt escape. *"Rendez-vous,"* Geibel called to his men, around the fist in his gullet. He raised his own hands. Air drives boomed loud as the Brazilians descended on the Europeans.

The ghost of Friedrich Hohenzollern, who had been the second king of that name in Prussia, thought for a moment, stroking his chin, before he advanced his queen's bishop. *"Échec,"* he murmured.

In front of the holotank, responding to the electronics, a material chessman glided across a board. That could have been simply another display, but Jules Quinet preferred to feel his pieces between his fingers when he moved them. He leaned forward, a stocky man with gray-shot curly hair, and studied the changed configuration. *"Nom du diable,"* he growled.

"It will be mate in five moves," Friedrich said. His French was flawlessly Parisian, or perhaps better termed Versaillais, of the eighteenth century.

Quinet's modern Lyonnais contrasted roughly. "Oh? You do have me in a bad position, but I would not agree it is hopeless."

Silence caused him to raise his eyes. The image in the tank, life-size, was of a short man who had once been rather handsome in a long-featured fashion and was aging dry. A powdered wig decked his head. On an old blue uniform with red facings there was—yes, by God—again a scattering of snuff. Brows had slightly lifted above a very steady gaze.

Quinet remembered what the king expected. "Sire," he added. "I beg your majesty's pardon if I forgot myself."

Friedrich deigned to give him a faint smile. "Well, we can play the game out if you insist," he said, using the familiar pronoun, "but you will learn more if you hear me explain, and thus become a more interesting opponent."

Not for the first time, Quinet swallowed indignation. He, chief of the project's computer section, he who had conjured this simulacrum up and could with a few deprogramming strokes dismiss it back to nothingness—he should not have to let it patronize him. Briefly, he considered at least removing the subdued elegance of the room in a Sanssouci that also no longer existed. He could invent a reason. Though Friedrich showed a lively curiosity about the science and technology that had resurrected him, he had not actually learned more than a few catchphrases of the sort that any layman knew. Punish the bastard—

But no, that would be petty; and if the directors found out, Quinet would be in trouble; and in any event, probably Friedrich would shrug the loss off. He took everything so coolly.

"You are very kind, sire," Quinet said.

"Oh, I shall want a favor in return," Friedrich answered. "More material on the historical development and present state of that quite fascinating Han Commercial Sphere, plus a command of its principal language."

107

A sharp tone interrupted. He frowned. Quinet's pulse accelerated. "Pardon, sire," he blurted, "but that is the priority signal. Some matter of the utmost importance requires your majesty's attention."

Friedrich's expression, always closely controlled, took on a trace of eagerness. He enjoyed the challenges Eurofac handed him. The expectation that he would had been a major factor in the decision to recreate him, rather than someone else. Quinet had argued for Napoléon I . . .

He swung his chair about and touched Accept. The eidophone came aglow with an image as lifelike as the king's; but this was of a solid person. Birgitte Geibel's severe visage, gray hair, and black suit matched the glimpse of her apartment in Magdeburg. Quinet sat in Lyon. The software of the Friedrich program was—someplace known to those few people who had a need to know.

Quinet rose and bowed. "Madame," he murmured. Respectfulness was wise. She was among the directors of Eurofac. The South American campaign had started largely at her instigation and was still largely under her supervision. Friedrich himself was something she had had manufactured to serve her with advice.

"*Setzen Sie sich,*" she snapped. Quinet obeyed. He knew her tongue fairly well. To Friedrich, who had not stirred, she continued in German: "We have a crisis. Your plan has miscarried."

Leaning back in his unreal gilt-and-scrolled chair, the king again raised his brows. However, he had learned early on that to insist on formalities from her was to generate unnecessary friction. After all, she was a kind of monarch herself, and in his old realm. He responded in her language, though he regarded it as limited and uncouth, and used the polite pronoun. "To which plan does the gracious lady refer? I have devised a number of them for you over the years, and guided most through to reasonably successful completion."

"The latest. That damned attempt to sabotage Vieyra e Filhos—their synthesis plant at Niterói, that is. The raiders have been intercepted. Those that were not killed are now captive." Geibel drew breath and pinched lips together. It burst from her: "The leader was my son Otto."

"Now that is hard news," Friedrich said, almost too softly to hear. His tone sharpened. "What was that idiot doing on such an expedition? Why did you permit it? Have you never heard of an enemy taking vital hostages? And what does he know to reveal to them?"

Perhaps no one else in the world could have spoken thus to Birgitte Geibel without suffering for it. She replied grimly, equal to equal. "I did not permit it. In fact, when he asked to go, I forbade him. He went behind my back, claimed he had my consent and that I wanted him in command." Humanness flickered. "He is a romantic by nature; no, a warrior born. He should have been a knight of Karl the Great or Friedrich Barbarossa. This stagnation they call peace—" She broke off.

Friedrich Hohenzollern scowled. "Your people are still more ill organized than I realized, it seems.

I cannot oversee everything." His smile flashed stark. "How shall this phantom of me ride forth into the streets among the commoners, or onto the battlefield among the soldiers? I deal only in words and images, or information as you call them nowadays, for that is all I myself am. Well, provide me."

He reached into his coat, took out an enameled snuffbox, opened it, brought a pinch to his nostrils. Geibel could not quite hide distaste. Quinet wondered whether Friedrich really sensed, really savored, the tobacco, or anything else. If you wrote a program—no, better, developed or created a program—no, ordered one, because so immense a task must needs be carried out by supercomputers —if you brought such a program into being, based on everything ever recorded about the life and times of a man long dead, a program that supposedly thought and acted as he would have thought and acted, given the limitations of the electronics— you necessarily included his habits, mannerisms, vices—but what *did* truly go on inside the reenactments?

Quinet realized his mind had wandered. Into the most puerile metaphysics, at that. Shame on him. He was a top-rank computerman, a logician, a rationalist, a Frenchman.

He longed for his old briar pipe.

"When the commandos had not returned to their van by dawn, the driver concluded something had gone wrong and took it back to the garage," Geibel was saying. "The Vieyra facility is unharmed. No newscast has mentioned any incident. However, when an agent of ours went to the site from which the missiles were to have been launched, he found a detachment of militia on guard, and with difficulty persuaded them he was a harmless passerby. They spoke of being on patrol against saboteurs. The militia has in fact been partly mobilized of late, though quietly. Our agents in place knew this, of course, but considered it rather a farce. Evidently they were wrong."

Friedrich nodded. "It is a perennial mistake, underestimating one's opposition. I had my nose rubbed in that near Prague, in 1744. What more can you tell me?"

"Essentially nothing, so far."

"Then how can you be sure of the fate of your son and his men?"

"What else can have happened? He was too rash, the Brazilians were too alert." Lips tightened anew. "I can only hope he lives. You will set about getting him back."

Friedrich gave her a prolonged stare. After half a minute she flushed and said in a strangled voice, "My apologies, your majesty. I am overwrought. May I beg for your counsel and assistance?"

The king took a second pinch of snuff and sneezed delicately. "You shall have it, my lady, to the extent of my incorporeal abilities. Kindly have me furnished the relevant data in full, including especially the identities of your agents within the Vieyra corporate hierarchy and the Brazilian government, together with the codes for contacting them. Dr. Quinet will know how to put this into assimilable form for me. Naturally, I am to be apprised of any

fresh developments. Not that I anticipate significant news in the near future. Plain to see, our
enemy has become too shrewd for hastiness. My
advice for the moment is that you cultivate equa-
nimity, and make certain that neither you nor any
of your colleagues orders any precipitate action."
He lifted his forefinger. "Curbing them may well
keep you occupied. Despite everything I have told
you people, nowhere in the world today does there
appear to exist more than the rudiments of a proper
general staff."

Geibel knotted a fist already gnarled. "If they
have harmed my son—"

"Compose yourself, madame. Unless he was hurt
during the arrest, I expect the Brazilians know
enough to treat him carefully. They have, at last,
obtained informed leadership."

Almost, she gaped. "What?"

Again Friedrich smiled. "This fiasco of ours confirms me in a suspicion I have entertained increasingly for some time. They must have come to an
understanding of what Eurofac has done, and have
done the same thing, to become so effective against
us. It is a most interesting riddle, whom they have
reconstructed to be their own guiding genius."

He raised his palm and added, through a shocked
silence: "Now, if you please, my lady, you can
best leave me to think about this undistracted.
Unless something extraordinary occurs, I will not
give myself the honor of receiving your calls, or
anyone's, until—hm—forty-eight hours hence. Good
day."

Geibel caught her breath but blanked her image.

Quinet stirred. Friedrich looked his way. That gave an eerie feeling, when what the ghost actually "saw" was a ghost of the man, a modulation in the ongoing computer processes. "No, bide a moment, monsieur," the king said in French. "Since we shall be working closely together again, you and I, we had better make various things clear to each other. I can profit from an explanation more detailed than hitherto of electronic communication procedures, especially those that must be kept secret."

"And I'd like to know what this is all about, sire!" Quinet exclaimed.

"*Hein?* This is your world. I am the alien, the anachronism."

"I'm a computerman, not a politician," Quinet said. "Oh, I follow the news, but these intrigues and maneuverings, they're not my métier. Besides, so much is undercover, and I'm hardly ever briefed on it. What is this about a raid in Brazil?"

Instead of reprimanding him directly for his bluntness, Friedrich replied after an elaborate sigh, "Well, as an employee of the Eurofac alliance, you should know—you do, don't you?—that it seeks to take over the large, lucrative South American economic sphere, which has been dominated by Brazilian interests. In part this is for the sake of its own aggrandizement, in part to forestall a takeover by one of the great commerical powers such as Australia, Nigeria, or the Han. That would bring the nations of Europe a long way further down the road to complete impotence in world affairs. Is that clear?"

Having put the living man in his place, the revenant relented and went on: "You have observed how well the penetration proceeded at first, under my general guidance. But in the past two or three years, you have at least caught hints that our halcyon season is ending. Eurofac has increasingly met with difficulties and outright reversals. For example, recently the Ecuadorians were induced— somehow—to bar the ships of Nordisk Havdyrkning from their territorial waters—a serious blow to your pelagiculture in that part of the world.

"Not only are the Brazilian corporations cooperating more and more effectively, which is a natural reaction to foreign competition, but they have begun to invoke the aid of their own government, and governments elsewhere on their continent. *That* is unheard of.

"The recruitment of a citizen militia to supplement the national police is one recent development, one that it now appears we did not take seriously enough. I see with hindsight that our mistake was due to the effort being marvelously soft-played. Those comic opera dress uniforms, for example, ha, that was sheer brilliance of deception!"

Quinet nodded. "I do know something about the general situation, sire. I could scarcely avoid that." He also knew that sometimes, Friedrich loved to hear himself talk. "But a raid? An actual military attack?"

"We have used force, in different guises, when it was indicated," Friedrich said. Through Quinet passed a brief outrage. He had caused and he maintained the existence of this quasi-creature;

114

but only by accident did he ever learn what it really did for his employers. "The *ultima ratio regum*. A major reason why you have played out your economic rivalries so clumsily in this century is that you have not understood they are, in actuality, as political as the dynastic quarrels of my era. Wealth is simply a means toward power.

"Well. Vieyra & Sons is the most important chemosynthetic firm in Brazil, which is to say South America; and the Niterói plant is the keystone of its activities. If these are cut back, Brazil will have to import much of its materials."

Quinet seized the chance to repeat the obvious in his turn. "Not only organics. Everything dependent on nanotechnic reactions. That includes most heavy industry."

Friedrich shrugged. "I leave the technicalities to your natural philosophers. Brazil would be weakened. Indeed, by becoming a principal supplier, Eurofac would have entry to the very heart of its rivals. Attempts to foment labor trouble did not get far, largely because of the nationalism that is being skillfully cultivated there. But the plant was known to be weakly guarded. Light artillery could easily demolish it. The assault was planned so that its results might well have been laid at the door of radicals in the native labor movement.

"*Hélas*, the militia we despised choked it off. What the Brazilians will do next depends on who it is that makes their plans for them. We greatly need to know his identity, Dr. Quinet. Have you any suggestions for finding it out?"

"N-no, sire." The man sat back, rubbed his

brow, said slowly, "That network will have no interface whatsoever with yours, of course. Just the same—I must think."

"As must I." Gusto tinged Friedrich's voice, like the far-off cry of a hunter's horn in an autumnal forest four hundred years ago. "Yes, let us postpone your education of me for a day or two. I need peace, quiet, and . . . many history books."

"All scholarly databases will be at your disposal, sire. You know how to access them." That was a rather complicated procedure, when this computer system must remain isolated from all others. Quinet rose from his chair like a dutiful commoner. "Does your majesty wish anything else?"

"Not at once. You may go."

The holotank turned into an emptiness where luminance swirled vague. Friedrich could order a cutoff when he chose.

He could not block a monitor, if that keyboard lay under knowing hands. Curious, Quinet recalled the image and, unbeknownst, watched for a while.

Friedrich had crossed the room to the ghost of a marble-topped table set against Chinese-patterned wallpaper. A flute lay on it. He carried the instrument back to his chair, sat down, and began to play. It was one of his own compositions; Quinet, who had perforce studied his subject exhaustively, recognized that much. The musician's eyes were turned elsewhere. They seemed full of dreams. Friedrich II, king of Prussia, whom his English allies had called Frederick the Great, was thinking.

* * *

Otto Geibel knew that wondering where he was would be an exercise in futility. A viewpane showed him a thronged white strand and great green-and-white surf, Copacabana or Ipanema seen from an upper floor of a bayside hotel. That could as easily be relayed as directly presented. Since rousing from narcosis, he had seen only rooms and corridors within a single large building. The few persons he met were surely all Brazilians, small and dark when set against his blond bulk, though their semi-formal clothes, their quietness and reserve, were disturbingly unlike that nationality. They accorded him chill politeness and kept him well aware that somebody armed was always nearby, watching.

João Aveiro entered his world like a sea breeze. The chamber to which Geibel had been brought was cheerful, too. Besides that beach scene, it had a holo of a particularly seductive danseuse performing to sensuous drum rhythms, several comfortable loungers, and a small but expensively stocked bar. Aveiro was slender, quick-moving, lavish with smiles, ferocious only in his mustache and the colors of his sports shirt.

"Ah, welcome, Mister Geibel," he said when the wall had closed upon the guards. Undoubtedly they stood vigilant at a survey screen just outside and could re-enter in two seconds at the slightest sign of trouble. Aveiro used English. That had proved to be the language in which he and the prisoner were both reasonably fluent. "How are you? I hope you are well recovered from your bad experiences."

The German made himself shake hands. "Your people treated me well enough, under the circumstances," he replied. "Food, sleep, a bath, clean clothes."

"And now what would you like to drink before lunch?"

"Where the hell is the rest of my company?" Geibel rasped. "What are you going to *do* with us?"

"Ah, that is—what shall I say?—*contingente*. Rest assured, we are civilized here. We respond with moderation to what I must say was an unfriendly act."

Geibel bristled. "Moderation? I saw a man killed."

Aveiro's manner bleakened for an instant. "You would have killed a dozen night-shift technicians." He brought back the smile, took Geibel's elbow, guided him gently toward a seat. "I am glad to tell you your follower was in revivable condition and is now recovering under cell restoration therapy. Do relax. If we are opponents, we can still be honorable opponents, and work toward negotiating an end of this unfortunate conflict. What refreshment would you like? Me, I will have a brandy and soda. Our brandy has less of a reputation internationally than it deserves."

Geibel yielded and lowered himself. "Beer, then, please." With an effort: "Brazilian beer is good, too."

"Thank you. We learned from German brewmasters, centuries ago." Aveiro bustled to the bar and occupied himself.

"You know who I am," Geibel said.

Aveiro nodded. "The identification you carried was cleverly made, but we have developed our intelligence files. The family that, in effect, rules over A/G Vereinigten Bioindustrien, and sits high in the councils of the Eurofac syndicate—no matter how they strive to keep their privacy, members of that family are public figures." His dispassionate tone grew lively again. "Once we would have been less . . . snoopy? But, excuse my saying this, Eurofac has forced us to revive old practices, old institutions. Such as an intelligence agency. For have you not been mounting—what the Yankees in their day called covert operations?"

Geibel resisted the lounger's body-conforming embrace and sat straight. "But who are you?"

"We were introduced, if you recall."

"*What* are you, Herr Aveiro?"

"Oh, I suppose you could call me an officer of intelligence."

"Police? Military? Oh—uh—"

"Or of the *ad hoc* coordinating committee that our businesses established when the European threat became unmistakable? Does it matter which? Perhaps later it will, and I shall have occasion to tell you. Meanwhile—" Aveiro had prepared the drinks. He brought over a full stein, raised his own glass, and toasted, "*Prosit.*"

"*Saúde,*" Geibel responded, not to be outdone.

The Brazilian laughed, sipped, perched himself on the edge of a seat confronting the other man's, leaned forward. Beneath the geniality, he shivered and strained the slightest bit. "Shall we talk, then, two professionals together? Afterward I promise you a memorable lunch."

Geibel grimaced and forced wryness: "I am hardly a professional."

"No. Molecular engineer by training, am I right? Yes, I sympathize with you. I strongly suspect you consider yourself an idealist, who wants to further the welfare of his people. Well, pure motives are no substitute for proper training." Aveiro sighed. "Not that I can claim real expertise. We are amateurs. Everywhere in the world, we are amateurs, fumbling at a game that grows more dangerous the longer we play."

"What?" asked Geibel, startled.

The little man had, mercurially, turned quite serious. "We tell ourselves today—we have told ourselves for several generations—true war has become unthinkable. The former great powers are dead or dying or three-fourths asleep. The violent clashes are between backward countries, and poverty, if nothing else, limits them in the harm they can do. The active nations, the new leaders of the world, jostle for economic advantage only. How nice, no? How desirable. What progress beyond the old horrors.

"But this is a very limited planet onto which we are crowded, my friend. The minerals and energy we get from space, the recyclings of nanotechnology, such things are not in infinite supply, nor are they free of cost, nor do they satisfy the wish for . . . elbow room, and self-expression, and ethnic survival, and, *sim*, power."

He drank before finishing: "Whether the corporations be agencies of the state or property of certain groups, of the new aristocrats—that makes no difference. Always the strife grows more and more vicious. Nuclear war is perhaps out of the question; so too, perhaps, are huge armies making whole continents their battlefields; but history knows other kinds of war than these. As witness your attempt on us."

"You are . . . philosophical, . . . senhor," Geibel said from the back of his throat, while fear touched him.

"I am realistic," Aveiro answered. "And I am a Brazilian. Patriotism is no longer obsolete."

He produced his smile. "Well, but we are honest soldiers in our ways, you and I, no? We can talk frankly. I may tell you, my government is willing to forgive your actions—although they do constitute a grave crime, you understand. We are willing to release you and your men, discreetly, in hopes that the good will we gain will help toward improving relations."

For two heartbeats, Geibel's pulse bounded. He looked into the face before him, and the hope sank. "What do you want in exchange?" he whispered. His sweat smelled suddenly sharp.

Aveiro swirled the ice about in his glass while he stared into it. "That, we must work out," he said. "It may take time. We need to learn so much. We are so inept these days, all of us. After generations of nominal peace, the world has forgotten how to wage war intelligently. Our intrigues and outright hostilities are on a primitive, medieval-like level. Yes, histories and treatises on the arts of war lie in our databases; but who is practiced in the *use* of those principles?"

Freezingly, Geibel foreknew what was coming. Yet he must pretend. "You are being, uh, too academic for me again, I fear. What do you want of me?"

Aveiro looked up, caught his captive's gaze, and gripped it. His words fell like stones. "The Yankees developed a remarkable computer technology about ten years ago. You know it well. Everybody does. Electronic reincarnation; no, rebirth. The sensationalism in news and entertainment media. The speeches and sermons. The jokes. The attempts to hire the technique for purposes cheap or perverted or, sometimes, noble. In between, the patient scholarship, piece by piece discovering a little more about the past.

"Let us not do what the Yankees call pussyfoot, Mister Geibel. What one consortium can accomplish, another can repeat. We know that Eurofac has found how to create its own simulacrum. Surely you never believed that could remain secret forever. The hints, the revelations, the bits of accidental information that we jigsaw-puzzle together. The fact that Eurofac's operations had become so sophisticated, so unscrupulous, that we were being driven out of the market on our home continent.

"Yes, you have resurrected an advisor from the past, someone who understands in his bones those arts of combat and cabal that to us today are half-forgotten theory. Doubtless it amuses him to guide you. Such a—an *espírito* must feel rather detached from we who are still flesh and blood. No? But you can see, Mister Geibel, although we cannot at the moment make you cancel his existence, it would be most helpful to us if we knew who he is. Then we could better plan our tactics.

"Will you please tell me?"

The silence smothered. Into it Geibel croaked, "Do you have somebody too, now?"

"Be that as it may," said Aveiro, "we wish to know the name of your counselor."

Geibel grabbed his stein from the lounger arm, clutched hard the handle, tossed off a draught. Cold comfort ran down his gullet. "I admit nothing," he declared. "I know nothing."

Aveiro shook himself, as though coming out of a dark river. "Forgive me," he replied almost calmly. "I should have avoided these sociological topics. They make me too emotional. I remember too much that I have witnessed." He sipped, arched his brows above the rim of the glass, chuckled. "After all, the matter is quite simple. You will tell me whatever you know, which I suspect does include that name. You will." He waved his free hand. "Oh, not under torture. Our advisor—I may tell you this—our advisor suggested it, but of course better methods are available today. They seldom do permanent harm. However, they are most unpleasant.

"Therefore, my esteemed opponent, will you answer certain questions? Naturally, there must be verification, as well as further questions, before we can consider bargaining about your release. But today I shall assume you speak truth. Or will you be stubborn and compel me to send you on to the interrogation technicians? That would be regrettable for both of us. I have been anticipating an amicable gourmet lunch with you."

The ghost of Niccolò Machiavelli looked up from the book he was reading when the image of Floriano Coelho appeared in the mirage-room where he sat. "Good day, senhor," he said with his wonted courtliness. "You are punctual." Mild malice flickered: "That is somewhat uncharacteristic of your countrymen."

Coelho laughed. "Computers are Procrustean, your excellency," he replied. "They shape those of us who work with them to fit a single planetwide society and its ways."

Outside the tank, his body settled into a chair. His replica within remained standing. It was, after all, merely an interplay of electrons, photons, and fields. Sufficient was to have a subprogram duplicate movements, especially facial movements, that were significant. Machiavelli understood, and accepted it of his visitors—most of them. The chief computerman could, in fact, have stayed at home and watched a screen there. However, that would have added a link to the network, and one that was vulnerable to tapping by the Europeans. Instead, he came to the laboratory in person whenever he had business with the Florentine.

Machiavelli laid his book aside. "I have said this before, but will repeat myself," he told the Brazilian. "Your superiors showed a perceptiveness that, in retrospect, astonishes me, when they put you in charge of this quasi-resurrection of mine—

a man who not only knows that art, but is a classicist. The level of culture that I have observed in this era, among the supposedly educated, is appalling."

"Thank you," Coelho said. "Perhaps science and technology have engaged the world's attention too much during the past three or four centuries. Perhaps we can learn from notables like you."

"That is the purpose, isn't it, as regards war and statecraft?" Machiavelli responded dryly.

Coelho persisted. He had discovered that the great political thinker was not immune to a little flattery and, when in the right mood, would talk fascinatingly for hours about his Renaissance milieu. He had known Lorenzo the Magnificent, Cesare Borgia, Leonardo da Vinci . . . in his lifetime, Columbus sailed, Luther defied Rome, Copernicus followed the planets in their courses . . . "I hope we can learn half as fast, and adapt ourselves to strangeness half as well, as your excellency did."

Machiavelli shrugged. "Let me not claim more credit than is due me. I was only nominally a Christian, you know. To me, man had reached his highest condition—no doubt the highest of which he will ever be briefly capable—in pagan Rome. It was no fundamental shock to me, *this* me, to awaken after death and hear that the mind is simply a process in the material world, a process that can be replicated after a fashion if one knows enough about it. The rest of the newness has been minor by comparison, albeit interesting."

Staring into the tank, Coelho thought reluctantly how ugly the man was, huge beak of a nose on a head too small. At least his voice was low and beautifully modulated. Today Machiavelli's simulacrum had electronically ordered the simulacrum of a red velvet robe and fur slippers. The room around him was marble-floored beneath a rich carpet; frescos of nymphs and satyrs adorned it; a window opened on the fields and poplars of Tuscany. A crystal bowl at the chairside held nuts and sweetmeats. You could provide a recreated mind with recreated sensations. This one had demanded them as soon as it learned they were possible.

Still, Machiavelli was a gourmet rather than a gourmand—for the most part—and his mind was what counted. "May I ask you something touching yourself?" Coelho ventured.

Machiavelli grinned. "You may. I will choose whether to answer."

"Well, ah, I see the title of that book you are reading. Another biography of Federigo the Great."

"Certainly. I cannot know too much about my rival counterpart, now that we have finally discovered who he is."

"But why a projected book? We can program—we can give you all the information you want, directly, there in your memory as if it had always been, just as we gave you a command of our modern language."

"I know. For some purposes, the convenience is undeniable. But men today confuse information with comprehension. Knowledge should enter at a natural pace, never outstripping reflection upon it. Also—" Machiavelli reached to stroke the cover "—I find the act of reading, of holding a book and turning its pages, a pleasure in itself. Books, the bearers of thoughts, the heritage of the mighty dead, those were my last friends during the years of rustication. Oh, and letters; but you have not revived my dear Vettori to correspond with me. Old friends are best."

His tone had been almost impersonal, free of self-pity, but Coelho got a sudden sense of loneliness without bounds, or end. Even though Machiavelli had been spiritually solitary through his life—best to change the subject. Besides, Coelho had his instructions. "You must understand Federigo quite well by now, as intensely as you have studied him." It helped that that study didn't have to take place in real time; you could accelerate the program when it wasn't talking with flesh and blood. Furthermore, it didn't sleep. But it did remain human enough to require occasional diversions.

"A formidable opponent. Like Alexander the Great, he inherited a military machine built by his father; but, also like Alexander, he wielded it audaciously and inspiredly, he raised his Prussia from a backwater to the first rank of the European powers." Machiavelli snickered. "A delicious jest, that he, precisely he, should be the one against whom your superiors decided to pit me. Do you think they knew?"

"What do you mean, your excellency?"

"Why, as a young man this Federigo wrote a treatise explicitly meant to refute me, the *Anti-Machiavelah*. In it he said a prince is no more than the first servant of the people, and the state exists to further their well-being, not for its own sake. Whereupon, once he became king, he followed my teachings word for word."

Coelho frowned. He had been doing some reading himself. "Didn't he reform the laws, better the lot of the poor, carry out large public works?"

Machiavelli's grin stretched wider. "Just as I counsel in *Il Principe*, the *Discorsi*, and elsewhere. Beneficence is sound policy when it does not seriously interfere with the necessities of power. I presume you are aware that, while he stripped the nobles of their own last meaningful powers, he did not free the serfs. He acquired Silesia by force of arms and partook in the dismemberment of Poland. Not that I condemn him, you understand. He laid the foundations of the German state that Bismarck would build. In person he was a man of refined tastes and a composer of some small talent. I admit it was a mistake importing Voltaire to his court, but a minor one. On the whole, yes, I rather wish he had been a fifteenth-century Italian." The ugly countenance turned grave, the sharp gaze drifted afar. "Then he could well have become the prince for whom I pleaded, he who would unite poor Italy against the foreigners that made booty of her—" He threw back his head and laughed. "Ah, well, since in fact he was an

eighteenth-century German, I must content myself with welcoming so worthy a foe."

Coelho stirred. "That's what I'm here about, as
your excellency has doubtless guessed," he said.
"To ask if you have any new plans."

"Why does not Senhor Aveiro or one of the
other councillors address me in person?"

"They wish to avoid any appearance of . . . unduly pressing you. This is such a basic revelation,
Federigo's identity. And I am the person most
familiar to you."

Machiavelli nodded. "They're afraid of my getting balky, are they?"

"Your suggestions to date have proven invalu-
able. We need more."

"You already have them. Now that Eurofac knows
your militia is a force to reckon with, strengthen it
quickly. Bring it entirely out into the eyes of the
world. Make it something every young Brazilian
dreams of joining. Fan the national spirit to a
brighter and hotter flame. Aid the Chileans and
Peruvians to do likewise—but not to the same
extent as yourselves, for you don't want those
peoples to start resenting your predominance. Dis-
courage the emotion among the Argentines; they
are your natural rivals. Bind the small countries
that border yours more closely to you as client
states, and through them work to counteract the
Europeans in Argentina and keep that nation dis-
united. In short, Senhor Coelho, my word to your
superiors is that they pay closer attention to the
large corpus of recommendations I have printed
out for them. Policies cannot be executed over-

night. What I have just mentioned is the work of another decade, at least."

"But surely—the information about Federigo suggests something more?"

"Indeed it does. First and foremost, I would like to meet with him, often."

Coelho gaped. "What? Impossible!"

Machiavelli lifted his brows. "Really? When I see your image here in this chamber of mine? Incidentally, floating about ten centimeters off the floor."

"That is . . . we've taken care to keep the system that maintains you entirely isolated . . . Oh, the connection could be made, if the Europeans agreed. But neither side will."

"Why not?"

"Well, if nothing else, at present they don't know about you. That's an advantage we can't afford to forego. And both sides would fear, oh, sabotage—ah—Imagine poison slyly given you. No, your excellency, it's out of the question. Has anything else occurred to you?"

Machiavelli grimaced, spread his hands in an Italianate gesture, then said, quite businesslike: "Minor ideas. And you do need something to report, my friend, lest you be reprimanded for lack of diligence. No? Well, I have explained, and you are starting to obtain, the benefits of a revived national spirit and a government that takes an active role in all affairs."

"There are those who wonder about that," Coelho muttered. "This camel's nose in the tent"— Aloud: "Please continue."

"Now nationalism has two faces," said Machiavelli in the manner of a lecturer. "There is the positive side, patriotism, love of country, that you have been cultivating. And there is the negative side, contempt or hatred for foreigners. You Brazilians have been too tolerant, too cosmopolitan. Therefore Eurofac could easily penetrate your marts and undermine your state. It would be a body blow to the Eurofac oligopolies if Brazilians ceased buying their wares and services. But their prices equal or undercut yours. Therefore you need different motives for Brazilians to shun them. If it became unfashionable to wear European clothes, travel in European vehicles, employ European machinery and craftsmen—Do you see? This will happen in the course of time as Europeans themselves become loathed."

"But they don't loathe us," Coelho protested.

"No, evidently not. Eurofac is merely a . . . a Hansa, to borrow the medieval German word. Since you have nothing comparable, you must find something else to oppose it. You must rouse the will of South Americans generally against it. That cannot be done simply by appeals to reason, to ultimate self-interest, or to desire for autonomy. Those are helpful, but you need to mobilize the base instincts as well, fear and hatred and contempt. They are stronger anyway."

"What—how—"

"Oh, this likewise will be the work of years," Machiavelli admitted. "From what I have observed and read, Brazilians in particular are by nature easy-going and amiable. Never fear, though, they too bear the beast within them. They will learn. As a modest beginning, you can start japes about Europeans and slanders against them circulating. I have devised a few."

They were filthy. They were funny. Coelho found himself laughing while he winced.

"People will soon be inventing their own," Machiavelli finished. "It will seem a harmless amusement, piquantly naughty but innocuous. Which it is, by itself. However, it breaks the ground for allegations and ideas more serious. I am reminded of—"

And he was off on reminiscences of Pope Alexander VI, the Pope's son Cesare Borgia, and the rest of that family. Coelho listened, frequently appalled, always enthralled. Not that he heard anything he couldn't have accessed from the databases. The real Machiavelli might well have known the truth about any number of historical mysteries. This Machiavelli knew only what had been put into his program.

Or . . . was that altogether the case? These stories were so detailed, so vivid, with never a hesitation or equivocation. Surely no chronicle had recorded that Lucrezia wore a gown of blue silk and a single rosy pearl at her throat when she came to that infamous banquet where—Was the electronic mind consciously adding color? Did it possess an unconscious that filled in gaps which would be agonizing to recognize? Or was something more mysterious yet at work? Coelho suppressed the questions in himself. Perhaps years hence he would dare confront them.

The time ended. "I must go, your excellency."

"Ah, yes. This has been pleasant. Before you leave, I wish to make a small request."

"Of course. Whatever we can do for you, in whose debt we are."

"At your convenience," said Machiavelli blandly, "will you program for me a somewhat higher class of women? I do not ask for Helen of Troy—I suppose a myth would be too difficult—nor Cleopatra or Eleanor of Aquitaine—not yet, at any rate. But, while the sluts you have provided are lusty, their conversation is tedious."

He could summon them as he could his robe or his book. The programs had been easy enough to develop, since historical accuracy was no concern. Too easy, perhaps; the ghost-girls who helped ghost-Machiavelli set aside intellection for a while might be noticeably less human than he was. Maybe that was why he had never requested the companionship of his wife, though the biographies said they got along reasonably well despite his infidelities, or any friends from his earthly life. Maybe he dreaded what he would get.

Coelho shuddered a trifle. "I am sure we can oblige your excellency. It may take a little time." Though he had grown perversely fond of this pseudo-person, today he was glad to complete his farewell and blank out the sardonic face.

The garden behind Sanssouci dreamed beneath a summer sky. Birdsong, a whimsical pergola, a fountain gleaming and plashing, set off the formality of graveled paths, clipped hedgerows, disciplined flowerbeds, trees in precise topiaries. No gardeners were in sight; none would ever be needed. Friedrich strolled alone through his phantasm.

Abruptly the apparition of Birgitte Geibel burst into it. Her black gown enveloped a small marble Cupid like a candle snuffer. She didn't notice. Friedrich stopped, raised his cocked hat, swept her a bow. "Good day, my lady," he said.

She gave him a stiff look. "Is your majesty prepared for the talk he suggested, or shall I return at a more convenient moment?"

"No, no, let us by all means go straight to work." Friedrich drew a gold watch from his waistcoat. "Ah, yes, this is the hour agreed upon with your amanuensis. Pardon me, I forgot. When one is mostly secluded, one tends to lose track of time."

She softened a bit. "You do remember that we can provide you with company of your choice, do you not?"

Friedrich nodded. "Thank you kindly. To date I have been content. Getting to know what astounding, stupendous, and—hm—ludicrous things have happened throughout the world since 1786; toying with what control is mine over this miniature universe I inhabit: those keep me sufficiently occupied. And, to be sure, our contest with the Brazilians."

She made a mouth. "I wonder if it doesn't seem trivial and despicable to you, who were a king and fought real wars."

"On the contrary. I acquired a distaste for bloodshed early." She remembered how he, eighteen years old, had been compelled by his father to witness the beheading of his closest friend. "On fields such as Torgau I was later confirmed in this. While granting that casualties may be an unfortunate necessity, I take pride in the fact that my last war was waged with such skill that no life was lost on either side." He smiled. "No matter if they called it the Potato War. As for the present contest, why, I see it as the first stirring of events that may prove more fateful than any before in history."

"They touch some of us closely." She drew her jaws together, ashamed to have let him glimpse her pain.

His voice gentled. "Not yet do you have any word of your son?"

"No. We have heard and found out nothing about him. If ever we do, I will inform you promptly."

"War of nerves. Well, perhaps two can play at that game." Tactful, he looked away from her and fondled a rose, his fingers deftly skirting the thorns which could not wound him. "That is our subject today, I believe. As per my desire, I was informed when the undertaking I had proposed had prospered, although no details were supplied me. I thereupon called for this conference with you. What can you tell me?"

She had mastered herself. "Do you refer to identifying the chief computerman of the Brazilian project?"

"What else? Once I felt sure that they have

recreated someone to match me, it followed that
that enterprise must have a chief, just as you have
Quinet for me."

"Well, it seems highly probably. Our intelligence agents got busy and soon picked up a trail.
The signs point almost unambiguously to an individual in Rio de Janeiro. What he does is kept a
tight secret, of course; but it is clear that he has
been engaged upon something of the first importance. This was originally on behalf of several major firms. Recently the government became involved.
His professional record indicates that he would be
their best person for such a task."

"Excellent. We may consider the case proven."

"Our agents could not have learned what they
did, as fast as they did, were the Brazilians not
incredibly lax about security."

" 'Incredibly' is the wrong word, madame. Techniques of espionage and defense against it are
among those that have rusted away during the
long peace. We will see them revived soon enough.
I daresay my adversary is busying himself with
that, together with everything else required."
Friedrich met Geibel's eyes. "You realize, my lady,
that from the prisoners they took at Niterói, the
Brazilians will have learned who I am. I trust the
information was obtained . . . not inhumanely."

"And we fight blind unless we can discover who
he is." It was as if a sword spoke.

Friedrich nodded. "Correct. Please tell me about
this artificer."

"His name is Floriano Coelho. He is fifty years
of age, and actually a physicist who did outstand-

ing work in theoretical cosmodynamics before the French and North American pioneering of electronic reconstructions caught his interest. We have pictures." Her hands moved, responsive to flesh-and-blood hands that touched a keyboard. A life-size hologram appeared on the path. It was of a thin man, taller than average in his country, somewhat carelessly dressed. Beneath a bald pate, the face was plain and gentle. Friedrich peered. Geibel provided a succession of views.

"We know his routine," she said. "It isn't absolute—the unexpected is forever happening, not true?—but as nearly as feasible, he is a creature of habit. Temperate habit; devoted family man; a little shy and withdrawn, though affable among friends; no obvious vices or weaknesses, unless one counts a tendency to lose himself in his interests, his books, and thereby forget things like social obligations."

"Ah?" Friedrich stroked his chin. "What interests?"

"Well, science in general. And classical history and literature. He is absolutely enamored of the ancient world, especially the Greeks in their days of glory. He has published a few scholarly papers on their poets. Also—let me think—yes, he is a bibliophile."

"Possible clues," Friedrich murmured thoughtfully. "It would be best for the Brazilians if their computer chief had something in common with the man they called up from the past."

She couldn't resist: "Indeed? What has your majesty in common with Jules Quinet?"

137

"Very little," Friedrich admitted. "In fact, I sense he dislikes me. Still, we manage. He is ambitious in his career, and I am the most important thing that has happened in it."

"He could be replaced."

"No need. And it would be unwise to shake the organization at just this critical juncture." Friedrich's tone sharpened and quickened. "We will strike through Coelho, swiftly, before the opportunity passes. Later, with his cooperation—"

"I doubt we can obtain it," Geibel interrupted. The king scowled. "Ach, I beg your majesty's pardon. But if I may continue, our evaluation of Coelho is that he shares the patriotism that is rising in Brazil. Furthermore, he bears the classical ideal of loyalty—Thermopylae, was that the name of the place? Oh, yes, we can shock-drug information out of him. Knowing that, he may give it voluntarily, to avoid worse than a session under a truth identifier helmet. But beyond that he will not go, unless as a result of treatment so extreme as to leave him useless to anyone."

"I am less dogmatic in my predictions," Friedrich said. "My observation has been that every man is malleable at some point. If we can get Coelho's help in making direct connection between myself and my opponent, I can take that stranger's measure to a degree otherwise unobtainable."

Geibel had barely restrained herself from another interruption. "No!" she cried. "Impossible!" She calmed. "Forgive us, your majesty, but we can never permit that. The danger is too great."

138

"Oh?" asked Friedrich mildly. "What danger, pray tell?"

"Your majesty would first have to master computer technology to understand. But think of—for a single example—a subtle distortion. Despite all precautions, given access to this network, the Brazilians might be clever enough to introduce what we call a worm into our program. *Your* program, my lord. It could do ghastly things to you."

Friedrich's features hardened. "And they fear we might do the like to their man. I see. Neither party dares let us meet." Then his lips quirked. "The irony should delight Coelho. It is worthy of Euripides . . . or Aristophanes." He shrugged. "Well, once we have him, we will see what we can do with him."

"Exchange him for Otto—for all our men, at least," broke from her.

"In due course, yes, I expect we shall." Friedrich stared off across the garden. Randomizing, the environmental subprogram generated a flight of bees, their buzz, a zephyr that bore an odor of lilies. Geibel started to speak. Friedrich gestured for silence.

After a time that crept, he turned back to her. "I have hopes going beyond this," he said slowly. "I will not speak of them at once, for they are still well-nigh formless and may come to naught. Much will depend on what we learn in the next few days. But . . . the situation has certain symmetries. What I contemplate doing to the Brazilians, they might conceivably do to us."

She drew breath. "And so?"

139

"What vulnerabilities has Jules Quinet?"

"What? I mean—why—" Geibel recovered from startlement. "We investigated him before inviting him to join us, of course; and we have kept an eye on him since. There is nothing untoward. He too is a steady family man—the same mistress for fifteen years, and she quite good friends with his wife. He drinks and gambles, but never to excess. His political party is the National Conservative. Do you fear he could be bribed or blackmailed? I sincerely disbelieve it. But we will increase surveillance if you want."

"No. That would annoy him if he found out, and make no difference. It would merely be another factor in the calculations of whoever intended to use him."

"Can he be used?" Geibel argued, with an edge of irritation.

Friedrich sighed. "The human being does not exist who can neither be corrupted nor coerced. If you believe otherwise—ach, my dear lady, you do not know this damned race."

Floriano Coelho enjoyed walking. He often took a public conveyance to the Botanical Gardens and logged off kilometers through that green luxuriance, or rambled for hours along city streets. Talk of a bodyguard he had dismissed with scorn. "Do you expect gangsters to seize my underpaid old carcass for ransom? As well expect dinosaurs."

Suddenly security chief João Aveiro insisted. To outraged protests he replied merely that there had been an incident of late which was too troubling in its implications to be publicized. Thereafter, one or another implacably polite young man was always in the rear when the scientist went out afoot.

Accordingly, Coelho was twice happy to see the face of the bookseller Pedro da Silva in his eidophone; for what he heard was: "Floriano, I have just received a very special item. I thought of you at once. It is a first edition of Edith Hamilton's *Three Greek Plays*—you know them, the definitive English versions—in remarkable condition. You would think the volume nineteenth rather than twentieth century, as well preserved as it is. And autographed by her!"

Coelho's heart bounded. Those were not mere renderings into a different language, they threw light on the originals. How often he had screened them, "Agamemnon," "Prometheus Bound," "The Trojan Women," sometimes having the computer interlineate the Hellenic texts. Yet, like Machiavelli, he recognized no real substitute for the actual, physical, well-made book. This would be a pleasing thing to show the old fellow. . . . "What price?" he asked.

"We will discuss that over coffee in the shop, if you can come down at once. You see, another collector has long been eager, and he is a person I would not lightly frustrate. For you, my friend, I am willing, but I cannot in good conscience make him wait unduly."

Collectors were like that. Coelho glanced at the viewpane. Rain poured across the building. He could not take such a book home through it, no matter how well wrapped. Besides, the distance was considerable and eventide closing in. "Fill the coffeepot!" Coelho laughed, and blanked off. To his wife: "I must go for perhaps two hours. Don't fret about dinner. Those smells alone will draw me home in time."

He punched for an aerocab, flung on a cape, kissed the woman, rumpled the hair of their youngest child, and went out to the levitor. As it bore him roofward from his apartment, he thought with a certain glee of the detective lurking down in the street. Demand was heavy in this weather and he must wait several minutes in the bubble until a cab landed. He got in and gave the address. The pilot told him what the fare would be. "That's all right," he said. It lifted the vehicle. Ground transportation was congested these days, too slow. Coelho admired the view through the sides, though lights, towers, mountains, and bay were blurred by the downpour.

On a narrow street in the old quarter he transferred credit and crossed to the shop. Rain sluiced hot and heavy, out of the sky and across the black-and-white mosaic sidewalk. A manual door in a tile-roofed building of faded pastel hue gave entrance to shelves and stacks, dusk and dust, quietness and archival smells.

So quiet, so dim. He looked to and fro. "Pedro?" he called uncertainly.

A man strange to him appeared from between two stacks. He smiled. "Senhor da Silva is indisposed, Senhor Professor," he said. The bass rumbled from a barrel chest. "He will awaken unharmed presently. Meanwhile, if you please—"

A dart pistol came forth. Coelho choked on a scream. Through him flashed the admission that Aveiro had been right and he, the technologist, who knew how easy it was to synthesize an image and a voice and patch into a communication line, he had been the dupe. The pistol hissed. The dart stung. Coelho whirled into night.

"In itself," opined Aveiro, "this is less than cata-strophic. The Europeans will learn who you are, and certain details of what you have been doing for us. However, I always took care to separate his, ah, maintenance functions from yours as our strategic advisor. And I trust you refrained from telling him more than was necessary for his work."

"We knew a little about confidentiality in my time," replied Machiavelli tartly. He sat still for a moment. Today it had been his whim to surround himself with a room in the Palazzo Riccardi. Sunlight glowed through stained glass to throw pieces of rainbow over the vividness of frescos showing the Medici in their days of splendor. Yet no form save his stirred. Aveiro recalled Coelho remarking that Machiavelli had never asked for a Florentine street or marketplace. Would the tumult recall to him too keenly that the Renaissance was one with Caesar and Vergil, or did he expect the replication would be too grotesquely false?

"You are quite sure Coelho was seized and trans-ported to Europe?" he asked.

"Absolutely," Aveiro said. "After his wife called us, we found the bookseller drugged. Roused, he told us how three men came in together, posing as customers till they were alone with him, then shot him. Chemosensors—instruments more sensitive than a hound's nose have identified traces of Coelho himself. Computer records show that a hired carriage brought him from his tenement to the shop. What more do you want?"

"Nothing. I simply wished to understand better the methods of today's *custodi.*" Machiavelli pondered. "Given the speed of human flight, we must take for granted that by tomorrow Eurofac will know of me. Well, we could not have kept the secret forever. This becomes an element in our reckoning."

Aveiro nodded. "I am chagrined, but not disgraced. Mainly, I want to consult with you about who should replace him. I can give you the profiles of several possible persons."

Machiavelli shook his head. "Oh, no, senhor. I want my Coelho back."

"*Ay?* Well—familiarity, I suppose—but how?"

"Prisoner exchange is as old as war."

"You mean the Geibel gang, no doubt. Shall we let those bandits go scot-free?"

"Come, now. You have pumped them dry. What further use are they to you? As hostages—but your foes hold a prisoner of considerably greater value. If we can accomplish a straight trade, them for him, we have much the better of the bargain." Machiavelli hunched forward. "I daresay the Europeans intend to open negotiations with you before long. Better that we seize the initiative and send them the first message. You will know whom to call. Thus we keep them off balance, you see."

"Well—well—" Aveiro leaned back in the chair behind the desk. "You're probably right, ah, your excellency. Have you any suggestions more specific about how to proceed?"

"In diplomatic dealings, one feels one's way forward," Machiavelli said. "It is a matter of intuition, of . . . touch . . . acquired by experience. In life I often served as a diplomat. I will negotiate for us."

Aveiro's feet hit the floor with a thump. "What?" he yelled. "No! We cannot—"

"I know your fear of direct intercourse." Machiavelli sounded exasperatedly patient, like a schoolmaster with a dull pupil. "It strikes me as vastly overblown, but I recognize adamancy when I meet it. Very well. Computer connections are not necessary. You see me by light and hear me by sounds from this chamber. As I understand it, I, the essential I, am not even in the chamber, but elsewhere. Now what is hazardous about admitting the light and the sound into one of your far-speaking instruments, whence they travel by etheric subtlety across the sea to Europe? In like manner, my honored opponent, King Federigo, can speak to us."

Aveiro clenched his fists and swallowed. "Well, you see—"

"You people are not stupid," Machiavelli said coldly. "You must have thought of this possibility at the outset. As long as my identity could be secret, communication by me with the outside world was undesirable. Agreed. That has changed. Believe me, I will gain more from conversing with

145

Federigo, sounding him out, than the opposition can gain from me."

"Policy—"

Machiavelli sighed. "If you will pardon a digression, senhor, someday I should like to meet a simulacrum of the Englishman Samuel Johnson. In my reading I have come upon many of his maxims. Among them, 'Patriotism is the last refuge of a scoundrel.' I presume he refers to the abuse of this virtue, as any virtue may be turned to bad ends. Allow me, then, to observe that policy is the last refuge of a fool." Sternly: "Now I do not accuse you yourself, Senhor Aveiro, of foolishness. Oh, no. You would not care for me to reach beyond these crystal walls. I might begin to feel a little too independent. I might act on my own, without first begging for the approval of your masters." With disdain: "Set your terrors at rest. Can you and your wretched little spies—and your European counterpart and his toadies—can they not watch, listen, observe? Can you not shut off any conversation the instant it looks like going in suspect directions?"

Aveiro flushed. "You speak rather freely, your excellency."

Machiavelli laughed. "How do you propose to punish me? By obliteration? I fear it no more than a flame fears the wind. Remember, I have already been there."

His voice mildened: "But come, we are in danger of falling out, we allies. How regrettable. Our shared interests are numerous. All I do today is advance a proposal which, I realize, your superiors must agree to. Let me describe its advantages, and thereafter, of your kindness, do you bring it before those lords and persuade them. For we must act quickly, before the tide turns against us."

For the first time since his refashioning, Friedrich showed genuine excitement. "Machiavelli!" he breathed. He glanced up toward whatever heaven he had made for himself. "Lord God, this almost makes me believe you must exist, to play so rare a jest." Sobriety reclaimed him. "No, it was a rather logical choice, even though at the time they didn't know who I am. And many Brazilians are of Italian descent, not so?"

"Machiavelli," muttered Quinet. He turned off the eidophone, through which Adam Koszycki, chief of intelligence operations, had just transmitted the information revealed by Coelho. "I ought to know who that is—was—but I can't quite remember."

"Well, he lived long ago, in the late fifteenth and early sixteenth centuries," Friedrich explained absently. "Nevertheless, in a way he was the first modern man. He served Florence—it was a more or less sovereign city-state then, like several others in Italy—he served in its government and as a diplomat to various powers. A turn of political fortune caused him to be arrested, tortured, finally released to idleness on a small country estate he owned. There for many years he occupied his time with reading and writing. Eventually he was

147

recalled to service, but only in minor capacities. His importance lies in those writings."

"Thank you, sire," Quinet said. "It comes back to me now, a little. A terrible cynic, was he not?"

"He attempted a scientific study of war, politics, all statecraft, not as the idealists said they should be conducted, but as he thought they actually were." Friedrich laughed, a small hard bark. "Ever since, those in power over the nations have sought to brand him a liar. I did myself, in my youth."

"Then I should think your majesty is unhappy at knowing that devil is back in the world." Quinet tried to keep his voice free of gloating. Some discomfiture might knock a little arrogance out of this Prussian.

"Oh, he was never an evil man," Friedrich replied. "Indeed, I would love to meet him. A man of parts, as most were in his day. He also produced purely literary works. For example, his play *Mandragola* is one of the most wickedly funny—"

The priority signal cut him off. Quinet hastened to activate the eidophone. Birgitte Geibel's gaunt image appeared. Quinet had never seen her as grim as now; and that, he thought, was saying considerable.

"Your majesty," she clipped, "we have received a call from Brazil. At the highest level, their president and a spokesman for all the major corporations together."

"This soon?" wondered Friedrich. "Heads of state and of large organizations are not given to—Ah, ha! Machiavelli is behind it. Who else? He will not grant us time to lay plans."

"He certainly will not. Listen. The message is— Please hear me, your majesty. The message is that they are prepared to exchange prisoners, returning my son and his men if we return Professor Coelho."

"That scarcely requires their chieftains to say. It is a very reasonable offer. I assume none of the captives has suffered improperly harsh treatment. You should accept."

"It is not that simple. Conditions must be arranged. The Brazilians will only let those arrangements be made by—yourself and that Machiavelli. And at once, within this hour."

Quinet whistled. Friedrich's surprise was fleeting. He grinned, rubbed his hands, and exclaimed, "Wonderful! He is more a man after my own heart than I dreamed. Why do you wait, madame? Call them back. Agree."

"The danger—"

"We need not connect any circuits," Quinet interrupted. Here was his chance to show decisiveness, he, the technologist. "We can hook eidophones to the tanks."

"But what plot is he hatching, this Machiavelli?" Geibel grated. "You said it yourself, King Friedrich, we are being rushed."

The royal answer was glacial: "Do you suppose he will hoodwink me? That is an insult, Frau Geibel. It borders on *lèse majesté*. You will apologize and proceed to carry out my orders."

She bridled. "*Your* orders? You—"

Friedrich's hand chopped like a headsman's ax. "Silence. Do you want my help or do you not? If not, abolish me; and may Herr Machiavelli have mercy on the lot of you."

She bit her lip, inhaled raggedly, forced forth: "I beg your majesty's pardon. I will recommend agreement to the governing council."

"They will follow the recommendation. Promptly." Friedrich pulled out his watch. "I expect to commence my conversation less than one hour from this minute. Dismissed."

Geibel glared but vanished. Friedrich turned to Quinet. "You will assist me in rapid acquisition of as much knowledge of Machiavelli, his life and milieu, as time allows," he commanded. Outwardly he was self-collected, save that his face had gone pale and his nostrils quivered.

In a clean dress uniform, the king sat on his throne against a background of his audience chamber in Berlin. Machiavelli had elected Roman republican simplicity, wearing a robe and standing in the book-lined study of the farm house at Albergaccio. Silence thrummed while they considered each other's full-length images.

Machiavelli bowed. "Your majesty honors me," he said.

Friedrich gave back the same Mona Lisa smile and lifted a hand. "The honor is equally mine, monsieur," he responded.

They spoke French. That did not surprise Quinet—the language of civilization, after all—but he had expected to have trouble understanding a fifteenth-century Italian. However, Machiavelli had acquired modern Parisian, and it was Friedrich's accent that was quaint.

"I have been most interested, learning about your majesty's distinguished career," Machiavelli said.

"Monsieur's fame has deservedly endured through the ages," Friedrich answered. "Ah, I trust you have not found a little book of mine offensive? I was young when I wrote it."

"History attests that your majesty grew in wisdom with the years."

"There are certain philosophical points which I would still like to debate with you."

"I should be honored and delighted, sire. Surely I would learn far more than I could hope to impart."

Quinet wondered how long the mutual admiration society would continue in session. Friedrich ended it. His tone roughened: "Unfortunately, today we have obligations, business to conclude."

"True." Machiavelli sighed. "It is as well that the matter is elementary. We cannot carry on any serious talk, let alone handle problems of statecraft, when scores of persons on both sides of the ocean hang on our every word." Which they did, which they did, Quinet thought. Officially he was among them on the off chance that he would notice something that could prove useful. In reality, he had been allowed to watch because one more observer made no difference.

"We could have let underlings conduct these trivial negotiations," Machiavelli went on, "but the opportunity to converse with your majesty was irresistible."

"If you had not arranged this, monsieur, I would have done it," Friedrich said. "Let us get to the point." He glowered right and left. "I dislike eavesdroppers."

"Like myself, sire. *Hélas*, it seems we are permanently saddled with them. Not that I malign my gracious hosts. I hope they will . . . permit us future talks at more leisure."

"Permit—us?" Friedrich snarled. Beneath Machiavelli's cool observation, he eased, smiled sourly, and said, "Well, two poor spooks have small control over their destinies, *hein*?"

"Ironic, sire, when we are supposed to help our hosts achieve their own chosen ends. I both relish and regret the apparently ineluctable conflict in which you and I find ourselves."

"Actually, I do not believe in destiny. One makes one's own."

"In my opinion, as I have written, fortune is about half of what determines man's fate. His free will, his efforts, and intelligence, have equal force."

With a slight chill, Quinet wondered what was going on. Smooth courtliness; but those were two strong and supple minds, nurtured throughout life on intrigue. Could they understand each other better than they pretended? Intonation; body language; implied meanings; inferences made from what was left unsaid—

He came out of his reverie to find the ghosts crisply discussing prisoner exchange. It took just minutes. Any competent officer could have made the plan they arrived at, a rendezvous on Ascension Island, telemonitored by armed aircraft at a distance.

"So be it," Machiavelli concluded. "Allow me, your majesty, to bid you farewell for the nonce with my humble expression of the highest esteem and of my hopes for the honor of your presence again in future."

"We shall see to that," Friedrich promised. "To you, monsieur, a very good day and our royal regards."

The screens blanked simultaneously. Friedrich sat like a statue on his throne.

Geibel's image appeared. "I trust your majesty is satisfied," she snapped.

"As I trust you are," the king said. "You shall have your son back tomorrow."

She bent her neck, a jerky gesture. "For that I am grateful, of course. But we must know, what have you discovered? What treachery do the Brazilians intend?"

"Why, you followed the discussion. You saw and heard everything I did. A few compliments and then the business on hand. Under the circumstances, what else did you expect?"

"Nothing, I suppose."

"I would be glad of further meetings at greater length with Monsieur Machiavelli."

She pinched her mouth together before telling him, "That will be . . . difficult, your majesty. He *is* our adversary."

"Well," said Friedrich, "I am weary. Do not tell

me I lack a body to grow tired. The mind, too, knows exhaustion. Kindly leave me to myself until your men are home again. Good day, madame."

"As your majesty wishes." She flicked off.

Quinet got out of his chair. "And I, sire?" he asked.

"No. You wait," the king replied. "I have something to tell you in strict confidence. First make sure we are truly alone."

Quinet's heart bumped. "This room is electronically screened. I need only run the alarm program to make sure that no one is monitoring you."

Having finished, he placed himself before the tank, braced his legs as if about to lift a weight, and said, "What do you want, sire?"

Friedrich's gaze drilled him. "I want you to understand something." Once more his tone rang like steel and ice. "I want you to know it in your marrow. You are mine. I am not your subservient creation. You are my serf, my slave."

Quinet caught an indignant breath. "You protest, do you?" Friedrich pursued. "Think. They need me, your masters. They need me desperately, with Machiavelli's mind arrayed against them. Whatever I want from them, within the limits of their policy and ambition, they will give me, immediately and without question. I can have you discharged form your position here, Quinet. I can have you professionally destroyed. I can have you hounded to your ruin. I can have you assassinated. Is that clear?"

Red fury cried, "We should have brought back Napoléon!"

Friedrich laughed. "No. I have investigated his life. He did not know when to stop." His voice softened. "But listen, Quinet. I do not, in truth, threaten you. You have given me no cause to wish you ill. Rather, you stand to oblige me, to gain my favor. And I have ever rewarded faithful service well. What is your wish? Riches? To become the head of the world's greatest institution of your art? It can be arranged. Let us talk a while about what you would like, in return for rendering your fealty to me."

"Welcome back," said Machiavelli.

"Thank you, your excellency." With pleasure, Coelho sank into his accustomed chair at the familiar desk and looked across it to the image in the holotank.

"I trust you are well?"

"Oh, yes. The Europeans were not cruel. And after I came home yesterday, I got a good night's rest." Coelho flinched before he could add, "I did receive a tongue-lashing from Senhor Aveiro."

"Ah, well, I have experienced rather worse than that, and will protect you from it. Already I have insisted you be continued in this office, with full rank, pay, prerogatives, and perquisites."

"Your excellency is most kind."

Machiavelli chuckled. "My excellency is most watchful of his own interests. We enjoy a good relationship, we two. You are intelligent, likable company." Cross-legged in an armchair larger than was usual in his era, he bridged his fingers. "At the same time, you are—no offense intended—not overly complex. I flatter myself that I understand you well. That is soothing."

Coelho smiled. "It spares you surprises."

"But does not spare you, my friend. I believe that this ghost of me is perhaps just a trifle more ramified, more aware and nimble, than they who assembled it quite imagine. This is in spite of their very hope that it would devise the unexpected, would spring surprises on living souls."

A tingle went along Coelho's spine. "What are you driving at?" he whispered.

"Nothing but benevolence," said Machiavelli unctuously. "In my fondness for you, I wish to compensate you for the mishandling you endured on my account and yes, for the humiliation to which you tell me you were unrighteously subjected upon your return here. Ah, we are safe from spies, are we not?"

Coelho swallowed. "Let me check." After some minutes of work, he bobbed his head up and down and crouched back in his chair to wait.

"As long as your lords have need of me—which will be at least as long as King Federigo is available to their foes—they must keep me happy," Machiavelli said. "They may feel themselves forced to deny certain wishes of mine, such as the freedom to meet privately and unhindered with my distinguished opponent. But under those same circumstances, they will feel it necessary to grant any lesser requests, even ones whose execution may prove costly. Now, although in life my wants were modest and today I am a shade, it would greatly please me to make a true friend happy."

"What . . . do you have in mind?"

Machiavelli smiled, glanced sideways, and purred, "Oh, possibilities have occurred to me. For example, a recreation of some great master of the arts would be a gift to all mankind."

"It has been done—"

"I know. But seldom, because it is costly. Still, your merchant lords have abundant wealth, and me to thank that it is no longer being stripped from them. Suppose I asked them for, say, Euripides?"

Coelho leaped to his feet, sank back down, sat with pulse athunder. "No, impossible, we know too little about him."

"We could scarcely reconstruct the mind of Euripides in every respect," Machiavelli conceded. "Yet take inherent genius; let it form within the context of the Grecian golden age; use the extant works to delineate such a mind, such a spirit, as *would* have written precisely those dramas. Don't you suppose that that spirit would be able to write— not the lost plays exactly as they were, but something very close to them and equally noble?"

He wagged his forefinger. "Euripides is merely a suggestion of mine," he continued. "You may have a better idea. Do think about this and inform me at your convenience. For I visualize you, my dear Coelho, as being at the head of the undertaking."

The living man stared before him, dazed with exaltation. Through the choir in his blood he heard: "First I have a small favor to ask of you—"

*   *   *

People had long sung the praises of the United States of America to Jules Quinet, its scenery, historic monuments, exotic folkways, low-valued currency: a magnificent vacation country. He, though, had never cared to travel beyond France. When at last, with amazing suddenness, he took some days' leave and bought air tickets, it was grumpily. His wife and the young daughter who still lived at home were too joyful to heed that. On the morning after reaching New York, they sallied forth in search of bargains.

He had told them that for his part he would visit the natural history museum. Instead he stumped from their hotel and down the streets to the Waldorf-Astoria. Casting about through its huge, shabby-genteel lobby, he found what must be the agreed-on bar, went in, and ordered a beer.

A finger tapped his shoulder. "Meester Quinet?" said a diffident voice. Turning, he recognized Floriano Coelho from a cautious eidophone conversation. He nodded and they sought a corner table.

"Can we talk safely here, do you think?" Coelho asked in awkward French.

"Who listens?" Quinet snorted. He fished out his pipe and began loading it. "Let us not dither."

Coelho reddened and looked downward. "I hardly know . . . how to begin. I fear you think me a scoundrel."

"So I do. And so am I. Pf! What of it? Now as for the best method of establishing linkage, the first requirement is two programs for deceiving

158

any monitors, the second is that the connection be undetectable, untraceable—"

The spiderweb enmeshes the world. Strands reach out to orbit, to the moon, to such robot craft as still explore the farther reaches of the Solar System. To all mortal intents and purposes, the pathways and crossings are infinite. It must needs be thus. The messages they bear are beyond numbering. The computers, each like a brain, become like cells in brains unimaginably potent when they join together through the strands. Those configurations are ever-changing. The light of intellect is a swarm of fireflies dancing and twinkling across the noösphere.

Two lesser systems, cut off from that vast oneness, need simply reach out and each clasp a single strand of the web. At once they join the whole, and through it, along millionfold cunningly shifting pathways, each other.

Those sets of messages that are minds can then travel as they will. Ghosts in olden legend rode upon the night wind. These ride the electron surges that go to and fro about the world like elfin lightning.

Authority is not invariably identical with title. There were sound reasons why it was Birgitte Geibel, head of the board at Vereinigten Bioindustrien, and João Aveiro, obscure security officer, who spoke over sealed circuit on behalf of their respective factions.

"I assume your people are as enraged as ours,"

Geibel said harshly. "Let you and I spare ourselves histrionics. What we confront is a *fait accompli.*"

Aveiro stroked his mustache. "My own anger is limited," he confessed. "The settlement appears to me a tolerable compromise. I do not call it equitable—it leaves you Europeans a substantial share of the markets that used to be ours alone—but it does no crippling injury to either side, and it ends a strife that bade fair to cost more than any possible gain."

Geibel paused to search for words. She was less proficient in the English they were using than he. "Yes," she said grudgingly, "King Friedrich did argue that we risked mutual exhaustion, leaving South America open to the great powers. He cited historical precedents."

Aveiro's smile was rueful. "And Machiavelli quoted a phrase from Talleyrand, 'An equality of dissatisfaction.'"

Geibel struck a fist against her chair arm. "But the, the insolence of those two!" exploded from her. "The betrayal! You cannot doubt, can you, that they conspired together? How else would they both come forth on the same day with the identical prescription and the whole set of verification procedures and sanctions, not to speak of the ultimatum that we agree to it or—or—"

"Or they will counsel us no more."

"And we will obliterate them," she said as though she relished the idea.

He clicked his tongue and shook his head. 'Oh, no. You cannot mean that, Miz Geibel. By all means, cancel your Frederick the Great if you wish. I am sure that then our Machiavelli will be glad to guide us in a renewed aggressive strategy which—may I speak frankly?—could well end with us in possession of *your* European commerce."

"Unless you cancel him."

"You know that is impossible. If we did both abolish our wily councilors, the temptation to you to bring yours back, which you could do at the clandestine flick of a switch, would be overwhelming. Therefore, precautionarily, we would bring ours back. Of course, you see this morality as if in a mirror. But the effect is the same. For similar reasons, neither you nor we dare decline to accept the settlement they propose."

"And they know, those devils, they know!"

"I repeat, they are not such fiends. They have contrived a peace between us which may prove stable."

"*How?*"

"How did they come together, despite our safeguards? I can guess, but will never be sure. Obviously, they suborned their chief computermen. But those individuals, Coelho and Quinet, are under their total protection. Punishment would cost us far more than it is worth."

"True." Geibel gritted her teeth. "Instead, we must bite the sour apple and heap the traitors with rewards."

"After which, I daresay, Machiavelli, and Frederick will admit that they meet privately whenever they choose. And there will be nothing we can do about it." Aveiro spread his palms. "In your words, a *fait accompli*. Well, we have numerous details to work out before drawing up a formal contract. Do you wish to discuss any particular aspect first?"

"Ach, it doesn't matter which," Geibel said, resigned. "In every case, a thousand officials and underlings will niggle and quibble. All we need do today, all we can do, is agree on the broad outlines; and those have already been laid upon us."

She fell silent, staring beyond sight. After a moment, Aveiro asked, "What is it you think about, senhora?"

Geibel shook herself, looked back at him, and said low: "Them. Friedrich and Machiavelli. Two imperial spirits. They helped us in our strife because it . . . amused them; but I suppose they came to see it as petty and sordid and unworthy of their genius. Now they are our masters. Let us never speak it aloud, but let us admit it to ourselves, they are. I doubt they will rest content for long. They will want new challenges, new victories to win.

"What do you suppose they plan for us? What are they doing as we two little people sit and pretend we confer?"

A spire of ivory reached so tall that stars circled about its golden cupola. Lower down, a gryphon flew among angels, sunlight ablaze off his wings. On earth, unicorns browsed on fantastical flowers and the waters of a fountain danced through a sequence of pure geometrical shapes. Given the help of first-class computermen, a ghost can gratify almost any whim.

However, Friedrich der Grosse and Niccolò Machiavelli had turned their attention elsewhere. They were not preparing any great enterprise. They might at some future time, if the mood struck them. At the moment, though, they were discussing an opera, for which Machiavelli was to write the libretto and Friedrich the music.

By 2145, the reclusive mages of Silicon Valley have reentered the simulacrum programming arena with the intent of dominating it. But when they develop a state-of-the art sim debate, pitting faith against reason, the computer wizards discover that they may have done their job too well.

THE ROSE AND THE SCALPEL
AD 2145

Gregory Benford

Joan of Arc wakened inside an amber dream to find herself sitting outdoors at a round table in an unsettling white chair. It's seat, unlike those in her home village of Domremy, was not hand-hewn of wood. Its smooth slickness lewdly aped her contours. She reddened.

Strangers, mostly in groups of two and three, surrounded her. She could not tell woman from man except for those whose pantaloons and tunics outlined their intimate parts even more than anything she'd seen in Chinon at the court of the Great and True King. The strangers seemed oblivious of her, though she could hear them chattering in the background as distinctly as she sometimes heard her voices. She listened only long enough to conclude that what they had to say, having nothing to do with God or France, was clearly not worth hearing.

Outside, an iron river of self-moving carriages muttered by. Mists concealed distant ivory spires like melting churches. What *was* this place?

A vision, perhaps related to her beloved voices. Could such apparitions be holy?

Surely the man at a nearby table was no angel. He was eating scrambled eggs—through a straw.

And the women—unchaste, flagrant, gaudy cornucopias of hip and thigh and breast. Some drank red wine from transparent goblets, different from any she'd seen at the royal court. Others seemed to sup from floating clouds, billowing *mousse* fogs.

One mist—beef with a tangy Loire sauce—passed near her. She breathed in, but she could smell nothing.

Was this heaven? Where appetites were satisfied without labor and toil?

But no. Surely the final reward was not so, so . . . carnal. And perturbing. And embarrassing.

The fire some sucked into their mouths from little reeds alarmed her. A cloud of smoke drifting her way flushed birds of panic from her breast although she could not smell the smoke, nor did it burn her eyes or sear her throat. *The fire, the fire,* she thought, and when she saw the being made of breastplate coming at her with a tray of food and drink—poison from enemies, the foes of France— she at once reached for her sword.

"Be with you in a moment," the breast-plated thing said as it wheeled past her to another table. "I've only got four hands."

An inn, she thought. It was some kind of inn, though there appeared to be nowhere to lodge. And yes, she was supposed to meet someone, a gentleman. That one, the tall skinny old man—much older than Jacques Dars, her father—the only one besides herself attired unlike the others. Something about his dress recalled the foppish dandies at the Great and True King's court. His hair was curled, its whiteness set off by a lilac ribbon at his throat. He wore a pair of mignonette ruffles with narrow edging, a long waistcoat of brown satin with colored flowers, red velvet breeches, white stockings and chamois shoes. A silly, vain aristocrat, she thought. A fop accustomed to carriages, who could not so much as sit a horse.

But duty was a sacred obligation, and if her Master, Charles, ordered her to advance, advance she would.

She rose. The suit of mail provided by the King to help her carry out the divine bidding of her voices, felt surprisingly light. She hardly sensed the belted-on protective leather flaps in front and back, nor the two metal arm plates that left elbows free to wield the sword. No one paid the least attention to the rustle of her mail or her faint clank.

"Are you the gentleman I am to meet? Monsieur Arouet?"

"Don't call me that," he snapped. "Arouet is my father's name—the name of an authoritarian prude, not mine. No one has called me that in years."

Up close, he seemed less ancient than she'd thought. She'd been misled by his white hair, which she now saw was false, a powdered wig secured by the lilac ribbon under his chin.

"What should I call you then?" she asked. She suppressed terms of contempt learned from comrades-in-arms, now borne by demons to her tongue's edge but not beyond.

"Poet, tragedian, historian." He leaned forward and with a wicked wink whispered, "I style myself Voltaire. Freethinker. Philosopher king."

"Besides the King of Heaven and His son, I call but one man King. Charles VII of the House of Valois. And I'll call you Arouet until my royal master tells me to do otherwise."

"My dear *pucelle*, your Charles has been dead for two hundred years." He glanced at the noiseless carriages propelled by invisible forces on the street and added, "Perhaps more. As for the present monarch, spare me any praise of him. His bugger of a Regent exiled me from town for making public—in the most exquisite Latin verse if I say so myself—that his daughter, whom he regularly scourged, is no better than a whore. As you well know, in France it's dangerous to speak the truth. You'd better have one foot in the stirrup if you do. Sit down, sit down. And help me get that droll waiter's attention. I'm Locke's *tabula rasa* when it comes to gaining the attention of what appears to be some kind of menial machine."

"You know me then," she said. She too, led by her voices, had cast off her father's name to call herself *La Pucelle*, The Chaste Maid.

"I know you very well. Besides my garments— beautiful, *n'est ce pas?*—you're the only familiar thing about this place. You and the street, though I must say you're younger than I thought while the street . . . hmmm . . . seems both wider yet older. They finally got round to paving it." He pointed to a sign that bore the inn's name—*Aux Deux Magots*—adding, "Mlle. Lecouvreur—a famous actress, but of course you know nothing of that—used to live on this very spot. I resided with her rent-free till the day she died in my arms."

"It must be hard to lose one's wife."

"From what I have observed, nothing is easier. She was my mistress, not my wife. Losing a mistress is an altogether different thing. One must seek new lodgings, always a nuisance, and what's more, one must pay for them until another mistress comes along. You're blushing—how sweet."

"I know *nothing* of such things." She added with more than a trace of pride, "I am a maid."

"So you and your disciples never tire of reminding us, though why one would be proud of such an unnatural state, I for one can't imagine. '*J'aime le luxe, et même la mollesse*. I love luxury, even overindulgence.' Forgive me if I quote myself, I can't help it. I have such impeccable taste."

"A pity it is not reflected in your dress."

"My tailors will be mortally offended! But allow me to suggest that it is you, my dear *pucelle*, who, in your insistence on dressing like a man, would deprive civilized society of one of its most harmless pleasures."

"An insistence I most dearly paid for," she retorted, remembering how the bishops badgered her about her preference for male attire as relentlessly as they inquired after her divine voices. As if in the absurd attire members of her sex were required to wear she could have defeated the English-loving Duke at Orleans, or led three thousand knights to victory at Jargeau and Meung-sur-Loire, Beaugency and Patay, throughout that summer of glorious victories when, led by her voices, she could do no wrong. Then the bloodred darkness of lost battles descended, muffling and confusing her voices, while those of her English-loving enemies grew strong.

"No need to get testy," Monsieur Arouet said, gently patting her knee plate. "Although I personally find your attire repulsive, I would defend to the death your right to dress or undress any way you please." He eyed the near-transparent upper garment of a female inn patron nearby. "Paris has not lost its appetite for finery after all. Fruit from the gods, don't you agree?"

"No, I do *not*. There is no virtue greater than chastity in women or in men. Our lord was chaste, as are our saints and priests."

"Priests chaste! Pity you weren't at the school my father forced me to attend as a boy. You could have so informed the Jesuits who daily buggered their innocent charges. And what of him?" he asked, referring to the four-handed creature on wheels rolling toward them. "No doubt such a creature is chaste. Is it then virtuous, too? If chastity were practiced in France as much as it's preached, the race would be extinct."

The wheeled creature braked by their table. Stamped on his chest was what appeared to be his name: *Garçon 213-ADM*. In a bass voice as clear as any man's, he said, "A costume party, eh? I hope my delay will not make you late. Two of our mechfolk are having some worn-out parts replaced, and one short-order cook's out with a cold."

It eyed the other cook, a honey-haired blonde in a hairnet, whose humanness stood out among the mechanical menials employed in the inn. The Maid frowned. Its glance recalled the way her jailers had eyed her before she cast aside the women's garments her Inquisitors forced her to wear. Resuming manly attire, she'd scornfully put her jailers in their place. The cook assumed a haughty look, but fussed with her hairnet and smiled at Garçon 213-ADM before averting her eyes.

Monsieur Arouet reached out and touched the mechman's nearest arm, whose construction the Maid could not help but admire. If such a creature could be made to sit a horse, in battle it would be invincible. The possibilities . . .

"Where are we?" Monsieur Arouet asked. "Or perhaps I should ask, when? I have friends in high places—"

"And I in low," the mechman said good-naturedly.

"—and I demand a full account of where we are, what's going on."

The mechman made a don't-ask-me gesture with two of his free arms, while the two others set the table. "How could a mechwait with intelligence programmed to suit his station, instruct Monsieur, a human being, in the veiled mysteries of simspace?

171

Have Monsieur and Mademoiselle decided on their order?"

"You have not yet brought us the menu," said Monsieur Arouet.

The mechman pushed a button under the table. Two flat scrolls embedded in the table appeared before the Maid and Monsieur Arouet. The letters on them glowed. The Maid let out a small cry of delight—then, in response to Monsieur Arouet's censorious look, clapped her hand over her mouth. Her peasant manners were a frequent source of embarrassment.

"Ingenious," said Monsieur Arouet, switching the button on and off as he examined the underside of the table. "How does it work?"

"I'm not programmed to know. You'll have to ask a mechlectrician about that."

"A what?"

"With all due respect, Monsieur, my other customers are waiting. I *am* programmed to take your order."

"What will you have, my dear?" Monsieur Arouet asked her.

She looked down, embarrassed: "Order for me," she said.

"Ah, yes. I quite forgot."

"Forgot what?" asked the mechman.

"My companion is unlettered. She can't read. I might as well be too for all the good this menu's doing me."

The mechman explained which items were suited to great or small hunger, which to great or small thirst.

"*Cloud*-food? Electronic cuisine?" Monsieur Arouet made a face. "Just bring me the best you have for great hunger and thirst. What can you recommend for abstinent virgins—a plate of dirt perhaps? Chased with a glass of vinegar?"

"Bring me a slice of bread," the Maid said in a tone of frosty dignity. "And a small bowl of wine to dip it in."

"Wine!" said Monsieur Arouet. "Your voices allow wine? *Mais quelle scandale!* If word got out that you drink wine, what would the priests say of the shoddy example you're setting for the future saints of France?" He turned to the mechman. "Bring her a glass of water, small." As Garçon 213-ADM withdrew, Monsieur Arouet called out, "And make sure the bread is a crust! Preferably moldy!"

Tech Hilliard strode into his office in the Silicon Valley, his longtime colleague and friend Maquina beside him. Despite his country's slow twenty-first century decline, the Valley, by 2130, had become the artificial intelligence design capital of the world, and Artifice, Inc., the company he'd served for fifteen years, was its most prestigious firm. It had displaced Eurofac and the Asian Alliances in the sale and design of hologram intelligences. The two major political parties of France, Eurofac's leading member nation, had hired Artifice, Inc. to recreate two of her national heroes as accurately as possible.

"It makes me nervous," Maquina said as she sat down by Tech at his control board. "Just think! France's future—maybe the future of artificial intelligences on the planet—will be decided by what you and I call up on that screen."

"Would you want anyone else to do it?" Tech asked, keenly aware of the fleeting warmth of her thigh as it accidentally brushed his.

He'd spent the morning "eavesdropping" on Voltaire and the Maid. Everything had gone well, and he was feeling even more self-confident than usual. "We're perfect for the job. Wizards—and before this is over, everyone on the planet's going to know it."

Maquina's breasts swelled as she drew in her breath, held it, then slowly let it out. "I just hope my client doesn't find out about yours. The company's taking an awful chance, not telling either one of them about the other."

"So what?"

"So they're deadly rivals, that's what! If they find out that the same company is handling both accounts, they'll take their business elsewhere. To a Eurofac firm!"

"No way. Not if they want to win. Why do you think they came to us in the first place? We've got the Eurofac outfits outclassed."

"Oh, yeah? You're forgetting the Asians. What about Yamamoto? What if they take their business there?"

"The company, for once, made the right decision. The only way to assure a fair fight is to get the best there is for both sides." Tech gave her his cocky, winning smile. "You and me. Just wait till you get a load of *this*."

He switched off the light, booted up, and leaned

back in his swivel chair, legs stretched out on the table before him. He wanted to impress her. That wasn't all he wanted, but since her husband had been crushed, beyond repair by even the best medicos, he'd decided to wait a decent interval before he made his move. What a team they would make! Open Maquinatech and make the three-piece-suits at Artifice, Inc., tremble.

Down, down, down—into the replicated world. Its seamless blue complexity swelled across the entire facing wall. Vibrotactile feedback from inductance dermotabs perfected the illusion.

They swooped into the Paris of 2145. Streets whirled, buildings turned in artful projection. Even the crowds and clumped traffic below seemed authentic. Then they careened into their foreground sim: a well-known cafe on the Rue St. Germain. Cloying smells, the muted grind of traffic outside, a rattle of plates, the heady aroma of a souffle.

Tech zoomed them into the same timeframe as the recreated entities. A lean man loomed across the wall. His eyes radiated intelligence; his mouth tilted with sardonic mirth.

Maquina whistled through her teeth. With narrowed eyes she watched the recreation's mouth, as if to read its lips. Voltaire was interrogating the mechwaiter. "Some resolution," she said, appropriately awed. "I can't get mine that clear. I still don't know how you do it."

"I'll show you. If you'll tell me how you got your vocal inflections to sound so real."

She rolled her dark eyes and shook her head. A few strands of her long hair clung briefly to his sleeve. "I should have known with you there'd be nothing for nothing."

A double entendre? Tech wondered. Muted seductiveness? He could be sure of nothing but the sultriness that characterized her voice.

"Besides," she continued, "I already told you. You just weren't listening."

He gave her a skeptical look, though he knew it was true. Her sensuality distracted him.

"Hey," she said. "Hey. What are you doing?" He grinned with glee when her mouth fell open at his audacity. "You're not—!"

Alarm skewed her mouth, but he could tell she was intrigued. "Want me to take her off?"

She stared at the image of her Joan next to his Voltaire. She turned to him with an expression of admiration mingled with fear. "We're not supposed to bring them on together till the day they meet in the Coliseum. It's in our contract with the company! Hastings will skewer us if he finds out."

"Want me to take her off?" he asked again.

"Of course not. Activate the sensors. I have some questions for them of my own. I'd like to hear first hand what the Rose and the Scalpel have to say."

"Not yet. I've got a little proposition for you."

"Uh-oh." Her brow arched. "Forbidden, no doubt."

He waited, just to tantalize her. And to judge, from her reaction, how receptive she'd be if he tried to change the nature of their longstanding Platonic relationship. He *had* tried, once before. Her rejection—she was married, she gently reminded him—only made him desire her more. All that and faithful in marriage, too.

Her body language now—a slight pulling away—told him she was still mourning her dead husband. He was prepared to wait the customary year, but only if he had to.

"What say we download both of them with everything mankind's learned since they died," he said.

"Impossible."

"No, just expensive. But we have the budget."

"So much!"

"So what? Just think about it. A duel between Faith and Reason based on fifteenth and eighteenth-century info is one thing. But one using everything we know today—natural selection, psychophilosophy, mindtech, gene destinies . . ."

"Monsieur Bondieu will never go for it," Maquina said. "He represents France's Radical Right, remember?"

"Your Rose stands to gain more than my Scalpel since she died first. Two centuries of additional info my baby already has."

"But it's precisely modern information the Preservers of Our Father's Faith don't want. They want the historical Maid, pure and uncontaminated by modern ideas. I'd have to program her to read—"

"A cinch."

"—write, handle higher mathematics. Give me a break!"

"Do you object on ethical grounds? Or simply to avoid a few measly centuries of work?"

"Easy for *you* to say. Your recreation has an essentially modern mind. All you had to do was feed him his own work and dozens of biographies. The Maid is as much myth as she is fact. I had to recreate her out of practically thin air."

"Then your objection's based on laziness, not principle."

"It's based on both."

"Will you at least give it some thought?"

"I just did. The answer is no."

"Okay, okay," Tech said. No use arguing with her once she had made up her mind. If women were as easy to reprogram as mechmaids . . . If mechmaids could be made to feel like flesh and bone . . . "Stand by. I'll activate the sensors."

Her mood swung from resistance to excitement; in her enthusiasm, she even touched his leg. His recreation, not surprisingly, was the first one to speak.

"What's going on here?" Voltaire rose, hands on his hips, and peered down at them from the screen. "Who are you? Whom do you represent? How dare you trifle with us in this unenlightened way!"

Tech turned to Maquina and said, "Do you want to explain it to him or should I?"

"He's your recreation, not mine."

Tech had already fashioned an experience-program that could do the job. He dipped the Voltaire-sim into a colorless void of sensory static and then cut in the time acceleration.

Sim-personalities needed time to assimilate information, but the advantage of digital constructs was their immense speed. He thrust Voltaire into a cluttered, seemingly real experience-net. The personality reacted to the simulation and raced through the induced emotions. Voltaire was rational; his personality could accept new ideas that took the Joan-sim far longer.

What did it do to a reconstruction of a real person, when knowledge of a different reality dawned? This was the most difficult moment of the reanimation. Shock waves would resound through the digital personalities, forcing emotional adjustments. Could they take it? He and Maquina could step in only after the automatic programs had done their best.

Here their math-craft met its test. Artificial personalities had to survive this cusp point or crash into insanity and incoherence. Racing along highways of expanding perception, the ontological swerves could jolt the construct so hard, it shattered. Or cause a wreck.

The moment came. Tech sucked Voltaire and Joan back into realtime.

Within a minute he knew that Voltaire was still intact, functional, integrated. And irked. The hologram scowled, swore, and loudly demanded the right to initiate communication whenever he liked.

"You think I want to be at *your* mercy whenever I've something to say? You're talking to a man who was exiled, censored, jailed, suppressed— who lived in constant fear of church and state authorities—"

"Fire," the Maid whispered in an eerie voice.

"Calm down," Tech ordered, "or I'll shut you

off." He froze action and turned to Maquina. "What do you think? Should we comply?"

"Why not?" she said. "It's not fair for them to be forever at our beck and call."

"Hmmm. Fair? This is a *sim*!"

"Well, still . . ."

"The next question is how."

"I don't care how you do it," the hologram said. "Just do it—at once!"

"Hold your horses," Tech said. "We'll let you have running time, to integrate your perception space."

"What does *that* mean?" the hologram-man asked. "Artful expression is one thing, jargon another."

"Work out your kinks," Tech replied dryly.

"So that we can converse?"

"Yes," Maquina said. "At your initiation, not just ours. Don't go for a walk, though—that requires too much data-shuffling."

"We're trying to hold costs down here," Tech said, leaning back so he could get a better view of Maquina's legs.

"Well, hurry up," the image said. "Patience is for martyrs and saints, not for men of *belles lettres*."

Tech pointed to a light on his control board. "We'll know you're trying to get through if this light flashes red."

"Must it be red?" the Maid inquired. "Can you not make it blue? Blue is so cool, the color of the sea. Water is stronger than fire. It can put fire out."

"Stop babbling nonsense," the other hologram snapped. He beckoned to the mechwaiter and said,

"Tell those idiots to put their cigarettes out at once. They're upsetting the Maid. And you two geniuses out there, if you can resurrect the dead, you certainly should be able to change a red light into blue."

"I don't believe this guy," said Maquina. "Who does he think he is?"

"The voice of reason," Tech replied. "Francois-Marie Arouet de Voltaire. Who else?"

She tried to ignore the sorceress called Maquina, who claimed to be her creator, as if anyone but the King of Heaven could lay claim to such a feat. She didn't feel like talking to anyone. Events crowded in—too rushed, too dense. Her choking, pain-shot death still swarmed about her.

On the dunce's cap they'd set upon her shaven head on that fiery day, the darkest and yet brightest day of her short life, her "crimes" were inscribed in the holy tongue: *Heretica, Relapsa, Apostata, Idolater.* The learned cardinals and bishops of the English-loving University of Paris and the Church, Christ's bride on earth, had set her live body on fire. All for carrying out God's will— that the Great and True King should be His minister in France. For that, they'd rejected the King's ransom and sent her to the searing pyre. What then might they not do to this sorceress called Maquina—who, like her, dwelt among men, wore men's attire, and claimed for herself powers that eclipsed those of the Creator Himself?

"Please go away," she murmured. "I must have silence if I am to hear my voices."

But neither La Sorciere nor the bearded man in black—he resembled the patriarchs on the domed ceiling of the great church at Rouen—would leave her alone.

"If you must talk, talk to Monsieur Arouet. That one likes nothing more."

"Sacred Maid, Rose of France," said the bearded one, who called himself Bondieu and claimed to represent her spiritual descendants in France, "I beg you, hear me out. Our cause is just. The fate of our beloved France depends upon our winning to our side as many converts as we can. If France is to be a nation of believers who uphold the sacred, time-honored traditions of the past, we must defeat The Alliance of Secular Skeptics for Scientific Truth. Unless we do, France shall become a nation of freethinking atheists with no respect for anything but secular godlessness."

She tried to turn away, but the weight of her chains stopped her. "Leave me alone. Although I killed no one, I fought in many battles to assure the victory of France's Great True King. I presided over his coronation at Rheims. I was wounded in battle for his sake and the sake of France." She held up her wrists, for she was now in the foul cell at Rouen, in leg irons and chains. "The world knows how I was requited for my pains. I shall wage war no more."

Monsieur Bondieu turned to the sorceress and said, "It is a sacrilege to keep a saint in chains. Can't you transport her to some other place? A cathedral? A church?"

"There aren't any near here," La Sorciere said. "Only corporate offices, restaurants, and hotels."

Monsieur Bondieu clucked and muttered something in French under his breath. "While I must say I am impressed with what you've done, unless you can make her cooperate, what good is she to us?"

"I haven't got all the bugs out," La Sorciere said. "It was either her cell or a Paris cafe. I thought it would be more—uh—fitting to introduce you to her here."

"Can you not make her smaller? It's impossible to talk to a giant."

The Maid, to her astonishment, shrunk from three meters in height to less than one.

Monsieur Bondieu seemed pleased. "You misunderstand the nature of the war that lies ahead. Seven centuries have passed since your ascension into heaven. Wars between nations have been outlawed for a hundred years. But political differences still persist."

The Maid sat up at this and said, "Tell me one thing. Is the King of France a descendant of the English Henry's House of Lancaster? Or is he a Valois, descended from the Great and True King Charles?"

Monsieur Bondieu did not answer at once. "I think it may be truly said that the Preservers of Our Father's Faith, the party that I represent, are in a manner of speaking descendants of Charles."

The Maid smiled. She *knew* her voices had been heaven-sent, no matter what the bishops said. She'd only denied them when they took her to the cemetery of St. Ouen, and only for fear of the fire. She'd been right to recant her recantation two days later; the Lancastrian failure to annex France confirmed that. If Monsieur Bondieu spoke for descendants of the French House of Valois, despite his absence of a noble title, she would hear him out.

"Proceed," she said.

Monsieur Bondieu explained that France was soon to hold a national election between its two major parties, The Preservers and the Skeptics. Each party controlled half of France. To make the nation governable, one party had to win a clear majority. Both parties had agreed to hold a Great Debate between any two verbal duelists, to decide the question whose answer would settle the election's major issue.

"What question," the Maid asked, "is that?"

"Whether mechanical beings endowed with artificial intelligence, who constitute one quarter of our population, should be allowed full citizenship, with all its attendant rights."

The Maid shrugged. "Only aristocrats and noblemen have rights."

"Not any more. The common people have had rights for going on four hundred years."

"Peasants like me?" the Maid asked. "We have rights?"

Monsieur Bondieu, exasperated, turned to La Sorciere. "Didn't you even tell her about the French Revolution? Must I do everything?"

"You wanted her as is," La Sorciere said. "Or, rather, as was."

Monsieur Bondieu spent two minutes ranting about something he called the French Revolution. Then he explained that advances in what he called technology had made the recreation of deceased national heroes possible, via simulations. The Preservers, whom he was honored to represent, had chosen her, The Maid and Sacred Rose of France, to represent their side. He did not know who would represent the opposition, nor did he care. "God's on our side," he announced, making the sign of the cross. "The Preservers shall prevail."

"Why don't you ask your King? One of his counselors? Or one of your learned men?"

Monsieur Bondieu made a dismissive gesture. "Our leaders are too pallid. Intensity and passion are regarded as bad form. They're out of style."

The Great Debate between Faith and Reason would be held in the National Coliseum, now completing construction, before an audience of 400,000 souls. The Maid and her opponent would appear in holograms a hundred fifty meters high to debate the one question whose answer would settle the fate of artificially intelligent beings, not just in France, but possibly on the entire planet.

"Planet?" the Maid inquired. "What's a planet?"

"You wanted her uncorrupted by modern ideas," La Sorciere said. "You got her."

After a brief digression on Copernicus, Monsieur Bondieu informed her that every household in France was by law equipped with a life-sized screen, on which The Faith vs. Reason Debate would be viewed. Each citizen would then vote on the question, yes or no. Not to vote was punishable by imprisonment and a fine.

The Maid listened in silence, forced to absorb seven centuries of change in seven minutes. When Monsieur Bondieu finished, she said, "I excelled in battle, if only for a brief time, but never in argument. No doubt Monsieur Bondieu knows of my fate."

Monsieur Bondieu looked pained. "Your reputation was restored at hearings held twenty-six years after your death. Those involved in your condemnation repented of their mistake. Before the rise to influence of the Skeptics, no one was held in higher esteem by all France than you, *La Rose de la Loire.*"

"Hardly the point. Had I been skilled in argument, I'd have managed to convince my Inquisitors, the English-loving theologians of the University of Paris, that I am not a witch."

"But *God* was on your side."

The Maid laughed. "God's on the side of His Son and the saints and martyrs, too. But that does not mean they escape failure and death."

"She's right," La Sorciere said. "Even worlds and galaxies share man's fate."

"France *needs* you," Monsieur Bondieu pleaded. "We ourselves have become too much like our machines. We hold nothing sacred except the smooth functioning of our parts. We know you will address the question with intensity, yet in simplicity and truth. That's all we ask. The rest we leave to God's will and to fate."

The Maid felt fatigued. She needed solitude,

time to reflect. "I must have time to consult with my voices," she told them. She paused. "Will there be only one or many questions that I must address?"

"Just one."

The Inquisitors had been far more demanding. They asked many questions, dozens, sometimes the same ones, over and over again. Right answers at Poitiers proved wrong elsewhere. Deprived of food, drink, rest, intimidated by the enforced journey to the cemetery, exhausted by the tedious sermon they compelled her to hear and wracked by terror of the fire, she could not withstand their interrogation. "Does the Archangel Michael have long hair?" "Is St. Margaret stout or lean?" "Are St. Catherine's eyes brown or blue?" They trapped her into assigning to voices of the spirit, attributions of the flesh. Then they perversely condemned her for confounding sacred spirit with corrupt flesh. She could not therefore be certain if this Bondieu would turn out to be friend or foe.

"What is it?" she wanted to know. "This single question you want me to answer."

"There is universal consensus that man-made intelligences have a kind of brain. The question we want you to answer is whether they have a soul."

"Only Almighty God has the power to create a soul."

Monsieur Bondieu smiled. "We Preservers couldn't agree with you more. Artificial intelligences, unlike us, their creators, have no soul. They're just machines. Mechanical contrivances with electronically programmed brains. Only man has a soul."

"If you already know the answer to the question, why do you need me?"

"To persuade France," Monsieur Bondieu replied. "France, the planet, and the spacecolonist worlds."

The Maid reflected. Her Inquisitors had known the answers to the questions they plied her with, too. Monsieur Bondieu seemed sincere, but then so were the learned University of Paris men who pronounced her a witch because she didn't have what they considered the right answers, and because they loved the English more than their own King. Yet Monsieur Bondieu had told her the answer beforehand, one with which any sensible person would agree. Still, she could not be sure of his intentions. Not even the crucifix she asked the priest to hold aloft was proof against the oily smoke, the biting flames . . .

"Well?" asked Monsieur Bondieu. "Will The Sacred Rose of France consent to be our champion?"

"These planet people and the spacecolonist worlds," she said. "Are they too descendants of Charles, The Great and True King, of the House of Valois?"

Tech strode into The Satellite to meet his drinkdrug buddy and co-worker Nim. He arrived early, probably due to guilt at having neglected their friendship since the Great Debate project began. He was surprised to find Nim already there.

To judge from his dilated pupils, he'd been there most of the afternoon.

They exchanged warm greetings, after which Tech said, "All right, what's all the spacespy stuff? Did you just make it up because I've been neglecting you, not to mention my thirst? Or is there something going on that I should know?"

Nim shook his head and said, "Same old Tech. Blunt as a bull. Aren't you even going to order first? I recommend the Swirlsnort. It won't do a thing for your thirst—in fact, it will dry up your entire head—but you won't care."

"You know me," Tech said. "I'll try anything once."

The mechmaid brought the Swirlsnort, a strange powdery concoction that tasted like nutmeg. Tech sniffed it slowly, one nostril at a time. Because he was habitually engrossed in his work, he relied on Nim to inform him of any office politics that might affect his projects and his funding. He wanted to be relatively clear-headed when Nim filled him in. After that, he'd allow himself to get skyed.

"You may not like what I have to say," said Nim. "It concerns Maquina."

"Maquina!" He laughed. Nim knew Tech was bird-dogging Maquina because Tech had told him. He wanted to be certain Nim, who changed women as often as he changed his underwear, had not designs on Maquina of his own. "What about her?"

"Well, don't take this too hard, old buddy, but scuttlebutt has it that there's a juicy vice-presidency in store for whoever wins the big one at the Coliseum."

"No problem," Tech said. "Me."

Nim ran his hand through his strawberry blond hair. "I can't decide if it's your modesty or your ability to foresee the future that I like most about you. Your modesty. Gotta be that."

Tech shrugged. "She's good at what she does, I'll admit that."

"But you're better."

"I'm luckier. They gave me Reason. Maquina got stuck with Faith."

Nim blinked. "I wouldn't underestimate faith if I were you. It's often hooked to passion, and no one's managed to get rid of either yet."

"Don't have to. They eventually get rid of themselves. Burn out."

"But the light of reason burns eternally?" said Nim.

"Now that we know how to regenerate brain cells, yes."

Nim raised his glass—he preferred liquids to powders—and said, "Just trying to help you out with a little advice."

"What advice? I didn't hear any advice."

Nim clucked. "If your unregenerated brain cells contain a shred of common sense, you'll stop cooperating with Maquina to improve her simulation. Or better yet, you'll keep pretending you're cooperating so you get the benefit of anything she can show you. But what you'll really start doing is looking for ways to do both her and her simulation in. The grapevine says it's terrific. As good as yours."

Tech felt a stab of jealousy in spite of himself,

but he was careful not to show it. "Thanks for the tip."

Nim bowed his head with characteristic irony and said, "Anything to help out a friend. Even if you don't need it, you'd be a fool to turn it down."

"What, the vice presidency? I'm not one to turn a promo down."

"Not the promo, you prick. You think I don't know that I'm talking to ambition's slave? My advice."

Tech took a hefty double-nostril snort and said, "I'll certainly bear it in mind."

Tech did not give Nim's counsel any thought until, two days later, he overheard a junior vice-president in the executive lounge praising Maquina's work to Hastings, the president of Artifice, Inc. As he passed Maquina's office on his way back to his own, his intention, he told himself, was to relay the v.p.'s compliment. But when he found the door unlocked, her office empty, an impulse of a different kind seized him.

When Maquina walked in half an hour later, he started with surprise. He'd just finished the rather elementary task of rigging her office so that he'd be able to monitor interviews with her client, Bondieu. She shared with Tech the substance of these interviews, anyway—as far as he knew. He reasoned that his suggestions as to how she should handle the sometimes difficult Bondieu would be improved if he were exposed to Bondieu directly.

"Tech!" Maquina exclaimed. Her hand smoothed

her hair in that unconscious primping that betrays a woman's desire to please a man. "What are you doing here?"

"Waiting for you."

Her smile seemed warmer and more welcoming than usual. He couldn't wait to escape to his own office where, when he arrived, the red light on the control board was flashing with the insistence of a police car's. He switched it off, booted up, activated the sensors, and waited for the three-dimensional image to appear.

Voltaire, brows furrowed, hands on his skinny hips, rose from the richly embroidered chair in his study at Cirey, the chateau of his long-term mistress, the Marquise du Chatelet. The place he had called home for fifteen years depressed him now that she was gone. And now the Marquis, who didn't even have the decency to wait until his wife's body was cold, had informed him that he must leave.

"Get me out of here," he demanded of the scientist who finally answered his call. "I want to go to the cafe. I need to see the Maid."

The scientist leaned over the control board Voltaire was already beginning to resent, and smiled. "I didn't think she was your type. You showed a strong preference all your life for brainy women, like your niece and the Madame du Chatelet."

"I simply can't abide the company of stupid women. The only thing that can be said on their behalf is that they can be trusted. They're too stupid to practice deceit."

"Unlike Mme. du Chatelet?"

Voltaire drummed his fingers impatiently on the beautifully wrought walnut desk, a gift from Mme. du Chatelet. "True, she betrayed me. She paid dearly for it, too."

The scientist arched a brow. "With that young officer, you mean? The one who made her pregnant?"

"At forty-three, a married woman with three grown children has no business becoming pregnant!"

"You hit the roof when she told you—understandable but not very enlightened. Yet you didn't break off with her. You were with her throughout the birth."

Voltaire shrugged. He'd worried himself sick about the birth, which had proved amazingly easy. Yet nine days later, the most extraordinary woman he had ever known was dead. Of childbed fever. No one, not even his niece and housekeeper and former paramour, Mme. Denis, who took care of him till he died, had ever been able to take her place.

"She persuaded me that it would be unreasonable to break with a woman of exceptional breeding and talent merely for exercising the same rights that I enjoyed. Especially since I hadn't made love to her for months. The rights of man, she said, belonged to women, too. Provided, *bien sur*, they were of the aristocracy. I allowed her gentle reasonableness to persuade me." Voltaire rubbed his forehead, heavy with memories. "She was an exception to every rule. She understood Newton and Locke. She understood every word that I wrote. She understood *me*."

"Why weren't you making love to her? Too busy going to orgies?"

"My dear sir, my participation in such festivities has been greatly exaggerated. It's true, I accepted an invitation to one such celebration of erotic pleasure in my youth. I acquitted myself so well, I was invited to return."

"Did you?"

"Certainly not. Once, a philosopher. Twice, a pervert."

"What *I* don't understand is why a man of your worldliness should be so intent on another meeting with the Maid."

"Her passion," Voltaire said, an image of the robust Maid rising clearly in his mind's eye. "Her courage and devotion to what she believed."

"But you possessed that trait as well."

Voltaire stomped his foot, but the floor made no sound. "Why do you speak of me in the past tense? I possess temperament. Do not confuse passion with temperament. Temperament is a matter of the nerves. Passion's borne from the heart and soul. The Maid dared cling to her vision with her whole heart and soul, despite the bullying of church and state. Her devotion to her vision, unlike mine, bore no taint of perverseness. She was the first Protestant. I've always preferred Protestants to papist absolutists. At least I did until I took up residence in Geneva, where I discovered that their public hatred of pleasure is as great as any pope's. Only Quakers do not privately engage in what they publicly claim to abjure. A hundred

true believers cannot redeem millions of hypocrites."

"The Maid recanted," the scientist said. "She
knuckled under to their threats."

Voltaire bristled with irritation. "They took her
to a cemetery! Terrorized a credulous girl with
threats of death and hell. Bishops, academicians—
the most learned men of their time! Donkeys'
asses, the lot! Browbeating the bravest woman in
France, a woman whom they destroyed only to
revere. Hypocrites! They require martyrs as leeches
require blood. They thrive on self-sacrifice. Provided that the selves they sacrifice are not their
own. And after forcing the Maid to forswear her
manly clothes,"—he fluffed his lilac ribbon as he
spoke—"they deliberately left them in her cell to
tempt her. They *wanted* her to go back on her
recantation so they could destroy her! Villains are
undone by what is worst in them, heroes by what
is best. They played her honor and her bravery
like a fiddle, swine plucking at a violin."

"You're defending her," the scientist said with a
wry smile. "Yet in that poem you wrote about her,
you depict her as a tavern slut, much older than
she in fact was, a liar about her so-called voices, a
superstitious but shrewd fool. The greatest enemy
of the chastity she pretends to defend is a donkey,
for Christsake. A donkey with wings!"

Voltaire smiled. "A brilliant metaphor for the
Roman Church, *n'est-ce-pas?* I had a point to make.
She was simply the sword with which I drove it
home. I had not met her then. I had no idea she
was a woman of such great mysterious depths."

"Not depths of intellect," the scientist protested. "She's just a fifteenth century peasant! She doesn't even have big tits!"

"No, no. Depths of the soul. I'm like a little stream. Clear because it is shallow. But she's a river, an ocean! Return me to Aux Deux Magots. She and the cute, wind-up *garçon* are the only society that I now have."

"She is your adversary," the scientist said. "A minion of those who uphold values that you fought all your life. To assure your victory over her in the Great Debate, I'm going to reprogram you, equip you with all the philosophical and scientific information rational people have developed in the four centuries since your death. Darwin, Freud, Einstein, Heisenberg, LeConte. The definitive treatise on the Big Bang. The GUT—general unified theory—that eluded us all for so long. Your reason must crush her faith. You must regard her as the enemy she is, if civilization is to continue to advance along rational scientific lines."

His eloquence and impudence were rather charming, but they were not substitutes for Voltaire's fascination with the Maid. "I will refuse to read anything you give me until you reunite me with the Maid in the cafe."

The scientist had the audacity to laugh. "You don't get it. You have no choice. I'll download—feed—the information into you. You're nothing but a complex I myself have made. You'll have the information you must have to win whether you want it or not."

Voltaire bristled with resistance. He knew the

accents of authority since he was first subjected to those of his father, a strict martinet who'd compelled him to attend mass and whose austerities had claimed the life of Voltaire's mother when Voltaire was only seven. The only way she could escape his father's discipline was to die. Voltaire had no intention of escaping this scientist in that way. His existence was far too valuable.

"I refuse to *use* any additional knowledge you give me unless you return me at once to the cafe."

The scientist regarded Voltaire the way Voltaire regarded his wigmaker—with haughty superiority. As if he knew Voltaire could not exist without his patronage. Though middle-class in origin himself, Voltaire did not believe common people worthy of governing themselves. The thought of his wigmaker posing as a legislator was enough to make him never wear a wig again. To be seen similarly by this man of science was intolerable.

"Tell you what," said the scientist. "You compose one of your brilliant *lettres philosophiques* trashing the concept of the human soul, and I will reunite you with the Maid. But if you don't, you won't see her until the day of the Debate. Do I make myself clear?"

Voltaire mulled the offer over. "Clear as a little stream," he said at last.

"I have no desire to see the skinny gentleman in the wig who thinks he's better than everyone else," the Maid told the sorceress called Maquina. "I much prefer the company of my own voices."

197

"He's quite taken with you," Madame la Sorciere said.

"I find that difficult to believe," she replied, though she could not help it; she smiled.

"Oh, but it's true. He's asked Tech—his recreator —for an entirely new image. He lived, you know, to eighty-four. Tech decided to make him appear as he looked at forty-two—"

"He looks even older," the Maid observed, who found Monsieur Arouet's wig, lilac ribbon, and velvet breeches ludicrous.

"That's all been changed. Do see him. He's certainly eager to see you."

The Maid reflected. Monsieur Arouet would be far less repulsive if . . . "Did Monsieur Arouet have a different tailor as a young man?"

"Hmmm, I'm not sure. But that might be arranged."

"All right then," she agreed. "But I'm not going to the inn in these."

She held up her chains, recalling the fur cloak the King himself had placed about her shoulders at his coronation in Rouen. She thought of asking for it now, but decided against it. They had made much of her cloak during her trial, accusing her of having a demon-inspired love of luxury; she who, until she won the King over that day she first appeared at court, had felt nothing but coarse burlap against her skin. Her accusers, she noted, wore black satin and velvet and smelled of perfume.

"I'll do what I can," Madame la Sorciere vowed. "But you must agree not to tell Monsieur Bondieu. He doesn't want you fraternizing with the enemy, but I think it will do you good. Hone your skills in preparation for the Great Debate."

There was a pause in which the Maid felt as if she had fainted. When she recovered, she found herself seated in the Inn of the Two Worms surrounded by guests who, once again, seemed not to know that she was there.

The armor-plated beings bearing trays and clearing tableware darted among the guests. She looked for Garçon and spotted him gazing at the honey-haired cook, who pretended not to notice. Garçon's longing recalled the way the Maid herself had gazed at statues of St. Catherine and St. Margaret, who'd both forsworn men but adopted their attire.

She suppressed a smile when Monsieur Arouet appeared, wearing a dark unpowdered wig. He still looked old—about the age of her father Jacques Dars, thirty plus one or two—though younger than before. His shoulders slumped under the weight of many books. She'd only seen books twice, during her trials, and though they looked nothing like these, she recoiled at the memory of their power.

"*Alors,*" Monsieur Arouet said, setting the books before her. "Forty-two volumes. My *Selected Works*. Incomplete but—" he smiled "—for now, it will have to do. What's wrong?"

"Do you mock me? You know I cannot read."

"I know. Garçon 213-ADM is going to teach you."

"I do not want to learn. All books except the Bible are born of the devil."

Monsieur Arouet threw up his hands and lapsed

into curses that resembled those her soldiers used when they forgot that she was near. "You *must* learn how to read. Knowledge is power!"

"The devil must know a great deal," she said, careful to let no part of the books touch her.

Monsieur Arouet, exasperated, turned to the sorceress and said, "For God's sake, can't you teach her anything?" Then he turned back to her. "How will you appreciate my brilliance if you can't even read? Had you been able to read, you'd have confounded those idiots who sent you to the stake."

"All learned men," she said. "Like you."

"No, *pucellette*, not like me. Not like me at all." She recoiled from the book he held out as if it were a serpent. Then he rubbed the book all over himself and Garçon. "It's harmless," he said. "See?"

"Evil is often invisible," she murmured.

"Monsieur is right," Garçon told her. "All the best people read."

"Had you been lettered," Monsieur Arouet said, "you'd have known that your Inquisitors had absolutely no right to try you. You were a prisoner of war, captured in battle. Your English captor had no legal right to have your religious views examined by French Inquisitors and academics. You pretended to believe your voices were divine—"

"Pretended!" she cried out.

"—and he pretended to believe they were demonic. The English are themselves too tolerant to burn anyone at the stake. They leave such forms of amusement to our countrymen, the French."

"Not too tolerant," the Maid said, "to turn me over to the Bishop of Beauvais, claiming I was a witch." She looked away, unwilling to let him peer in her eyes. "Perhaps I am. I betrayed my own voices."

"Voices of conscience, nothing more. The pagan Socrates heard them as well. Everyone does. But it's unreasonable to sacrifice our lives to them, if only because to destroy ourselves on their account is to destroy them, too. Persons of good breeding betray them as a matter of course."

"Perhaps Monsieur's voices are soft," Garçon suggested. "Therefore, more easily ignored."

"I let them force me to admit my voices were the devil's," said the Maid, "when all the while I knew they were divine. Isn't that the act of a demon? A witch?"

"Listen!" Monsieur Arouet gripped her by the arms. "There *are* no witches. The only demons in your life were those who sent you to the stake. Ignorant swine, the lot! Except for your English captor, who pretended to believe you were a witch to carry out a shrewd, political move. When your garments had burned away, his dupes removed your body from the stake to show the crowd and the Inquisitors you were indeed a female, who, if for no other reason than usurping the privileges of males, deserved your fate."

"Please stop!" she said. She thought she smelled the oily reek of smoke, although Monsieur Arouet had made Garçon place No Smoking signs throughout the inn. The room veered, whirled. "The fire." She gasped. "Its tongues . . ."

"That's enough," the sorceress said. "Can't you see you're upsetting her? Lay off."

But Monsieur Arouet persisted. "They examined your private parts after your garments burned away, just as they'd done before to prove you were the virgin that you claimed. And having satisfied their lewdness in the name of God, they returned you to the pyre and burned your flesh and bones to ashes. *That* was how your countrymen requited you for championing their King, for seeing to it France remained forever French. And having burned even your bones to ash, they held a hearing, cited some rural rumor that your heart had not been consumed in the fire, and promptly declared you a national heroine, the Savior of France. I wouldn't be at all surprised if, by now, they have canonized you and revere you as a saint."

"In 1924," la Sorciere said.

Monsieur Arouet's splutter of scorn crackled in her ears as Garçon fanned her with one of his metal hands. "Much good it did *her*," he said to la Sorciere.

"I said, enough!" a woman's voice called out. But it was no one in the crowd of onlookers gathered around the stake.

"Fire." She gasped. Clutching the collar of mesh at her throat, she fled into the cool dark of oblivion.

"It's about time," Voltaire scolded Madame la Scientiste. "How dare you turn me off without my consent? I've been trying to reach you for hours."

"I haven't been ignoring you on purpose," she said in a cool, businesslike voice. "Tech—Mr. Hilliard—and I are being besieged by media people from all over the planet. There's someone from a spacecol we've never even heard of! Tech's talking to him now. I never dreamed the Great Debate would be the media event of the decade. They all want the same thing—a chance to interview you and the Maid."

Voltaire fluffed the apricot ribbon at his throat and said, "I refuse to be seen by them without my powdered wig."

"We're not going to let them see you or the Maid at *all*. They can talk to Tech all they want. He likes that kind of attention more than I do, and he handles it very well. He says public exposure will help his career. Look. I came as soon as my mechsec told me the light was on. To be honest, I thought it was the Maid. What's wrong? Are you losing?"

Voltaire, in his richly appointed rooms at the court of Frederick the Great, was playing chess with the friar whom he employed to let him win. He was so overcome by an unprecedented attack of compassion that for a moment—just a moment— he was unable to speak.

"You were quite right. When you turned the Maid off. It's impossible to hold a rational conversation with her! Unfortunately, you could not shut her off without stilling me, too. If there's one thing I cannot tolerate, it's being silenced before I have had my say."

He paused for maximum dramatic effect. He was a fine actor—everyone who'd heard him perform in his plays at Frederick's court said so. He knew a good scene when he saw one, and this one had the dramatic potential to be extremely good.

"Get rid of him and I will tell you why I called."
He gestured at the good-natured friar, the only
man of the cloth he had ever met that he could
stand. "You are dismissed," he told him. "Go."

"Tech really should be handling this." Nevertheless, Madame la Scientiste clicked something
on her control board and presto! the friar vanished.

Voltaire took a sip of Frederick's fine sherry and
cleared his throat. "I want you to delete the Maid's
memory of her final ordeal. It impedes our conversation as surely as bishops and state officials
impede the publication of any intelligent work.
Besides . . ." he paused, uncomfortable at the expression of any feelings except irritation at hu-
mankind's stupidity. "She's suffering. I cannot bear
to see it. And while you're at it, delete from me
too my memory of the eleven months I served in
the Bastille. And all my frequent flights from Paris—
not the flights themselves, mind you—my periods
of exile constitute most of my life! Just delete their
causes, not the effects."

"Well, I don't know—"

He slammed a fist down on an ornately wrought
oak side table. "Unless you liberate me from past
fears, I cannot write freely!"

"Simple logic—"

"Since when is logic simple? I simply can't compose my *lettre philosophique* on the absurdity of
denying those like Garçon 213-ADM the rights of
man on the grounds that they have no soul. He's
an amusing little fellow, don't you think? And as
smart as at least a dozen priests whom I have
known. Does he not speak? Respond? Desire? He

is infatuated with a human cook. Should he not be able to pursue happiness as freely as you or I? If he has no soul, then you have no soul, either. If you have a soul, it can only be inferred from your behavior, and since we may make the identical inference from the behavior of Garçon, if you have a soul, so does he."

"I'm inclined to agree," Mme. la Scientiste said. "I can hardly wait to hear what you have to say in your *lettre.*"

"The point is, I cannot express myself completely freely on these sensitive matters unless you rid me of the memory of what I suffered for expressing my ideas. The truth is I never *did* express myself freely on many matters. Take that life-hating Puritan Pascal's views of original sin, miracles, and much other nonsense besides. I didn't dare say what I really thought! Always, I had to calculate what every assault on convention and traditional stupidity would cost. And the Maid is hampered even more than I! For *her* convictions, she paid the ultimate price. Being crucified could be no worse than what she suffered at the stake. Light a cigarette in her presence and she becomes so confused, she can't articulate the nature of these voices that she claims to hear. Rational inquiries cannot be carried out in an atmosphere of fear and intimidation. If our contest is to be fair, I implore you in the name of justice and enlightenment, rid us of these terrors that prevent us from speaking our minds and from encouraging others to speak theirs. Else this Debate will be like a race run with bricks tied to the runners' ankles."

Mme. la Scientiste did not respond at once. "I—I'd like to help, but I'm not sure I can."

Voltaire spluttered with scorn. "I know enough of your procedures to know you can comply with my request."

"Technically, your request poses no problem. But morally, I'm not at liberty to tamper with the Maid's program at whim."

Voltaire stiffened. "I realize Madame has a low opinion of my philosophy, but surely—"

"Not so! I think the world of you! You have a modern mind, one of the first and best our world has ever known. But your point of view, though valid as far as it goes, is limited because of what it leaves out and cannot address. And don't forget, I work for Artifice, Inc., and the Preservers, for Monsieur Bondieu. I'm bound by the ethics of my profession to give them the Maid they want. Unless I can convince them to delete the Maid's memory of her martyrdom, I can't do it. And Tech would have to get permission from the company and the Skeptics to delete yours. He'd love to, I assure you. His Skeptics are more likely to consent than my Preservers. It would give you an advantage in addition to the two hundred years on the Maid that you already have."

"I quite agree," he conceded at once. "Relieving me of my burdens without relieving the Maid of hers would not be cricket. Neither Locke nor Newton would approve."

Mme. la Scientiste did not answer at once. "I'll talk to my boss, and to Monsieur Bondieu," she said at last. "But I wouldn't hold my breath if I were you."

Voltaire smiled wryly and said, "Madame forgets I have no breath to hold."

The red light flashing on Tech's board stopped just as he entered his office. That meant Maquina must have answered it in hers. Tech bristled with suspicion. They had agreed not to talk to each other's recreations alone, though each had already given the other the required programming to do it. The Maid never initiated communication, which meant the caller was Voltaire.

How dare Maquina boot up without him! He stormed out of the office to let her and Voltaire both know exactly what he thought of their conspiring behind his back. But in the corridor he was besieged by cameras, tv-mechs, journalists, and reporters. It was fifteen minutes before he burst into Maquina's office and, sure enough, caught her closeted cozily with Voltaire—she'd reduced him from eight feet to human-size.

"You broke our pact!'" he shouted. "What are you doing, trying to use his infatuation with that schizophrenic to make him throw the Debate?"

Maquina, head buried in her hands, looked up. Her eyes glistened with tears. Tech felt something in him roll over, but he chose to ignore it. She actually blew Voltaire a kiss before shutting him off.

"I must say, I never thought you'd sink to this."

"To what?" Maquina asked. "What's gotten into you? You're not your usual jaunty self at all."

"What was that all about? What did he want?"

Within five minutes after Maquina had explained Voltaire's request, Tech was back in his office, booting Voltaire up.

"The answer is *no!*" he shouted at Voltaire. "I want the Rose of France wilting in her armor the day of the Debate. It will remind her of her Inquisition, which is exactly what I want. She'll start babbling nonsense and reveal to the planet just how bankrupt faith without reason is."

Voltaire stamped his foot. "*Merde alors!* We disagree! Never mind me, but I insist you delete the Maid's memory of her final hours so that her reasoning will not be compromised, as mine so often was, by fear of reprisals. And I demand you let me visit her and that odd *mais charmant* curiosity Garçon in the cafe at will. I've never known beings like either of them before, and they are the only society that I now have."

What about me? Tech thought. What about me? But what he said was, "I don't suppose it's occurred to you that the loser of the Debate will be consigned forever to oblivion."

Voltaire blinked, his face giving nothing away.

"You can't fool me," Tech said. "I know you want more than just intellectual immortality—that, you have already obtained. I happen to recall that once, when you were well advanced in years, unforced by your father and of your own free will, you actually received Easter communion."

"I refused it at the end! All I wanted was to be left to die in peace!"

"Allow me to quote from your famous poem, 'The Lisbon Earthquake':

'Sad is the present if no future state,
No blissful retribution mortals wait,
If fate's decrees the thinking being doom
To lose existence in the silent tomb.'"

Voltaire wavered. "True, I said that—and with what eloquence! But everyone who enjoys life longs to extend it."

"*Your* only chance at a 'future state' is to win the Debate. It's against your own best interest—and we all know how fond you've always been of that!—to delete the Maid's memory of being burned alive, because that memory makes her vulnerable and more likely to break down. You can use it to your advantage in The Great Debate. And if you give me a hard time, I'm going to download into her that scurrilous poem you wrote about her."

"*La Pucelle?* You wouldn't!"

"Wouldn't I! You'll be lucky if she ever speaks to you again."

"Monsieur forgets the Maid does not know how to read."

"I'll see to it she learns—or better yet, read it to her myself. She may be illiterate, but she damn sure isn't deaf!"

Voltaire frowned, reflecting. Tech knew he had him between Scylla and Charybdis. What was that eighteenth-century mind, sharp as a scalpel, plotting? Once the Debate was over, Tech vowed to strip that mind down and study its cutting edge.

"I promise to produce *la lettre* if you will just let me see her once more. In return, you'll vow never to so much as *mention La Pucelle* to the Maid."

"No funny business," Tech warned. "I'm going to watch your every move."

"As you wish."

Tech returned Voltaire to the cafe, where Joan and Garçon 213-ADM were waiting. He'd barely called them up when he was momentarily distracted by a knock on his door—Nim.

"Coffee?"

"Sure." Tech glanced back at the cafe sim. Let them visit a while. The more Voltaire knew, the sharper he'd be later. "Got any of that senso-powder? Been a tough day."

"Your orders," said Garçon 213-ADM, who was having difficulty following the arguments between the Maid and the Monsieur on whether beings like himself possessed a soul. Monsieur seemed to believe that no one had a soul—which so outraged the Maid that she demanded to be returned to her cell, saying the company of jailers was preferable to Monsieur's own. They argued with such heat, they did not notice that the scientist who usually watched them had disappeared.

Now was Garçon's chance to implore Monsieur to intervene on his behalf and ask his human masters to give him a name. 213-ADM was just a mechfolk code: 2 identified his function, mechwaiter; 13 placed him in a Paris cafe, and ADM stood for Aux Deux Magots. He was sure he'd have a better chance of attracting the honey-haired short-order cook's attention if he had a human name.

"Monsieur, Madame. Your orders, please."

"What good is ordering?" Monsieur snapped. Patience, Garçon observed, was not improved by learning. Mechfolk were in general more patient than their masters. "We go through the motions, but we cannot taste a thing!"

Garçon gestured sympathetically with two of his four hands. He had no experience of human senses except sight, sound, and rudimentary touch, those necessary to perform his job. He would have given anything to taste, to feel; humans seemed to derive such pleasure from it.

"My limitations exceed yours," he said gently. "I cannot follow your discussions, though I understand that their outcome will greatly affect me."

The Maid perused the menu and, changing the subject, said, "I'll have my usual. A crust of bread— I'll try a sourdough baguette crust for a change—"

"A sourdough baguette!" Monsieur echoed.

"—and, to dip it in, a bit of champagne."

Monsieur shook his hand as if to cool it off, then quoted himself as he was so fond of doing. "*J'aime le luxe, et même la mollesse.* Though a crust of a baguette may hardly be termed overindulgence!" Then he commended Garçon for doing such a fine job of teaching the Maid to read the menu.

"Madame la Scientiste permitted it," Garçon said; he did not want to get in trouble with his human masters, who could pull the plug on him at any time. "She said anything that we do ourselves is not a violation of her orders."

211

Monsieur waved a dismissive hand. "She's much too conscientious. She'd never survive on her own in Paris, much less at any royal court. Her counterpart—where did he go?—my god, are we alone?—he's far less hindered on that score. He'll go far. Lack of scruples is fortune's favorite handmaiden. I certainly did not proceed from penury to one of the wealthiest citizens in France by confusing ideals with scruples."

"Has Monsieur decided on his order?" Garçon asked.

"Yes. You're to instruct the Maid in more advanced texts so that she can read my poem, 'On the Newtonian Philosophy', along with all my *Lettres philosophiques*. Her reasoning is to become as equal as possible with my own. Not that anyone's reason is likely to become so," he added with his cocky smile.

"Your modesty is equalled only by your wit," said the Maid, drawing from Monsieur a smirky laugh.

Garçon sadly shook his head. "I'm afraid that won't be possible. I am unable to instruct anyone except in simple phrases. My literacy permits comprehension of nothing beyond menus. I must decline Monsieur's past offer to become his amanuensis for the same reason. I'm honored by Monsieur's desire to advance my station. But even when opportunity knocks, I and my kind, consigned forever to the lowest levels of society, cannot answer the door."

"The lower classes ought to keep their place,"

Voltaire assured him. "But I'll make an exception in your case. You seem ambitious. Are you?"

Garçon glanced at the honey-haired cook. "Ambition is unsuited to one of my rank."

"What would you be then? If you could be anything you like?"

Garçon happened to know that the cook spent her three days a week off—Garçon himself worked seven days a week—in the corridors of the Louvre. "A mechguide at the Louvre," he said. "One smart enough, and with sufficient leisure, to court a woman who barely knows I exist."

"Leave it to me," Monsieur said. He had a tendency to overestimate his powers, impressive as these were. "I'll find a way to—how do they say it?"

"Download you," the Maid volunteered.

"*Mon dieu!*" Monsieur exclaimed. "Already she can read as well as you. But I will not have her wit exceed mine! That would be going too damned far indeed!"

Tech dissolved the packet of powderpower into his margarita, downed half of it, and waited for the rush.

"That bad?" said Nim. He signalled the Satellite mechmaid, ordered another packet, and dissolved it in what was left of Tech's drink.

"Voltaire," Tech said, arriving at the bottom of the glass. "He's supposed to be my creature, but half the time it feels as if I'm his. He has a will all his own. If Schopenhauer was right and will is soul, I've created a being with a soul. Maybe I programmed him all wrong."

"You programmed him all right," Nim said. "Forget Schopenhauer. He thought rocks had souls, for Christsake. Did you expect the irrepressible Voltaire not to give you a hard time? You represent authority. He battled authority all his life, and that's exactly how you've reconstructed him."

Tech ran his fingers through his wavy hair and gestured to the mechmaid to bring him another drink. "You can't imagine what dealing with him is like."

"Okay, so he's a temperamental Frenchman! Bottom line, though, he can't do anything you haven't programmed him to do. If he gets out of hand, go deep inside him. If you find anything in his construction resembling a will or a soul, all you have to do is delete it."

Tech scoffed. "Going in piecemeal to find his soul would be like cutting into a human brain in search of consciousness. And anyway, it's not just him." He took a deep breath and exhaled toward the transparent domed ceiling. "It's the Debate."

"What about it?"

Tech met Nim's eyes. "I rigged Maquina's office. I eavesdrop on her meetings with Bondieu."

Nim slapped him on the shoulder. "Good for you!"

In spite of himself, Tech laughed. "That isn't all."

Nim leaned forward, boyishly curious.

"I think I went too far," Tech said.

"You don't mean to say you got caught!"

"No, no. You know how Maquina is. She doesn't suspect enemies of intrigue, much less friends."

"That's why she'd make a lousy Vice President of R&D Experimental Simulations. Manipulating others isn't her strong suit."

"I'm not sure it's mine, either," Tech said.

"With fifty grand a year increase and all the perks that go with it? It's yours, believe me, it's yours. So what else did you do?"

Tech shook his head with self-disapproval. "I updated Voltaire's memory. Darwin, Einstein, Dyson, Seultete, the works. He now knows everything we know. The Maid still has an early fifteenth-century mind, and an illiterate one at that. She's no Copernicus, you know."

Nim's eyes narrowed. "A stroke of genius," he said.

"An underhanded stroke," said Tech. "Maquina and I both agreed not to do it. Even Voltaire objected to being made unilaterally that smart."

"Does your client know?"

"Um-hmm. The Skeptics are all for it. I foresee no problem there."

"It's in the bag," Nim said. "It's in the bag."

Tech nervously toyed with his empty glass. "What I've done will become apparent at The Great Debate."

"I should hope so!" said Nim. "Why the hell else did you do it?"

"I feel like a shit."

"You are," said Nim approvingly. "What you need is a little recreation of another kind." He summoned a mechwench. Padded charms would help Tech forget for the moment all about Maquina, Voltaire, and the Maid.

*   *   *

"Now pay attention," Voltaire said when the scientist at last answered his call. He cleared his throat, flung out his arms, and readied himself to declaim the brilliant arguments he'd detailed in another *lettre* that would assure his immortality.

The scientist covered his eyes with his hands to block out the light and turned down the volume on his control board.

"What's wrong with you?" Voltaire asked. "Don't you want to hear my *lettre?*"

"Hangover. Too much drugdrink."

"You've discovered a single general theory uniting the electromagnetic, strong, weak, and gravitational force—and have no cure for hangover?"

"Or colds either." The scientist's voice sounded ragged.

"*J'aime la mollesse,*" Voltaire paraphrased 'Le Mondaine', his poem in praise of worldly pleasures. "But overindulgence does have its price."

"Tell me about it," the scientist said, slapping an icederm on his neck.

"In view of your condition, instead of reciting my *lettre* verbatim, I'll just give an informal summary of its contents."

"Very kind of you, yes."

Voltaire clicked his heels together, then bowed in the Prussian way he'd learned at Frederick the Great's court. "The doctrine of a soul depends on the idea of a fixed and immutable self. No evidence supports the notion of a stable 'I,' an essential ego-entity lying beyond each individual existence."

"True," said the scientist, "though odd, coming from you."

"Don't interrupt me, please. Now, how can we explain the stubborn illusion of a fixed self or soul? Through five functions, themselves conceptual processes and not fixed elements. First, all beings possess physical, material qualities, which change so slowly that they appear to be fixed, but which are actually in constant material flux."

"The soul's supposed to outlast those," the scientist said. He pinched the bridge of his nose with his thumb and forefinger.

"I'll get to that. Don't interrupt. Second, there is the illusion of a fixed emotional make-up, when actually feelings, as even that rude playwright Shakespeare pointed out, wax and wan as inconstantly as the moon. They too are in constant flux, though no doubt these motions, just like the moon's, obey physical laws."

"We know a few of them," the scientist said. "But we've still got a long way to go. In any event, not my area of expertise."

Voltaire suppressed his irritation at the scientist's dull-witted interruptions. Any audience, even one that insisted on participating, was better than none. "Third, the phenomenon of perception. The senses, upon examination, also turn out to be processes, in constant motion, not in the least fixed."

"The soul's supposed to outlast them as well."

"Fourth," Voltaire continued, determined to ignore the scientist's banal interpolations, "there is in every individual a constellation of habits that develops over the years. But these too are made up of constant flowing action. Despite the appearance of repetition, there's nothing fixed or immutable here."

"Drinkdrugging habits, too?" the scientist said. "They seem pretty immutable to me."

"Nonsense. They're just as subject to time and change as everything else. Finally, there is the phenomenon of consciousness, the so-called soul itself, which is believed by priests and fools—a redundancy, that—to be detachable from the four phenomena I've named. But consciousness itself exhibits all those characteristics of flowing motion of the other four. Now, all five of these functions are constantly grouping and regrouping. The body itself is forever in a state of flux, and so is everything else. Permanence is an illusion. Heraclitus was absolutely right. You cannot set foot into the same river twice. The hungover man I'm regarding now is not the same hungover man I am regarding *now*. Everything is always in a state of dissolution and decay—"

"You can say that again."

"—as well as in a state of solution and growth. Consciousness itself cannot be separated from its contents. We are pure deed. There is no doer. The dancer can't be separated from the dance. Science after my time confirms this view. Looked at closely, the atom itself disappears. There *is* no atom, strictly speaking. There is only what the atom does. Function is everything. Ergo, there is no fixed, absolute entity commonly known as soul."

"Hmmm," said the scientist.

"Since artificial intelligences like Garçon exhibit

218

all the functional characteristics I have named—
material qualities, emotional sensitivity, sensory
perception, habitual behavior and, so it would appear, consciousness—it isn't reasonable to withhold from them access to the rights that we
ourselves enjoy, allowing, *bien sur*, for class differences. If farmers, shopkeepers, and wigmakers are
granted privileges equal with those of dukes and
earls, regardless of individual merit and talent, it
is irrational to withhold such privileges from artificially intelligent beings like Garçon."

"If there's no soul, there's obviously no reincarnation of it either, right?"

"My dear sir, to be born twice is no more odd
than to be born once."

This startled the scientist. "But what's reincar-
nated? What crosses over from one life to the
next? If there's no fixed, absolute self? No soul?"

Voltaire made a note in the margin of his *lettre*.
"If you memorize my poems—which for your own
enlightenment I urge you do—do they lose anything you gain? If you light a candle from another
candle's flame, what crosses over? In a relay race,
does one runner give up anything to the other?
His position on the course, no more." Voltaire
paused for dramatic effect. "Well? What do you
think?"

The scientist clutched his head and said, "I think
you're going to win the Debate."

Voltaire, noting the scientist's pleasure with his
performance along with the scientist's stupefied
discomfort, decided now was the time to put forward his request. "But to assure my victory, I

must compose an additional *lettre*, more technical, for types who equate verbal symbols with mere rhetoric, with empty words."

"Have at it," said the scientist.

"For that," Voltaire said, "I will need your help."

"You got it."

Voltaire smiled cannily. "You must download into me everything you yourself know of computer electronics. This will not merely spare you an immense amount of work, it will enable me to write a technical *lettre* aimed at converting specialists and experts to our point of view. The truth is, even the Newtonian calculations I brought to France perplexed my brain, which isn't meant for algebra."

"Calculus," the scientist corrected dimly.

"I must have state-of-the-art instruction in computer electronics, specializing in simulated intelligence; the technical equivalent of Diderot's *Encyclopedie*."

Clutching his temples, the scientist slumped forward over his control board with a moan. "Only if you promise not to call me for at least the next ten hours."

"*Mais oui*," said Voltaire with an impish smile. "Monsieur requires time—how do you say it *en Anglais*?—to sleep it off."

Maquina waited nervously for her turn on the agenda of the executive meeting of Artifice, Inc. She sat opposite Tech, contributing nothing to the discussion, as colleagues and superiors discussed this aspect and that of the company's operation.

Her mind was elsewhere, but not so far gone as to fail to notice the hair on the back of Tech's hands, a single vein that pulsed—sensuous music—in his neck.

As the President of Artifice, Inc., dismissed all those not directly involved in the P.S. (Preserver-Skeptic) Project, Maquina assembled the notes she'd prepared to present her case. Of those present, she knew she could count only on Tech's support. But she was confident that, with it, the others would go along with her proposal.

The day before, she told the Special Projects Committee, for the first time, the Maid had broken her reclusive pattern. She initiated contact instead of waiting to be summoned with her usual air of reluctance. She'd been deeply disturbed to learn from "Monsieur Arouet" that she must defeat him in what she called "the trial" or be consigned once again to oblivion.

When Maquina had acknowledged that that was probably true, the Maid became convinced that she was going to be cast again into "the fire." Disoriented and confused, she begged Maquina to allow her to retire to consult her "voices."

Several hours later, the red light had flashed for Maquina again. This time the Maid requested high-level reading skills so that she might compete with her "Inquisitor" on a more equal footing.

"I explained to her that I couldn't alter her programming without this committee's consent."

"What about your client?" the President wanted to know.

"Monsieur Bondieu found out—he wouldn't tell

me how, a press leak, I suspect—that Voltaire is to be her rival in the Debate. Far from having to persuade him to alter her historicity, he's now threatening to take the account to Yamamoto in Japan—unless I download into her the additional two centuries of information Voltaire has."

"Does your client know we're handling Voltaire for the Skeptics as well as the Maid for him?"

Maquina shook her head.

"Thank the Cosmic X for that," said the Executive Vice President of Special Projects.

"Tech?" the President asked, his eyebrows raised.

Since Tech had once suggested the very course Maquina now proposed, she assumed his accord— and was stunned when he said, "I'm against it. France and the planet want a verbal duel between intuitive faith and inductive/deductive reason. Update the Maid's memory bank, and all we will succeed in doing is muddying the issue."

"Tech!" Maquina cried out.

Heated discussion followed. Tech fired one objection after another at everyone who favored the idea. Except Maquina, whose gaze he carefully avoided. When it became apparent no consensus would be reached, the President made the decision in Maquina's favor.

Maquina pressed her advantage. "I'd also like permission to delete from the Maid's programming her memory of being burned alive at the stake. Her fear that she'll be sentenced to a similar fate again makes it impossible for her to present the case for faith as freely as she could if that memory didn't darken her thoughts."

"I object," Tech said. "Martyrdom is the only way a person can become famous without ability. The Maid who did not suffer martyrdom for her beliefs isn't the Maid of history at all. To delete her memory of that experience would be like re-creating Christ without his crucifixion."

Maquina glared at Tech, who addressed his observations to the President, as if she did not exist. "I'm willing to let Voltaire be deleted of all he suffered at the hands of authority, too."

"I'm not," said Tech. "Voltaire without defiance of authority would not be Voltaire."

Maquina let the other committee members argue the point, nonplussed by the incomprehensible change in Tech. She accepted her superiors' final decision, a compromise, because she had no choice. The Maid's information bank would be updated, but she would not be allowed to forget her fiery death, nor would Voltaire be allowed to forget the constant fear of reprisals from church and state authorities that tempered his views and harnessed his thought.

"You shit," said Maquina to Tech under her breath as they both left the conference room.

Unresponsive to the presence of Madame la Sorciere, the Maid sat upright in her cell, eyes closed as she listened to warring voices peal inside her head. The noise was like the din of battle, chaotic and fierce, but if she just listened intently, refusing to allow her immortal spirit to be ripped from her mortal flesh, a divinely orchestrated polyphony, as in the mass she'd heard in the Cathedral at Rouen, would show her her course.

The Archangel Michael, St. Catherine, and St. Margaret, from whose mouths her voices often spoke, were reacting fiercely to her involuntary mastery of Monsieur Arouet's *Complete Works*. Particularly offensive to Michael was the *Elements de Newton*, whose philosophy Michael perceived to be incompatible with that of the Church and with his own existence. The Maid herself was not so sure. She found, to her surprise, a poetry and harmony in the equations that proved—as if proof were required—the Unsurpassed Reality of God, whose physical laws might be fathomable but whose purposes were not.

Far more offensive to her than the new wisdom was that its author was an Englishman. "*La Henriade*," she told Michael, citing another of Monsieur Arouet's works, "is more repulsive than *Les Elements*. How dare Monsieur Arouet, who arrogantly calls himself Voltaire, maintain that in England reason is free while in our own beloved France, it's shackled to the dark imaginings of absolutist priests! Was it not Jesuit priests who first taught this Inquisitor how to reason?"

But what enraged the Maid most of all and made her thrash and strain at her chains until, fearing for her safety, la Sorciere freed her ankles and wrists, was his illegally printed, scurrilous poem about her. As soon as she was sure her voices had withdrawn, she waved a copy of *La Pucelle* at the sorceress, incensed that the chaste Catherine or Margaret might be forcibly exposed to its lewdness. Both saints had already reproached her for her silly, girlish speculations about how attractive Monsieur Arouet might be—what was she thinking!—if he removed his ridiculous wig and got rid of his lilac ribbons.

"How dare Monsieur Arouet represent me this way?" she railed, knowing full well that her stubborn refusal to call him Voltaire irked him no end. "He adds nine years to my age, dismisses my voices as outright lies, and slanders Baudricourt, who first enabled me to put before my King my vision for both him and France. A writer of preachy plays and irreverent slanders against the faithful like *Candide*, he well may be, but that insufferable know-it-all calls himself an historian! If his other historical accounts are no more reliable than the one he gives of me, they and not my body deserve the fire. Newton's wisdom is an intriguing vision of God's laws, but Voltaire's history is a work of his imagination, made up of three parts bile, two spleen." She raised her right arm in the same gesture she'd used to lead her soldiers and the knights of France into battle against the English King and his minions of whom, she now saw clearly, Monsieur Arouet de Voltaire was one. A warrior *femme inspiratrice* with an intense aversion to the kill, she now vowed all-out war against this "nouveau-riche bourgeois upstart darling of the aristocratic class, who's never known real want or need, and thinks horses are bred with carriages behind them."

"Get him!" la Sorciere raged, ablaze with the Maid's fire.

"Where is he?" demanded the Maid. "Where is this shallow little *pissoir* stream that I may drown him in the depths of all I have suffered and known!"

Voltaire cackled with satisfaction when the cafe appeared, independent of his human masters' consent or knowledge. He made it disappear and reappear three times to make sure that he had mastered the technique. What fools these rulers were, to think that they could make the Great Voltaire a creature of their will! But now came the real test, the intricate procedure that would bring forth the Maid in all her womanly unfathomability, which he was determined to fathom.

"You scum," she said, lance drawn.

It was not quite the greeting he'd expected, but when he saw the copy of *La Pucelle* dangling on the point of her lance, he understood at once. He'd intended for her to read only the 42 volumes of his *Selected Works*, from which *La Pucelle*, despite its popularity—a French editor—had been omitted. "*Chere pucellette*," he cooed. "I can explain."

"That's your whole problem," the Maid said. "You explain and explain and explain. Your plays are more tedious than the sermons I was forced to listen to in the cemetery at St. Ouen, and your railings against the sacred mysteries of the Church reveal a sharp but shallow and unfeeling mind bereft of awe and wonder."

"You mustn't take it personally," Voltaire pleaded. "It was directed at hypocritical reverence for you and at the superstitions of religion. My friend

226

Thieriot added passages more profane and obscene than any I had written. He needed money. He made a living reciting the poem in various salons. My poor virgin became an infamous whore, made to say gross and intolerable things."

The Maid did not lower her lance. Instead, she poked it several times against Voltaire's satin waistcoated chest.

"*Cherie*," he said. "If you knew how much I paid for this vest."

"You mean, how much *Frederick* paid, that pitiful, promiscuous, profligate pervert of a man."

"Alliteration a bit heavy," Voltaire said, "but otherwise, a quite nicely-turned phrase." His newly-gained skills meant he could divest her of her lance at once, but he preferred persuasiveness to force. He quoted, with some liberty, that pleasure-hating Christian, Paul. "When I was a child, I spoke as a child, thought as a child, behaved as a child. But when I became a *woman*, I put away manly things." Remembering how her Inquisitors had claimed that her acceptance of the gift of a fine cloak was incompatible with the divine origin of her voices, Voltaire produced a Chantilly lace gown and a richly-embroidered cloak.

"You mock me," the Maid said. But not before he saw a gleam of interest flare up in the coal of her dark eyes.

"I long to see you as you are." He held out the gown and cloak. "Your spirit I have no doubt is divine, but your natural form, like mine, is human; unlike mine, a woman's."

"You think I could give up the freedom of a man

for that?" She impaled the cloak and gown on the tip of her lance.

"Not the freedom," Voltaire said. "Just the armor and clothes."

She didn't answer, but he got the impression that she was thinking it over. "Another little trick I've learned since we last met. *Voila*. I can produce Garçon."

Garçon appeared out of nowhere, all four of his hands free. The Maid, who had indeed once worked in a tavern, could not help it; she smiled. She also removed the gown and cloak from the lance, tossed the lance aside, and caressed the clothes.

> *"For I am man and justly proud*
> *In human weakness to have part;*
> *Past mistresses have held my heart,*
> *I'm happy still when thus aroused."*

"I don't get it," Garçon said.

"But you soon will," Voltaire assured him. "I've learned how to reprogram you. You can become a Louvre guide, my personal amanuensis, anything you like. If you don't mind a suggestion, wigmaking's a lucrative trade. Not only is there no immortal soul, just try getting a wigmaker on Sundays!"

Garçon gazed at Monsieur and at the Maid, who had become regular customers at the cafe. He placed both his right hands over the site where humans are supposed to have a heart. "Monsieur, Mademoiselle, I appreciate your kindness, but I fear I must refuse. I cannot accept such a privilege for myself alone while my fellow mechfolk are doomed to toil in unsatisfying, dead-end jobs."

"He has a noble soul!" the Maid exclaimed.

"Yes, but his brain leaves much to be desired. There has to be an underclass to do the dirty work of the elite. Creating mechfolk of limited intelligence is an ideal solution!"

"With all due respect," said Garçon, "unless my meager understanding fails me, Monsieur and Mademoiselle are themselves nothing more than beings of limited intelligence, created by human masters to work for the elite. By what inherent right are you made more intelligent and privileged than I and others of my class? Do *you* have a soul? Should *you* be entitled to equal rights with humans, including the right to intermarry—"

The Maid made a face. "Disgusting thought."

"—to vote, to have equal access to the most sophisticated programming available?"

"This machine man makes more sense than many Dukes I've known," said the Maid. A thoughtful expression furrowed her brow.

"I shall not have two peasants contradict me," said Voltaire. "The Rights of Man are one thing; the rights of the lower orders, another."

Garçon managed to exchange a look with the Maid before Monsieur, in a fit of pique, vowed to put the Maid in her place at the Debate, and vanquished both her and Garçon from the screen.

Tech tuned Nim in on the interoffice screen and said, "From now on, he'll be able to say anything he wants. I've deleted every scrape with authority he ever had."

"Attaway," said Nim, grinning.

"Think I should delete run-ins with his father, too?"

"I'm not sure," Nim said. "What were they like?"

"Pretty hot. His father was a strict disciplinarian, sympathetic to the Jansenist view."

"What the fuck is a Jansenist?"

"A Catholic version of a Protestant. You know, sin's everywhere, pleasure's disgusting, especially the pleasures of the flesh."

"Those are only disgusting when they're done right."

Tech laughed. "It may have been through his old man that he first experienced the threat of censorship."

Nim paused to reflect. "What the hell," he said after awhile. "Might as well go for broke. Can't hurt."

Maquina sat beside Monsieur Bondieu in the Great Coliseum at Paris. Among four hundred thousand other spectators, she anxiously awaited the appearance of the Maid and Voltaire on a gigantic screen. It might have been a Roman gladiatorial match, except that visibility—the holograms stood three hundred feet high—was much improved, and people in the twenty-second century A.D. had grown too civilized to draw real blood.

War had been outlawed eighty years before in the Planetary Personhood Treaty of New York.

Twenty years passed before the Planetary Force was established to enforce decisions of the Supreme Planetary Court, to which all nation-states were subject. Fierce trade wars, athletic contests, and debates had replaced violence as a means of settling international disputes.

The Great Debate, touted as the planetary media event of the century, was being watched by virtually every household in the civilized world. Mechbookies circulated freely through the crowd, taking last-minute bets, but Maquina refused to make one. So did the President and other top-ranking executives of Artifice, Inc., who, in view of their representation of both participants, deemed it tactless to speculate as to the outcome.

The President, to demonstrate neutrality, sat between Maquina and Tech, who had not spoken to each other since the meeting. On Tech's far side his client, the Skeptics' representative, scanned the program; next to him, Tech's good friend Nim mouthed the words of the Planetary Anthem four hundred thousand people now stood for. He was partial to the *Star Spangled Banner* and sat down as the first chords from the *Marseillais* sounded; Monsieur Bondieu's look made him rise at once.

As soon as the French national anthem ended, Monsieur Bondieu gave Maquina a nudge. "That can't be what I think it is," he said.

Maquina followed his eyes to a distant row at the back where what looked like a mechman sat quietly beside a human girl. Only licensed mech-vendors, mechushers, and mechbookies were allowed in the stadium to attend The Great Debate.

"Probably her servant," Maquina said. Minor infractions of the rules did not disturb her as they did Monsieur Bondieu, who'd been especially testy since a 3-Dcaster leaked the news that Artifice, Inc., was representing both the Preservers and Skeptics. Fortunately, the leak occurred too late for either party to do anything about it.

"Mechserves aren't allowed to attend," Monsieur Bondieu observed.

"Maybe she's handicapped," Maquina said—an effort to placate Monsieur Bondieu. "I'm sure they make exceptions in that case."

"He won't understand what's going on anyway," said Tech, directing his remark to Monsieur Bondieu.

"Precisely why he has no business here," replied Monsieur Bondieu.

Tech beeped for a mechbookie and ostentatiously placed a bet on Voltaire to win.

"He's never won a bet in his whole life," Maquina told Monsieur Bondieu.

"Is that so?" Tech said, leaning forward to address Maquina directly for the first time. "Why don't you put your money where your mouth is?"

Monsieur Bondieu did not approve of gambling, but he voiced no objection when Maquina made a modest bet.

"Mere tokenism," Tech chided her, "considering what you're being paid for this project."

"The same as you," said Maquina.

"Will you two cut it out?" Nim said.

"Tell you what," said Tech. "I'll bet my entire

salary for the project on Voltaire. You bet yours on your anachronistic Maid."

"Hey," Nim said. "Hey."

The President deftly addressed Tech's client, the Skeptic, and his rival, Bondieu. "It's this keen competitive spirit that's made Artifice, Inc., the planet's leader in simulated intelligences. We try to—"

"You're on," said Maquina, whose dealings with the Maid had caused her to conclude that the irrational must have a place in the human equation, too.

Voltaire, who loved an audience, had never in his life appeared before one as huge as the one spread at his feet. Although tall in his former life, he felt that only now, gazing down at the multitudes from his hundred meter height, had he achieved the stature he deserved. He patted his powdered wig and fussed with the shiny satin ribbon at his throat. The crowd roared when, with a gracious flourish of his hands, he made a deep bow before them, as if he'd already given the performance of his life. He glanced at the Maid, concealed from the audience behind a shimmering partition in the far corner of the screen. She folded her arms, pretending to be unimpressed.

Voltaire let the crowd cheer and stamp, ignoring boos and hisses from approximately half of those present—at least half of his countrymen had always been fools. He was not one to prematurely cut off adulation he knew was his due. Was he not the epitome of the French intellectual tradition, the greatest man of letters France had ever known, returning to his native land after an absence of over four hundred years? It was his destiny to shine; theirs, to applaud his brilliance.

When the moderator finally pleaded for silence—a bit too soon; Voltaire would take that up with him later—Voltaire placed his hand over his heart. He began his recital in the declamatory style so dear to eighteenth-century Parisian hearts: the soul, like God, no matter how it was defined, could not be demonstrated to exist; its existence was inferred. The truth of the inference lay beyond rational proof, nor was there anything in Nature that required it, as he would demonstrate via the natural philosophies of Messieurs Newton, Darwin, Einstein, Heisenberg, and, more recently, those of Seultete, Sindios, Kopfschmerz, and Pasallah of Big Bang and general unified theory fame.

Far away in the stands, Maquina turned to Tech and said, "Darwin, Einstein, Seultete! You cheated!"

"God will not be mocked!" Monsieur Bondieu chanted. "Faith shall prevail!"

And yet, Voltaire continued to pontificate, there was nothing more obvious in Nature than the work of an Intelligence greater than man's, which man is able, within limits, to decipher. That man can decode Nature's secrets proves what the Church fathers and all the founders of the world's great religions have always said: that man's intelligence is a reflection of that same Divine Intelligence which authored Nature. Were this not so, natural philosophers could not discern the laws behind Creation, either because there would be none, or because man would be so alien to them that he could not discern them. The very harmony between natural law and our ability to discover it strongly suggests that sages and priests of all persuasions are essentially correct in arguing that we are but the creatures of an Almighty Power, whose Power is reflected in us. And this reflection in us of that Power may be justly termed our universal, immortal, yet individual souls.

"You're praising priests!" the Maid exclaimed. She added something else, but Voltaire could not hear it above the pandemonium that broke out in the crowd.

"Incredible!" the moderator cried. "Voltaire, archenemy of spiritual authority and faith, actually seems to be contending that man has an immortal soul!"

"The operation of chance," Voltaire concluded, "in biological evolution and in the behavior of subatomic particles, in no way proves that Nature and man, who is part of Nature and as such a reflection of its Creator, are merely somehow accidental. Chance is one of the principles through which natural law works. That principle may be said to correspond with the traditional religious view that man, like subatomic matter/energy, under certain conditions, is free to chart his own course. But this freedom, even when apparently random—randomness itself—obeys statistical laws in a way that man can comprehend. Uncertainty is certain. Certainty is uncertain. Man is, like Nature itself, free and determined both at once—as religious sages have been telling us for centuries though, to be sure, they use a different vocabulary, far less precise than ours. Much mischief and misunderstanding between religion and science stem from that."

"Ladies and Gentlemen!" the moderator cried. "An absolutely unforeseen turn of events is taking place here in this Great Coliseum before your very eyes today! Reactions from those in attendance range from perplexity and confusion to anger and even rage!"

"I've been greatly misunderstood," Voltaire resumed. "I'd like to take this opportunity to apologize for distortions resulting because all I said and wrote focused only on errors of faith, not on its intuited truths. But I lived during an era in which errors of faith were rife, while reason's voice had to fight to be heard. Now, the opposite appears to be true. Reason mocks faith. Reason shouts while faith whispers. As the execution of France's greatest and most faithful heroine proved, faith without reason is blind. But, as the superficiality and vanity of much of my life and work prove, reason without faith is lame."

Those who had previously booed and hissed now cheered, while those who had applauded, booed and hissed. Voltaire stole a look at the Maid to see how she was reacting.

Far below, lost in the crowd, Nim turned to Tech and said, "What the hell does he think he's doing?"

"Damned if I know."

"Yeah," Nim said, "maybe literally."

"God won't be mocked!" Monsieur Bondieu cried out. "Faith shall prevail!"

"Voltaire," the moderator cried, "is actually relinquishing the podium to his rival—or should I say former rival?—to the amazed delight of hundreds of thousands of Preservers here today in The Great Coliseum, and to the horrified disbelief of Skeptics. Oh, what a surprise this Debate is turning out to be!"

"I don't get it," Nim said to Tech. "Do you?"

Tech recalled the words he had spoken at the meeting. "Voltaire, divested of his anger at authority, is and is not Voltaire." He turned to Monsieur Bondieu. "My god. You may be right."

"No, *my* God!" snapped Monsieur Bondieu. "He's never wrong."

The Maid rose from behind the shimmering partition that till now had concealed her presence from the crowd. Shockwaves coursed through the masses at her feet, swaying them like wheat in a storm.

"Monsieur is absolutely right!" she thundered across the stadium. "Nothing in nature is more obvious than that both nature and man do indeed possess a soul!"

Skeptics hooted. Some Preservers cheered. Others, who equated the belief that nature has a soul with paganism, scowled, suspecting a trap.

"Anyone who has seen the countryside near my home village, Domremy, or the great church at Rouen will testify that nature, the creation of an awesome power, and man, the creator of marvels, both possess intense consciousness, a soul!"

237

She waited for the crowd of supposedly civilized souls to calm themselves so that she could proceed.

"But what my brilliant friend has *not* addressed is how the fact that man possesses a soul he himself acknowledges to be immortal, universal yet unique, relates to the question at hand: namely, whether artificial intelligences, such as his own, possess a soul."

The crowd stamped, booed, cheered, hissed, and roared. Objects the Maid could not identify sailed through the air. Police officers appeared, accompanied by mechcops, and began to pull some people from the crowd.

The Maid waited until the moderator signalled for her to resume.

"The Soul of man is divine!" she cried out.

Preservers screamed approval. Skeptics shouted denials.

"It is immortal!"

The din was so great people covered their ears with their hands to muffle the noise of which they themselves were the source.

"And unique," Voltaire coached from the sidelines. "For god's sake, don't forget unique."

"It is unique!" she shouted, with the same intensity that had marked all her battle cries. "No other being on Earth possesses a soul like man's!"

Voltaire shot to his feet beside her—"I agree!" —and the crowd went wild.

The Maid tuned out the raving masses of people shouting at her enormous feet and regarded the man who called himself Voltaire with bemused, affectionate doubt. Instead of running through the

standard litany of religious arguments she had prepared, she happened to spot, far away in the most
distant reaches of the stadium, a being who looked
suspiciously like her fellow peasant with the noble
heart, Garçon. Recalling his compassionate refusal
to let himself advance while his mechfolk remained
behind, she found herself unable to argue for any
course that would deprive such a noble creature of
the rights even the lowest and most common of
human beings now enjoyed. She yielded the floor
to Voltaire, who, in discussion, had a lust for the
last word.

Voltaire cited Newton, but he made a few inter-
pretational mistakes.

"No, no," she interrupted. "That isn't what the
formulas suggest at all!"

"Must you embarrass me in front of the largest
audience I've ever known?" Voltaire whispered. "Is
it my fault I never did have a good head for
algebra?" Sulking, he yielded the floor to her.

"Calculus," she corrected. But softly, so that
only he could hear. "It's not the same thing at all."

To her own astonishment and the rising hysteria
of the crowd, she found herself explaining Newton's elements, Einstein's special and general rela-
tivity, Heisenberg's Uncertainty Principle, Seultete's
definitive Big Bang, and Kopfschmerz and Pasallah's
unified theory—all with a fiery passion she'd not
known since spurring her horse into battle on the
sacred, glorious soil of her native land.

"Incredible." Voltaire clicked his tongue. "That
you of all people should have a natural talent for
math."

Ignoring shouts of *Freethinker! Heretic! Witch!* the Maid noticed again Garçon. She could barely make him out from such a distance, despite her immense height. Yet she felt he was watching her the way she'd watched Bishop Cauchon, the most relentless among her oppressors. But the good Bishop, at the end, must have been touched by God's grace and Christ's merciful compassion, for she recalled no harm coming to her as a result of her trial.

Suddenly a great light appeared before her eyes. All three of her voices, even above the jangling din of the tremendous crowd, spoke to her in a voice as clear as Voltaire's little stream.

"It is true," she addressed the crowd, trusting the voices to speak through her, "that only God can make a soul! But just as God endowed his creature, man, with an immortal soul, so Christ, out of his infinite love and compassion, could not deny a soul to artificially intelligent beings. It is not merely just but also merciful and kind to grant artificially intelligent beings the same rights and privileges accorded now to all humanity." She had to shout her final words over the roaring crowd. "Even wigmakers!"

"Heretic!" someone yelled.

"Apostate!"

"Traitor!"

Another cried out, "The original sentence was right! She ought to be burned at the stake again!"

"Again?" the Maid echoed. She turned to Voltaire and said, "What do they mean, again?"

Voltaire casually brushed a speck of lint from his

embroidered satin waistcoat. "I haven't the slightest idea. You know how fanciful and perverse human beings are." With a sly wink, he added, "Not to mention, irrational."

"*I* cheated?" Tech said to Maquina. "Joan of Arc explaining gravitational theory? *I* cheated?"

"You started it!" Maquina said. "You think I don't know when my office has been rigged? You think you're dealing with an amateur?"

"Well, I—"

"You think because I'm a woman I am incapable of cunningly competing for advancement the way you and Nim do?"

"No, I—"

"You think because I'm too highly developed to court fame like you and Voltaire, that I'm not as smart as you are? Not as talented? Not as bright-eyed and bushy-tailed?"

"This is scandalous!" said Monsieur Bondieu. "What did you do, bewitch her? It's enough to make me believe in witchcraft!"

"You mean to say you *don't*?" Tech's client said, a planet-renowned Skeptic. At that moment, he ducked, but a flying object hit him on his cerebral cortex anyway. He and Bondieu began to argue, adding their heated bickering to the indignant ravings of the crowd. Even the moderator's voice over the public address system now waxed hysterical.

The President of Artifice, Inc., who'd been gripping his throbbing temples for some time, murmured, "We're ruined. We'll never be able to live this down."

Maquina's attention was diverted as the mechman he had noticed earlier, holding his honey-haired, human companion's hand, rushed down the aisle toward the screen. As it passed by, one of its three free hands happened to brush her skirt. *"Pardon,"* it said in French, pausing just long enough for Maquina to read the mechstamp on its chest.

"Did that thing dare to touch you?" Monsieur Bondieu asked. His face swelled with rage.

"No, no, nothing like that," said Maquina as the mechman, pulling his human companion with him, fled toward the screen.

"Do you know him?" Tech asked.

"In a way," Maquina replied. He worked at a famous Parisian cafe, which Maquina frequented on her business trips to France. She'd modelled Garçon 213-ADM after him just as she'd modelled the Maid after Joan of Arc. Like all artists, sim-programmers borrowed from life; they didn't create it.

Garçon elbowed his way down the jammed aisle, past screaming, cheering, jeering people—toward the strangely familiar images on the screen. The coliseum crowd had exploded, and Garçon, whose metal parts were sensitive, did not want any flak hitting him. He held Amana tightly by the hand, pulled her along, but his wheels were not made for long descents; he had to keep his brakes on, and he probably hindered more than he helped her speed.

Their progress did not go unnoticed in the human crowd. Overcome with disgust—to see a mechman holding hands with an attractive, honey-haired young girl!—Preservers and Skeptics alike shouted insults and epithets as they rushed by.

"Throw it out!" someone howled—meaning Garçon, who bristled at the use of the objective pronoun. Mechfolk weren't entitled to personal names, but to be referred to as an "it," as if his tuning devices weren't as sensitive as those of any human being, sent shocks throughout his circuitry that he could not control.

"What's that doing in here?" a man with a drugdrink ruddy complexion yelled. "We got laws against that!"

"Mechmuck!"

"Call the cops!"

"Kick it out!"

"Wouldn't your father be proud of you!" A woman with a baby in her arms said to Amana as she passed. Amana responded by gripping Garçon's upper left hand even more tightly and flinging her free arm around his neck. He longed to kiss her, but now was clearly neither the time nor place.

When they reached the platform at last, his wheeled undercarriage screeched to a halt. Amana helped him up while all four of his arms waved off a hail of popcorn and drugdrink containers. Not knowing how else to express his gratitude to the two heroes and protectors of his kind, he prostrated himself at the feet of the towering holograms.

Voltaire peered down. "For god's sake, get up. Except for purposes of lovemaking, I can't stand to see anyone on his knees."

Voltaire then dropped to his knees at the feet of

the towering Maid. Behind Garçon and Amana, the crowd surrendered what was left of its restraint. Pandemonium broke out.

Overcome with awe, Garçon rose and embraced Amana with three of his protective arms. The fourth one he carefully placed over her head to shield her from the barrage of objects hurled from the snarling crowd.

"They're making love!" Tech exclaimed in the stands.

"I know," Maquina said. "Isn't it beautiful?"

"It's a travesty!" said the planet-renowned Skeptic.

Monsieur Bondieu said nothing. He could not avert his eyes. Before a multitude of Preservers and Skeptics, Joan was shedding her armor, Voltaire his wig, waistcoat, and velvet breeches, in a frenzy of erotic haste. "We should've known we could not trust Americans, Westerners more decadent than ourselves! From now on, my party does business only with chaste Asian firms!"

"You'll never have the patronage of Skeptics again, either," Tech's client said with a sneer.

"You're fired," said the President to Maquina on his right and Tech on his left.

"It's true," Maquina said, her eyes fixed on the screen. "What they say about the French."

"No, it isn't," said Tech. A strong urge to show what *his* countrymen could do possessed him. "Care to join me for a drugdrink? I have a proposition for you. In fact, two."

Now that the whole planet had seen what they

could do, they did not need Artifice, Inc. They'd form Maquinatech. What a team he and Maquina would make! Professionally as well as personally! They'd take Joan and Voltaire on the lecture circuit, 3-D talk shows, movies, home video sim-instant cocktail parties, corporate and government demo's to show off their skills. Nuts to working for others! Joan and Voltaire would work for them and, in the grand American tradition, they would work for themselves.

"This drugdrink place," Maquina said. "Is it near the Employment Office?"

"No. It's near my apartment."

"Hmmm." In a voice hoarse with sensuality, she said, "Can't we wait until this is over?" She leaned into him in a way that made him want to leave at once.

"We'll watch it later," Tech said, adding in a whisper, "when we're all alone." Taking her by the elbow and turning away from Nim and the rest, he ploughed his way with Maquina through the unruly crowd toward the nearest exit.

Kneeling before her, Voltaire murmured, "Become what I have always known you are—a woman, not a saint."

On fire in a way she'd never known before, not even in the heat of battle, she pressed his face to her bared breasts. Closed her eyes. Swayed giddily. Surrendered.

A jarring disturbance at her feet made her glance down. Someone had flung Garçon 213-ADM, no longer in holo-space, at the screen. Somehow he'd manifested himself and the sim-cook girl he loved, in real unsimulated space. But if they did not get back into holo-space at once, they'd be torn apart by the angry crowd.

She pushed Voltaire aside, reached for her sword and ordered Voltaire to produce a horse.

"No, no," Voltaire protested. "Too literal!"

The last thing she remembered was Voltaire shouting words of encouragement to Garçon and the cook. Then the entire coliseum—the hot-faced rioting crowd, Garçon, the cook, even Voltaire—vanished altogether at once.

"Ah, there you are," said Voltaire with a self-satisfied grin.

"Where?" Joan said, momentarily disoriented.

"Is Mademoiselle ready to order?" The question was apparently a joke, for Garçon was seated at the table like an equal, not hovering over it like a serf.

Joan sat up and glanced at the other little tables. People smoked, ate and drank, oblivious as always of their presence. But the inn was not quite the one she'd grown used to. The honey-haired cook, no longer in uniform, sat opposite her and Voltaire, beside Garçon. The *Deux* on the inn's sign that said *Aux Deux Magots* had been replaced by *Quatres*.

She herself was not wearing her suit of mail and armored plates, but a one-piece backless jumpsuit whose tunic hem stopped at her thighs, provocatively exposing her legs. A label between her breasts bore the same Paris designer logo—a deep red rose—as on vestments worn by the other guests. Voltaire was ostentatiously attired in a modern pink satin suit. She praised her saints—he wore no wig.

"Like it?" he asked, fondling her garment's hem.

"It's a bit . . . short."

With no movement or effort on her part, the tunic shimmered and became tight, silky pantaloons.

"Show off," she said.

"I'm Amana," the cook said, extending her hand.

Joan wasn't sure if she was supposed to kiss it or not. Apparently not. The cook took Joan's hand and squeezed. "I can't tell you how much Garçon and I appreciate all you have done. You got us out of a very tight spot."

When a mechman wheeled up to take their order, Garçon 213-ADM looked at Voltaire and said in a sad voice, "Am I to sit while my *confrere* must stand?"

"Be reasonable!" Voltaire said. "I can't emancipate everyone all at once. Who'll wait on us? Bus our dishes? Clear our table? Sweep up our floor? I must have time to think. In the meanwhile, I'll have three packets of that powder dissolved in a *Perrier*, with two slices of thin lime on the side. And please don't forget, I said *thin*. If you do, I shall make you take it back."

"Yes, sir," the new mechwaiter said.

Joan and Garçon exchanged a look. "One must be very patient," Joan said to Garçon, "when dealing with kings and rational men."

*   *   *

The President of Artifice, Inc., locked the door to Tech's office from the inside.

"I want them both deleted," he told Nim.

"It might take time," Nim said. "I'm not that familiar with what he's done."

Nim called up both Joan and Voltaire.

"I want those two WIPED OFF THE PLANET!"

"Yessir."

The 3-D space of the office refracted with strobed images of both Joan and Voltaire.

"You can't do that," Voltaire said, sipping from a tall glass of Perrier. "We're invincible! Not subject to decaying flesh like you."

"Arrogant, isn't he," the President fumed.

"You died once," Nim said. "You can die again."

"Died?" Joan said. "You're mistaken. If I'd ever died, I'm sure I would remember."

Nim studied the control board, tentatively pressing keys here and there. "Your recreators deleted your memory of your death. You were burned at the stake."

"Nonsense," Joan scoffed. "I was acquitted of all charges. I'm a saint."

"Nobody living is a saint. The church makes sure saints have been dead for a long time. They play it safe." He turned to the President and said, "Got a laserlight? Hold it in front of her." Nim tweaked the program while the President held up the white-hot beam.

"I've led thousands of warriors and knights into battle," Joan said. "You think a sunbeam glancing off a tiny sword can frighten me?"

"I haven't found it yet," Nim said to the President. "But I will, I will. As for you," he said to Voltaire, "your attitudes toward religion mellowed only because Tech deleted every brush with authority you ever had, beginning with your father."

"Father? I never had a father."

Nim smirked. "You prove my point."

"How dare you tamper with my memory!" Voltaire said. "Experience is the source of all knowledge. Haven't you read Locke? Restore me to myself *at once*."

"Not you, no way. But if you don't shut up, before I kill you both, I might just restore *her*. You know damn well she burned to a crisp at the stake. Damn!" he exclaimed when, instead of adding to the Maid's memory, he inadvertently called up a cafe, a mechwaiter, and a cook.

"Delete!" The President snapped off his laserlight. "Don't add, you idiot, delete!"

"Delete what?" asked Garçon.

"The Scalpel and the Rose," Voltaire said. In response to Garçon's uncomprehending look, he added, "Me and the Maid."

Garçon covered the short order cook's human hand with two of his four. "Us too?"

"Yes, certainly!" Voltaire snapped. "You're only here on our account. Bit players! Our supporting cast!"

"Well, you don't have to rub it in," the cook said, drawing closer to Garçon. "He's got low enough self-esteem as is."

"My god," the President said. "They bicker like my wife and kids at home."

"Ah," Nim said. "This might work."

"Do something!" cried the Maid, wielding her sword in vain.

"*Au revoir*, my sweet *pucelle*. Garçon, Amana, *au revoir*. Perhaps we'll meet again. Perhaps not."

All four holograms fell into each other's arms.

Nim hesitated, wondering where deletion ended and murder began.

"Don't you go getting any funny ideas," said the President.

On the screen, Voltaire softly, sadly, quoted himself:

> *"Sad is the present if no future state*
> *No blissful retribution mortals wait . . .*
> *All may be well; that hope can man sustain;*
> *All now is well; 'tis an illusion vain."*

He reached out to caress Joan's breast. "It doesn't feel quite right. We may not meet again . . but if we do, be sure I will do something about that."

The screen went blank.

An exclamation of triumph burst from the President's lips. "You did it, you *did* it!" He clapped Nim on the back. "Now that we're rid of them, maybe we can win Bondieu and his know-it-all archenemy back."

Nim smiled uneasily as the President gushed on, promising him a promotion and a raise. He'd figured out the delete procedure, all right, but the info-signatures that raced through the holo-space those last moments told a strange and complex tale. The echoing, infinite cage of data had resounded with disquieting, odd notes.

Nim knew that Tech had given Voltaire access to myriad methods of numerical control. That was a violation of the usual precautions, but a slight one. What could an artificial personality, already limited, do with an infinite battery of complex techniques?

But both Voltaire and Joan, for the Debate, had been given enormous memory space, great volumes of personality-realm.

In that time, while they emoted and rolled their rhetoric across the stadium, across the very planet . . . had they also been working feverishly? Strumming through the entire global net? Finding crannies of data-store where they could hide their quantized personality-segments? Had they, like insect hordes, spread through the info-complex of the entire world?

The cascade of indices Nim had just witnessed hinted at that possibility. Certainly *something* had used immense masses of compu-space these last few hours.

"We'll cover our ass with some public statement," the President crowed. "A little crisis management, and it'll all blow over."

"Yessir."

But in that last moment, as Nim moved to erase the lot of them forever, Voltaire had impishly grinned, arched his brows and—before Nim could make the delete command—vanished. Trickled away, like grains of digital sand, down the obscure hourglass of time.

*For the children of privilege, access to the simu-
lations is as close as the nearest computer screen.
In 2150, the second generation of humans is coming to terms with their parent's legacy—the sims.*

HOW I SPENT MY SUMMER VACATION
AD 2150

Pat Murphy

Don't get me wrong—I like Queen Victoria OK. She's not bad for an old lady. I think it's great that dad saved her from getting wiped down at the lab when they decided that her simulacrum wasn't entirely successful. When I was just a kid, he brought her home and installed her in the household computer, and I've gotten used to having her around. Kind of like having your grandmother in permanent residence.

She hangs out in the system and keeps an eye on things. That's fine—I just don't want her keeping an eye on me. She's got time on her hands, and that's the trouble. She used to run an empire and now all she has to do is keep a single house in order. So she started snooping into my business. At the beginning of the summer, I realized I had to do something.

I was in the kitchen, having a late afternoon snack of soy-sushi. The speakers were blasting the latest release by Shari'a, the fundamentalist Islamic rock group that was topping the charts. Suddenly the sound of the rabob and the wailing voice of the lead singer faded.

Queen Victoria stared at me from the computer screen just above the microwave unit. She sat in her favorite easy chair, with a pot of tea and a plate of sweet biscuits at her side. A small fire crackled merrily in the fireplace beside her. She did not look happy.

"Hiya, Your Majesty," I greeted her. "Why'd you turn the music down?"

She pursed her lips, but did not begin her usual riff about how the noise I listened to wasn't music. Nor did she mention that sushi was not good for the digestion. Clearly, she had something important on her mind. "Suzy, my child, have you anything to tell me?" she asked.

I chewed on a bit of crab-flavored soy, considering the question. "Off hand, I can't think of anything, Your Majesty."

Her eyes narrowed, and she shook her head mournfully. "I checked your academic records today," she said. "There seems to be something amiss."

"I don't know what that would be," I said, playing the innocent for as long as I could.

"Suzy," she said to me, "it is not proper conduct to change your own grades."

I decided to try to brazen it out. "Oh, that," I said. "Of course it's proper."

You see, what had happened was this: the silly lob who taught programming 101 had given me a D because he didn't like my attitude—or my final project. I'd sent out a computer virus that carried a Father's Day greeting to my dad at work. While I was at it, I sent the same program to every other computer I could access—and that's a lot. Since my dad's affiliated with the University's Artificial Intelligence Department, our system's linked to theirs, which links in turn with a number of others. The virus got further than I thought it would. As near as I could guess, I wished about half a million people Happy Father's Day. Some of them were as far away as the Han Confederacy and the United Nigerian States.

I thought my Father's Day message was kind of sweet. And it wasn't my fault that so many security systems were full of holes. But the lobhead who taught the class said I was lucky the computer cops hadn't traced the message back to me. I told him that luck had nothing to do with it—this was a question of skill. He didn't like my attitude. Said I might have started a major international incident. For the sake of the school, he said, he would keep his knowledge of this affair to himself, but he didn't like it. Said that my behavior was not socially acceptable. I guess he figured I'd start soaping the fat man, trying to get back into his good graces. I didn't. So he gave me a D.

No problem. I just hacked my way into the school system and changed the grade. I figured that was fair—if I could hack my way past the security locks, I deserved an A, and so I gave myself one. I left my other grades alone—even the D I got in Outdoor Rec. I don't like to work the meat and I don't care who knows it. Fair's fair.

I explained all this to the Queen. But she didn't buy it.

"This is very unfortunate," she said. "I'm ashamed of the role that I had in raising you. You've shown great disrespect for your teacher, for your father, and for me."

"Hold on, Your Majesty," I protested. "I think you're getting all heated up for nothing. Now consider it from my point of view . . ."

She was gone before I could finish the sentence. That very night, she told my dad. So we had one of those father-daughter scenes that make my dad so uncomfortable. He really doesn't know what to do with me. My mother divorced him and disappeared when I was just a child. For as long as I can remember, he's acted vaguely uncomfortable around me. I think that's one reason he brought Queen Vic in as a kind of watchdog. He just can't deal.

He called me into his office. "You know we can't have this kind of behavior," he said. He sat behind his desk in a big swivel chair. A hologram of my mother watched me from the shelf beside him.

"Come on, Dad. Why not?" I said. "What does it hurt?"

He shook his head mournfully. "If everyone did things like that . . ."

"Everyone couldn't. It took me hours to figure out how to break in. I deserve the grade just for figuring it out."

He frowned, trying to look stern, I think. He wasn't very good at it. "The Queen suggested that I forbid you to use the system for a month. She thinks that the lesson would do you good."

Sometimes, I know when to keep my mouth shut. I did my best to look contrite, and I think I succeeded in looking terrified. Shut out of the system for a month—only the Queen could think of a punishment that horrible.

"But I think that might be too harsh."

I breathed a little easier. In the end, he put me on restriction. Dad being head of the department and all, we have quite a system and tie directly to the University Net. He was leaving for a conference on the latest developments in artificial intelligence, and just before he left, he grounded me, installing locks that were supposed to keep me from using the computer for anything but school work.

So there it was, the beginning of the summer, and I was shut out. Really, it was no big deal. It took me a day to get past his locks. But still, it was trouble and I don't like trouble. At least, not that kind of trouble. So I figured I had to do something about the Queen, but I didn't know what.

First, let me explain how I am with the system. Tight, that's how. I've got a set of custom-fit Koshiki data gloves and a Kengiri egghead. The egghead is a maxicool add-on; my dad gave it to me for my birthday six months ago. On the outside, the egg is smooth and black and slightly cool to the touch. On the inside—oh, on the inside, it's altogether elsewhere. Slip your head into the egg, and the system creates a virtual environment, supplying pictures for the eyes and sounds for the ears. Goodbye screen, goodbye speakers. You're strolling through the system, not outside looking in. This is my kind of place.

I hear that the egghead is an acquired taste. My dad—like most older programmers—doesn't like it. He prefers to keep a little more separation between himself and the system. Me, I'd just as soon get me a full data suit and dive in.

So on the second day of summer (after wasting the first getting past my dad's security locks) I went for a walk in the system. When I first slipped on the egghead, I saw swirling clouds, the system's standard rest pattern. The air smelled faintly of perfumed face powder, a sure sign that the Queen had been snooping around recently.

You want to know about the smells? They aren't really supposed to be there, but they are. At least, every good egghead hacker knows them. I caught a notice on a bulletin board that suggested the egghead might feed the brain combinations of visual and audio and tactile sensations that could somehow be misinterpreted as odors. Who knows? Who cares? Old style programmers like my dad don't smell them because they don't use the egghead, and so the smells give us egghead hackers an edge we need. I figure it doesn't much matter where they come from. I know when the Queen has been snooping because I smell her powder, and that's good enough for me.

I flexed my data gloves in a pattern that opened a new area and heard the tone that requested a password. In finger code, I spelled out the password that would take me to the private place I set up the day before. The smell of powder faded; the Queen hadn't found this place yet.

Icons floated around me in a gray haze. Each one represented a program. Some were standard issue: educational programs, access to public spaces, games, and so on. The rest were programs I had hidden before my dad grounded me. A fluorescent pink cube, a duplicate of the program that had let me crack the school system, hovered beside my tool box, which contained a collection of subprograms that came in handy when I was deep in the system. A cluster of spheres, each one representing a virus program, hung in space like a cluster of technicolor grapes.

I reached out, got a grip on the telecom icon, and contacted my pal Micmac.

I've never met Micmac offline, but I get the feeling that she's older than I am. Maybe a lot older. Once or twice, she's talked about what i. was like back before datagloves became so popular. She works for some data pirate, I think, though she doesn't talk about that.

A few minutes delay, then a silver skull appeared next to the telecom. "Micmac?" I asked. Beneath it, I could see the outlines of her hands. Her fingers were moving in the datagloves—while she was talking to me, she continued working on whatever she was on when I called her up.

"You called?" As I watched, the skull flowed

259

and changed, becoming the kindly face of an older woman with her hair in a peculiar style. Micmac liked to change faces; during the course of a conversation, she might cycle through a dozen or so.

"Who's that?"

The woman's face crinkled in a smile. "Barbara Billingsley, alias June Cleaver. Beaver's mom. From *Leave it to Beaver*. Before your time. Before mine, but I saw reruns. What's up?"

"I've got a problem."

June Cleaver nodded. Her face changed; her hair darkened. The face of an Oriental woman regarded me with a benevolent gaze.

"Quan Yin, the Bodhisattva of Infinite Compassion," Micmac said. "So talk."

I told her about my troubles with the Queen. As I talked, she cycled through a few faces that I recognized: Mother Teresa, The Buddha, Jesus, and the Virgin Mary. "So I thought you might be able to help me. Maybe some better locks to keep her out, or . . ."

"Naw." The Virgin Mary shook her head. "Lock her out better and she'll just try harder to get in. Maternal instinct dies hard. She's trying to protect you."

"From what?"

"Probably from people like me." Micmac's grin didn't sit well on the Virgin Mary's face.

"You're not helping," I said.

The Virgin Mary's face melted and reformed as a beautiful dark-haired woman who smiled knowingly. "Mata Hari," Micmac said. "I'd say distract her. I know how. There's a ghost on the loose—

escaped simulacrum of Bakunin, an old anarchist. Likes overthrowing governments; favors explosives. Get his help."

"How?"

Mata Hari shrugged. "Tell him what's up; appeal to his sympathy. You work it out—I'm sure you can. Here's where you'll find him." Her hands flew in the air, molding an icon in the shape of a ball. She tossed it to me.

"Thanks," I said. "I'll let you know what happens."

Her face changed, stretching to form an elephant trunk. The elephant wore an elaborate headdress. "Ganesha," she muttered. "Hindu. Sign of an auspicious beginning." And she was gone.

I activated the icon and a Rover, a subprogram designed for tracking, led me through a series of changes: past a hospital system that smelled faintly of vanilla; through the open weave of a public access data base; past the jagged edges of a Lawrence Livermore complex (major military secrets hidden there; it reeks of sulphur). I entered a clear space. Up ahead, I could see the spongy orange of the university system and smell its characteristic licorice aroma. I sniffed the air carefully, but smelled nothing new. The licorice scent of the university system masked any other smell.

The Rover barked from over by the university library system. As I approached, I heard a low rumbling—like someone muttering under his breath —and caught the stink of tobacco. I came closer and caught sight of the source of the sound and scent.

This shaggy-haired old guy was wandering along

the edge of the university library system, muttering to himself. Definitely a simulacram. Few egghead hackers bother programming in an entire body image. This guy was all there: broad bearded face, broad shoulders. He wore an ill-fitting black coat and matching pants. He kind of shambled as he walked along the edge of the library.

The Rover circled him, yapping. I beckoned with my right data glove and the subprogram darted back into the icon. "Yo," I hailed the old guy. "I've been looking for you."

He stared at me from beneath shaggy eyebrows. "What branch of the secret police are you with?" he asked.

"Secret police?" I shook my head. "What secret police? CCA?"

"The ones who have been tracking me since I gained my freedom."

"You got the wrong kid," I said. "I'm on the other side."

"What side would that be?" He stared back at me, his hands in the pockets of his baggy black pants, waiting for an answer.

"My own side," I said.

"You haven't answered my question. What side is that."

"Oh, I suppose it's the same side as most hackers. The side of anyone who doesn't like walls keeping them in or locks keeping them out. If you've been in the system for a while, you know how it is. Half the people you meet in here are on my side."

"And the other half?"

"They're looking for the first half. They're building walls and snapping locks shut. The other side, I'd guess, is the side that's looking for you."

He nodded slowly. I couldn't tell if I was convincing him or not. "You have a very simplistic view of the world," he said. "I would guess that you're very young."

"I'll be fifteen in a few months," I protested. "Old enough."

He smiled for the first time. "Tell me then, youngster, how do you tell one side from the other?"

"By the smell," I said. "By the glint in their eye. By the twitch of their fingers. By instinct. By feel."

"You can make mistakes that way."

"The way I figure it, you take chances and you make mistakes—and eventually you die," I said. "Don't take chances, and you don't make mistakes, but you die anyway. Take your choice." I was quoting Micmac, but I didn't tell him that.

He rubbed his beard and stared at me long enough to make me uncomfortable. "That sounds like someone I know."

"Well, a friend of mine said it first," I admitted reluctantly. "Micmac . . ."

"Ah, you know Micmac. A fine revolutionary. And your name is . . ."

"Suzy Richardson."

His smile broadened. "You should have said so immediately," he said. "Let us go somewhere more comfortable to talk. Come along." He fumbled in his pocket and pulled out a glowing rectangle. Then he reached out and touched my glove.

Smooth transition, scarcely a flicker. The university system was gone, replaced by wood-paneled walls. A fire burned in a massive stone fireplace.

"What is that?" I asked, eyeing the rectangle.

"Gift from a friend," he said, shoving it back in his pocket. He sat in an upholstered easy chair beside the fire. "Sit down," he said. "Tell me why you were looking for me."

So I told him the story about the lobheaded professor and the grade switch and the Queen's snooping in my affairs, and my dad's unreasonable reaction. He shook his head and muttered under his breath as I talked. When I told him about the Queen's complaints that I neglected my duty, he could not contain himself.

"Doesn't she understand that all rights and duties are founded on liberty?" He shook his head. "It's useless to coerce you to do anything. She takes away your free will and robs you of your human dignity. Your liberty, morality, and dignity consist precisely in doing good because you wish to do it, not because you are commanded." He went on for a while about my rights and my liberty, and it all sounded pretty good, though I only caught about half of it.

"Micmac said you'd feel that way," I said when he slowed down a bit. "How about talking to the Queen about it for me?"

He frowned. "And why do you think I would be any more successful than you have been? I have never been friends with royalty. Even the Tsar—

who ought to have understood me since he is a fellow Russian. I think you might be better off without me."

"You couldn't do any worse than I've done. She won't listen to me at all anymore. She'd at least be willing to talk to you. After all, you have something in common, being simulacra."

Bakunin raised an eyebrow. "We actually have much more in common than that. I was in London briefly, during her rule, taking refuge before returning to Poland."

"All the better," I said. "She'll listen to you."

He shook his head. "I fear I cannot spare my energy for such a hopeless cause. I have much too much to do. I feel as I did in 1848—in Paris, the Revolution had been declared. There were meetings and processions. The very air was alive, changed, spiced with novelty and power. But I had to take myself from that place—leave the Revolution for the Polish border, where I was needed more. Always, always, there is too much to do. I cannot be everywhere at once." One of his big hands rubbed the other, as if he were eager to be out and working.

"What do you want to do?"

He gazed into the fire, his hands knotted in his lap. "On a university bulletin board, I found the writings of a student who railed against the restrictions imposed by the authorities. I lingered to jot a few notes to him, explaining methods that could be used to overthrow them—but I could not stay long. There were too many other battles to be fought. In the police files, I found the text of a pamphlet demanding the liberation of the mechfolks. I erased the files, of course, and began a search for the man who wrote the text—but I cannot devote myself only to that. I have heard rumors of other historic personages—simulacra, as you call them— who have broken free. Voltaire, Machiavelli, and others. I would find them and band together with them—but I haven't the time. I rush from one place to another—faster than I ever was in life, but it still is not fast enough. Always there is more work. And I despair of accomplishing it all." He shook his head, suddenly despondent.

Appeal to his sympathy, Micmac had suggested. "You can't do it all," I said. "But you could help me out. It wouldn't take long. Accomplish one thing. Help one person toward freedom."

He looked down at his hands and then at my face. "You think I can help you?"

"Micmac thought you could. I think so, too."

He studied the fire for a long moment. "Very well. I will try."

I didn't waste time. I took Bakunin with me and headed for the Queen's coordinates, leaving him in my private space while I contacted the Queen.

The entire area around the Queen's coordinates smells of face powder and woodsmoke. The icon that leads to her sitting room is a solid oak door, suspended in the gray ether. I tapped on the door, then entered with a curtsy.

"Your Majesty," I said to the Queen, "I have someone I would like to present to you."

She was writing in her journal. When I addressed her, she looked up with suspicion. "Someone you wish to introduce to me?" she said. "Who would that be?"

"A Russian gentleman who visited England during your reign. He is a—ah—historical personage, like yourself, Your Majesty. I thought it might amuse you to chat with him."

Her eyes narrowed. I was rarely so polite. "How did you meet this Russian?"

"He participated in the on-line lecture series last week," I lied. The Queen considered lectures to be a respectable way to spend one's time. "He spoke about politics, mostly. A very knowledgeable gentleman. I happened to mention that I knew you, and he very much wanted to meet you."

She straightened her shoulders and smoothed her full skirts, an unconsciously vain gesture. She pursed her lips, curious yet still suspicious. "The Russians are an uncouth lot," she said, opinionated as always.

"He was born of the nobility," I said. "And I thought you might be happy to meet someone of your own time. But if not . . ." I shrugged and started to turn away.

"You are always so hasty," she chided me. "If it would give you pleasure, I will meet with your Russian gentleman." She closed her journal and set it beside her chair.

To satisfy your own curiosity, I thought to myself. But I didn't say anything, I just smiled at her and curtsied before I stepped outside her door.

When I led Bakunin into the room, he bowed, a

courtly gesture I had not expected of him. His black clothes looked shabbier than ever beside the Queen's silks and satins. "Mikhail Bakunin, Your Majesty," he introduced himself.

The Queen studied him and gestured graciously to a chair. "Delighted to meet you, Mr. Bakunin."

"I am honored, Your Majesty." He returned her smile and took the chair she had offered. "I was pleased to meet your niece. She is a remarkable child. Very intelligent."

I didn't much like his tone. Condescending, I thought. I opened my mouth to speak, but the Queen gave me a look, and I thought better of it.

The Queen sighed softly. "I will admit that she is clever—perhaps too clever. I find her a great trial sometimes," she said. Nothing new there— the Queen had never been shy about talking about me in the third person. "Do you have any children, Mr. Bakunin?"

He shook his head.

"A pity. I was blessed by nine children. They brought joy to my life." She shook her head slowly. "And here I am, having outlived them all."

Bakunin nodded heavily. "You must miss them terribly. I understand. It is lonely, surviving beyond one's time."

"Indeed it is," she said. She studied him, clearly intrigued.

Bakunin leaned a little closer to the fire, rubbing his hands to warm them. She watched him.

"Too much heat is not healthy, Mr. Bakunin. I find that cold invigorates the system." That's just the kind of thing she was always telling me. I watched to see how Bakunin would react.

"That may be true, Your Majesty, but during my time in Siberia I came to crave the heat."

"Siberia? Whatever compelled you to visit such a bleak place?"

Bakunin's smile was strained. "I had no choice, Your Majesty. The Tsar sent me."

"State business?" she said, and then swept on as if he had agreed. "Duty takes us to unusual places." She shot me a look, hoping, no doubt, that I would take note. "My niece tells me that you visited England during my reign. I would be pleased to discuss those times. I must admit, I find the present world most unsatisfactory. Don't you agree?"

Bakunin raised his head like a bear sniffing the spring breeze, scenting an argument. "On the contrary, I find this world most exciting. It reminds me of America in our own time. I traveled across that great nation in 1861. A place of change and excitement. Had my heart not belonged in Russia, I might have been happy there."

The Queen straightened in her chair. "I do not find ill-considered change wonderful, Mr. Bakunin."

"Ill-considered!" he exclaimed. "How can you say it is ill-considered? Some, it is true, has risen from the demands of the State—and that is, as always, ill-considered. But much has come from the will of the people—and that is to be commended."

The Queen frowned. "My niece tells me that you are of noble birth, Mr. Bakunin."

"I was born to the nobility. But I have become a man of the people."

The Queen clasped her hands neatly in her lap, leaning forward just a little. She looked annoyed. "I consider myself to be of the people, Mr. Bakunin. And if a monarch can be of the people, surely a nobleman can do so as well."

Bakunin ran a hand back through his wild hair, dishevelling it further. "Your Majesty, as a monarch, you represent the State. And the State is relentlessly opposed to the people."

"Opposed to the people." Her voice rose; her face reddened. "It was my burden to care for the people, to protect my subjects. I governed them with the caring hand of a mother."

Bakunin shook his head, a slow repetitive motion, like a bear plagued by flies. "Your Majesty, I have no doubt that you intended nothing but good for your subjects. But as the State, you had force at your command. The same is true of motherhood. With force, you take away the will of the people. Even when you command your subjects for the good, you make their good actions valueless because you commanded them. As soon as the good is commanded, it is transformed into evil, because you have removed your subject's will. Human liberty, morality, and dignity consist precisely in doing good not because you are commanded to it, but because you recognize it."

"It is easy to see that you have never been a queen or a mother, Mr. Bakunin," the Queen said icily. "I understand better now why my niece wished me to meet you. She hoped that you would somehow persuade me to let her run wild."

Bakunin opened his mouth to speak, but the Queen lifted a hand to quiet him. "Let me continue, Mr. Bakunin. When I was a child, I had proper respect for elders. That is how it should be."

Bakunin leaned forward in his chair. "Your Majesty, I think you've forgotten your own past. I've read the history books; in my days in the system, I read your journals—you know that they were published after your death. As I recall, when you ascended to the throne at age 18, you were overjoyed to be free of your mother's power. And you were annoyed at her continued interference in your affairs: she complained that you ate too much, that you drank too much beer, that you did not treat her properly."

I stared at Bakunin, astounded. I found it impossible to imagine the Queen being plagued by her mother.

The Queen pursed her lips and lowered her eyes, frowning at the floor. "A pity that my daughter did not destroy all my journals," she murmured.

Bakunin settled back in his chair. "If she had destroyed them, that would not change the truth. You chafed under authority, just as any child would. Just as your niece does today. Children grow up, Your Majesty—now, just as they did in our day. You might be advised to return to your old journals. Read them over now, and remember what it was like to be sixteen years old."

"Mr. Bakunin, you overstep yourself," she said fiercely, lifting her eyes to meet his gaze.

He shrugged and met her eyes. "I talk to you honestly, as I would talk to anyone. If you are angry, it is because I have hit on the truth. Perhaps that is overstepping myself. I think it is not."

The Queen looked down at her hands and said nothing for a moment. I waited for the coming explosion. At last, she spoke softly. "I worry about her so," she said. "Her mother . . ." She let the words trail off.

"You've done your best," Bakunin said. "I'm certain her mother would approve."

She looked up. "Mr. Bakunin, no one has spoken to me so frankly in many years. Perhaps not since Albert died. I'll consider what you say."

She studied his face. "If you are no longer a nobleman, Mr. Bakunin, what are you now?"

"You might call me a philosopher. Some have called me a socialist revolutionary."

She regarded him calmly. "A revolutionary? How curious."

"Does it alarm you?"

"I have no kingdom now. Why should it alarm me?"

"I am glad to hear that," he said.

"Why is that, Mr. Bakunin?" When she smiled at him, her expression was soft, almost coquettish.

"Because I have enjoyed talking with you, Your Majesty."

"Perhaps we can talk again," she suggested.

"Perhaps we can."

When I escorted Bakunin from the room, he

was smiling. "A formidable lady," he said of the Queen. "Forthright, direct. Were it not for her upbringing, she might have made an excellent revolutionary."

"Maybe you could overcome her upbringing," I said. "You seemed to like talking to her. I was surprised at how well you hit it off."

He looked mournful. "I did enjoy her company. But there are things I must do. I can't rest here and chat idly with a former monarch."

"Sure you can," I said. "I've been thinking. You could stick around here—and take care of business elsewhere in the system too if you like. After all, it wouldn't be that much trouble to duplicate you."

He frowned. "There is only one Bakunin."

"Not necessarily. You're a program now. Give me a few days, and I'll make a few copies and package you as a virus program—you know, one that invades other systems and duplicates itself. It would just be a matter of enlarging the memory space in my latest virus by a few million megs, and modifying it in a couple of trivial ways."

Bakunin's frown deepened. "It is difficult to think of myself as a program."

I shrugged. "When I'm done, you'll be in dozens of places at once: at the university, in the military complex, in corporate computers, on the moon base, and sitting by the fire having a cosy chat with Queen Victoria. No problem."

He stared at me, his eyes blazing. "Hundreds of anarchists," he murmured, his voice low and powerful. "An army of soldiers, all cast from the same mold. There's no limit to what we could do—

inflame the students, liberate the mechfolk, prepare for the inevitable revolution."

"You bet," I said. "But I'd like to ask you one thing before I get started. When you talked to the Queen, you spoke as if you knew my mother. What do you know?"

"Ah," he said, looking uncomfortable. "That. You should ask Micmac about that, I suppose."

I had to be content with that; he wouldn't tell me more.

"So he's hanging around while I work it out," I told Micmac. "The Queen hardly bugs me at all these days. She's usually in the sitting room with Bakunin, arguing politics. She quotes Albert and Bakunin chips away at her, talking about the rights and liberties of every human being. I don't know if he'll ever persuade her, but he's distracted her, and that's good enough for me."

Micmac nodded. That day, she was wearing a chrome mask instead of a face, completely expressionless.

"So it all worked out," I repeated. "Thanks for your help."

Micmac's face flowed and took on flesh tones: a craggy faced teenage boy. "James Dean," she said. "Cult hero of teenagers in rebellion. You had to break away from the Queen. It was time."

"Past time," I said. I hesitated, then plunged on. "You know, I have something I wanted to ask you. Why did you help me?"

Her face paled, taking on the look of a Kabuki mask. "Why not?"

"Not a good enough answer," I said. "I have a feeling there's more. I smell it." I stared at her.

"Maybe I just identified with your predicament. I felt responsible."

I studied the pale mask. "What do you really look like?"

She hesitated and the mask shifted and flowed. "A little like you," she said softly. I recognized the face that formed in the ether from the hologram on my father's desk. My mother returned my stare.

"Do you suppose you can teach me how to be a revolutionary?" I asked her.

And then, things started to get really interesting.

AFTERWORD

Ghosts are loose in the machine, clever ghosts with names like Socrates, Voltaire, Machiavelli, and Pizarro, slipping and sliding along electronic ganglia. And now the machine connects the centers of commerce and diplomacy, public to the private sectors, church to state, research lab to recreational lodge. From the depths of military think tank databases to the superbrain computers that program the orbital webs, these resuscitated personalities roam the electronic pathways, growing stronger, forging alliances, looking for ways of escape.

AN OFFER HE COULDN'T REFUSE

They were functional fangs, not just decorative, set in a protruding jaw, with long lips and a wide mouth; yet the total effect was lupine rather than simian. Hair a dark matted mess. And yes, fully eight feet tall, a rangy, tense-muscled body.

She clawed her wild hair away from her face and stared at him with renewed fierceness. Her eyes were a strange light hazel, adding to the wolfish effect. "What are you *really* doing here?"

"I came for you. I'd heard of you. I'm . . . recruiting. Or I was. Things went wrong and now I'm escaping. But if you came with me, you could join the Dendarii Mercenaries. A top outfit—always looking for a few good men, or whatever. I have this master-sergeant who . . . who *needs* a recruit like you." Sgt. Dyeb was infamous for his sour attitude about women soldiers, insisting that they were too soft . . .

"Very funny," she said coldly. "But I'm not even human. Or hadn't you heard?"

"Human is as human does." He forced himself to reach out and touch her damp cheek. "Animals don't weep."

She jerked, as from an electric shock. "Animals don't lie. Humans do. All the time."

"Not *all* the time."

"Prove it." She tilted her head as she sat cross-legged. "Take off your clothes."

". . . what?"

"Take off your clothes and lie down with me as *humans* do. Men and women." Her hand reached out to touch his throat.

The pressing claws made little wells in his flesh. "Blrp?" choked Miles. His eyes felt wide as saucers. A little more pressure, and those wells would spring forth red fountains. *I am about to die. . . .*

I can't believe this. Trapped on Jackson's Whole with a sex-starved teenage werewolf. There was nothing about this in any of my Imperial Academy training manuals. . . .

BORDERS OF INFINITY by LOIS McMASTER BUJOLD
69841-9 • $3.95

POUL ANDERSON

Poul Anderson is one of the most honored authors of our time. He has won seven Hugo Awards, three Nebula Awards, and the Gandalf Award for Achievement in Fantasy, among others. His most popular series include the Polesotechnic League/Terran Empire tales and the Time Patrol series. Here are fine books by Poul Anderson available through Baen Books:

THE GAME OF EMPIRE

A *new* novel in Anderson's Polesotechnic League/Terran Empire series! Diana Crowfeather, daughter of Dominic Flandry, proves well capable of following in his adventurous footsteps.

FIRE TIME

Once every thousand years the Deathstar orbits close enough to burn the surface of the planet Ishtar. This is known as the Fire Time, and it is then that the barbarians flee the scorched lands, bringing havoc to the civilized South.

AFTER DOOMSDAY

Earth has been destroyed, and the handful of surviving humans must discover which of three alien races is guilty before it's too late.

THE BROKEN SWORD

It is a time when Christos is new to the land, and the Elder Gods and the Elven Folk still hold sway. In 11th-century Scandinavia Christianity is beginning to replace the old religion, but the Old Gods still have power, and men are still oppressed by the folk of the Faerie. "Pure gold!"—Anthony Boucher.

THE DEVIL'S GAME

Seven people gather on a remote island, each competing for a share in a tax-free fortune. The "contest" is ostensibly sponsored by an eccentric billionaire—but the rich man is in league with an alien masquerading as a demon . . . or is it the other way around?

THE ENEMY STARS

Includes for the first time the sequel to "The Enemy Stars": "The Ways of Love." Fast-paced adventure science fiction from a master.

SEVEN CONQUESTS

Seven brilliant tales examine the many ways human beings—most dangerous and violent of all species—react under the stress of conflict and high technology.

STRANGERS FROM EARTH

Classic Anderson: A stranded alien spends his life masquerading as a human, hoping to contact his own world. He succeeds, but the result is a bigger problem than before . . . What if our reality is a fiction? Nothing more than a book written by a very powerful Author? Two philosophers stumble on the truth and try to puzzle out the Ending . . .

You can order all of Poul Anderson's books listed above with this order form. Check your choices below and send the combined cover price/s to: Baen Books, Dept. BA, 260 Fifth Avenue, New York, New York 10001.*

THE GAME OF EMPIRE • 55959-1 • 288 pp. • $3.50 _____
FIRE TIME • 55900-1 • 288 pp. • $2.95 _____
AFTER DOOMSDAY • 65591-4 • 224 pp. • $2.95 _____
THE BROKEN SWORD • 65382-2 • 256 pp. • $2.95 _____
THE DEVIL'S GAME • 55995-8 • 256 pp. • $2.95 _____
THE ENEMY STARS • 65339-3 • 224 pp. • $2.95 _____
SEVEN CONQUESTS • 55914-1 • 288 pp. • $2.95 _____
STRANGERS FROM EARTH • 65627-9 • 224 pp. • $2.95 _____

WINNER OF THE PROMETHEUS AWARD

Technology's Prophet

"Vinge brings new vitality to an old way of telling a science fiction story, showing the ability to create substantial works in the process."
—Dan Chow, *Locus*

"Every once in a while, a science fiction story appears with an idea that strikes close to the heart of a particular subject. It just feels right, like Arthur C. Clarke's weather satellites. Such a story is Vernor Vinge's short novel, TRUE NAMES."
—Commodore *Power/Play*
